Forget Me Not

Cupid's golden arrow

Delivers a lasting sting!

By

Joan McSweeney

ACKNOWLEDGEMENTS
The list of individuals who supported me throughout
this journey is long, including those who offered
encouragement and served as beta readers, the
computer engineer who saved my material more than
once, and members of the Henderson Writer's Group.
I value the guidance my editor, Lyn Robertson,
offered during the process.

ISBN # 9798718533873

Editing by Lyn Robertson
Cover design by Kathleen Cleary

<u>Dedication:</u>

Farolyn McSweeney

Daughter and Caretaker

Introduction:

FORGET-ME-NOT is loosely based on the folklore of
Rose de Lima Hospital in Henderson, Nevada, during
the 1950s. The story is inspired by two individuals -
Sister Anne Wasco, Adrian Dominican Catholic nun
who baked Angel Bread and Al Freeman, a Jewish
man, and publicist with the Las Vegas Sands Hotel and
Casino, who was at the hospital recuperating from
war-related injuries.

While many historical events are true to the time, other
facts are rearranged for a more compelling read.

Part 1:

Giana

Italian Campaign

Chapter 1

"**H**ey! What the hell you doing round here?" yelled Lieutenant Roger Atkins walking around the new surroundings. He wasn't looking for drama, but it caught up with him on that day.

Two years ago, the Japanese bombed Pearl Harbor. Roger enlisted in the pilot training program and graduated as a commissioned officer. Last month, he and his crew received orders from the North Africa front to join the Italian Campaign in Bari, Italy.

Poor visibility scrubbed the daylight bombing raid over the enemy's target. Roger left the Mess hall for a breath of fresh air. He passed military buildings and continued to the outer perimeter of the base. Narrowing his eyes, he focused on a large olive grove with twisted tree trunks. Some appeared as individuals crippled with age. He made out a small figure that weaved as it advanced with brisk steps.

"Stop. Damn it!"

The intruder sprinted, tripped and landed face down in the dirt.

Roger tapped the side of his flight boot, fingered the knife concealed in a secret pocket. He held the sharp blade at the ready, in case enemies lurked about.

He looked around the immediate vicinity for co-conspirators. Spotting none, he tucked the knife back in its place.

Roger ran and reached a motionless figure. He jabbed at the small form. Germans sometimes used youngsters as spies. He yelled, "If you're a German plant, your number's up! Now, damn it. Get up!"

No response. He scooped up and examined the limp body.

The young face already showed signs of a bruised eye. Roger pushed back a bushy crop of black hair. He reached inside his vest and fished out two handkerchiefs to absorb the blood trickling from the boy's hairline.

An uncomfortable awareness swept over him. Dropping explosives from 25,000 feet over an enemy zone, bomber pilots remained removed from the mangled, human wreckage far below. He returned the small body to ground.

In the distance, Roger heard the whine of a troubled engine. It sounded like a Jeep making short runs forward, jerking in reverse, and forward again. He stood, waved his hands, and hollered, "Help. Over here. Help!"

Responding, the driver made a quick U-turn and braked at Roger's side. The private sprung from the vehicle and saluted smartly. "Sir, making a test run ... just checking the transmission." Roger handed the boy to the private and jumped in the passenger seat.

"I was a Boy Scout," the private said directing his attention to the kid's injuries. He cleared his voice and proclaimed, "There's not much damage. He'll be knocked out for a while, a black eye, needs a few stitches. Kids always get hurt like that."

"Give him to me, Scout. Head to the city for medical attention."

The private placed the kid in the crook of the lieutenant's arm and settled into the driver's seat. The Jeep bounced down the ill-defined road washed away by previous rains.

"Can't wait to wipe out 'em Krauts."

"Hey. Take it easy!" The lieutenant bobbed up and down in the light-weight Jeep. "I've got an injured kid here!" He lowered his voice. "Hopefully, not a spy."

"Yeah! We just may have gotten one!" The private sneaked a look. "But keep the kid's head higher than his heart. As a scout, I know about these things."

Roger stared at the child in his arms. *He looks more like a curious kid.*

The truck swerved. "Me, I'm new to this place." The private maneuvered the vehicle through mud puddles.

"Learn the lay of the land, Scout, or you'll end up on KP."

"Kitchen Patrol? Never. Gitty-up, old Bronco, gitty-up!"

§ § §

Motorized traffic increased. Roads grew tight with trucks going to and from the port. The Jeep caught up with a Red Cross ambulance and followed it to a large medical facility, The Polyclinic. The health care complex was a 2000 plus bed facility. One of the massive public works orchestrated by Benito Mussolini, Italy's disgraced prime minister who tried to flee the country.

The private helped Roger from the vehicle and continued with his unsolicited advice, "Sir, you need to keep the kid's head elevated."

"Thanks, Scout."

The private saluted, hopped back in the Jeep. He beeped as he clanked down the road.

Roger paused and studied the front of the medical facility. Tradesmen with saws, blades, masonry, and painting tools, continued their mission—convert the grounds to meet the demands of the Allied military forces. A team of gardeners with shovels and wheelbarrows planted Italian cypress trees around the large horseshoe acreage.

Clergy strolled freely around the grounds with their heads bowed. Their hands remained hidden inside the extended sleeves of the black habit. An elongated strand of wooden rosary beads made a belt, the only accessory.

Though a different religion from Roger, their demeanor reminded him of his father. *Sober, somber, probably humorless, too.*

Roger's grip on the kid stiffened. The kid grew heavier as he inched through the hospital's entrance. He stood under the canopy in front of double doors, top half with glass windowpanes, bottom with wooden panels. He saw a long, wide passageway. Signs strategically placed above the doorways indicated various departments.

The antiseptic smells triggered memories of the day his young sister lay dying in an isolated New York hospital ward.

Doctor, help her breathe. Please make her take a breath! Roger remembered yelling. His pleading went unheeded.

The Polyclinic

Chapter 2

Roger continued through the corridor's newly painted white matte wall on one side. The opposite wall waited for a fresh coat.

"Excuse me," a workman called. His overalls were splattered with paint. He held a bucket as he made a wide circle around the lieutenant.

Roger mumbled apologies for blocking the way, then continued down the hall.

Nurses spoke with Italian, British, and American accents as they attended their chores. Patients made their way down the hall. Some on gurneys, in wheelchairs, or crutches, as others used walking sticks.

Roger avoided looking at the red-stained handkerchiefs resting on his chest. The sight of blood made him edgy. Eyes straight ahead, he resumed the immediate mission to get attention for the kid. He spotted a sign hanging over an alcove

—

Staff Surgeon

Mediterranean Theatre of War Operations

It was an active scene as military personnel rushed in and out the commander's office. Straight ahead, he noted signs for medical departments: Orthopedics to his left, followed by Heart Surgery. On his right, he passed markers for the Neurosurgery and Plastic Center.

A nurse with files clasped to her chest slowed her walk. "Mamma mia! Guiseppi, okay?" She didn't wait for an answer and pointed to General Surgery. "You go, quick. I get his mama."

"Mama," the kid muttered.

Roger wasted no time and hurried through the double doors. "It's okay. We're here. You'll be okay."

His facial muscles relaxed when the medical staff took charge. They immediately tossed the blood-stained handkerchiefs into the laundry hamper. An attendant with a damp towel made his way toward the lieutenant, and wiped at the splattered bloodstains on his jacket.

"Guiseppi! My bambino!" a sobbing nurse barged into the room. She looked at the American doctor and lieutenant and cried out, "My little boy!"

"Lieutenant, please escort the nurse to the waiting area so I can focus on the patient."

Roger took her by the elbow. She gasped for breath between sobs. Roger tried to assure her, "Boy, okay."

She stared at him with big, brown, teary eyes. "Uh … bambino, okay."

He pantomimed stitching his forehead. "A few stitches." She must have understood because she relaxed and slumped in his arms.

"My Guiseppi." She made the sign of the cross and uttered, "Too much hurt in my country… my husband … dead … why?" She buried her head in Roger's chest, her tears streaked the leather jacket. "Please, sweet Jesus, not my little boy, my little Joey."

Roger walked her to the waiting area, turned her toward an empty chair. He balanced the weight of her small frame between his arms, guiding, almost carrying her to the seat.

A slight smile crossed his face. Military life did strange things to a man. Momentarily, the close feel of a warm lady's body distracted him.

The nurse dropped into the chair while Roger stared at her for a few moments. He blurted out, "So, you're a nurse?"

Before she responded, an older couple rushed into the waiting room. The woman, beige cotton stockings rolled down to her ankles and apron around her waist, stretched her arms to the nurse. The old man wore trousers held by frayed suspenders and a belt looped around his waist.

The nurse embraced both, and the trio began a conversation in Italian. The woman's tears rolled down her cheeks.

They hushed to watch Roger pace the area. The threesome eyed his every movement. He fingered his jacket pocket, located his cigarettes, and lit up.

Roger could speak a few words of Italian, but could not judge if the group accepted or rejected Allied presence. They might view him as an unwelcome intruder.

Roger felt compelled to wait to be sure the little guy was okay, and not a spy. Self-conscious, he sauntered to an ashtray stand, stamped out his half-smoked cigarette, and cast them a sidelong glance.

He noticed a pattern as their talk continued. Each time they said *American*, their expressions softened.

The man stretched himself tall and gestured as if holding an invisible rifle. He marched in place. "Soldato?"

"A pilot." Roger swept an opened hand up to the sky.

"A pilot," the gentleman copied his words. Next, the man pointed upward and threw kisses to the ceiling. Roger took that as a good sign.

The trio regrouped. Roger heard an Italian word, *eroe*. It sounded like *hero* to him and he bit his lip. He was puzzled.

They didn't seem to have ill will toward him, but they should not think of him as a hero. *I'm the reason their young fellow was injured in the first place.*

Upon hearing *eroe* again, Roger used gestures to protest. That seemed to only endear him more. They smiled at Roger's embarrassment.

He walked to the ashtray, lit another cigarette, and tossed the match.

"Ah, the Puglia family." The medic entered with a broad smile. "Hello, Papa and Nonna and Giana."

Giana assumed the role of translator. "Your boy is fine. Has a black eye, few stitches, and will be okay soon. Not serious." She shot Roger a knowing look as if to say, *you knew it all along. My boy would be fine.* She made him feel like a true hero, or at least good about himself … the magic of a pretty lady's smile.

"Lieutenant, I'm Ted Cleland. Guess you know the handkerchiefs are done with."

"Roger Atkins, and, I understand," he said as he offered him a cigarette.

The women exchanged glances. Giana understood the meaning of this quick exchange. The pilot had used his handkerchiefs to clean up her little boy.

The doctor informed the family their boy would be fit to go home soon. He instructed them to keep him awake for the rest of the day.

"Hey, lieutenant. You Flyboys have a day off?"

"Blame it on the weather—poor visibility so our daylight raid got scrubbed."

"And have you seen the jam up at the port where all my medical supplies are laid up?"

"I admit, near the port, we started following a line of traffic before we got here. I hope some of it will be carrying your material."

"It's bullshit. I've been hoping that for days, but god damn it…." The doctor noted the family's surprised faces. Ted apologized and moved on to a different topic.

"How did you meet Joey?" He smiled at the family.

"Saw him early this morning just roaming about. Thought he might be a German spy. In fact, next time he may end up shot if he's mistaken for a spy."

"No! No! No shoot." Giana ran and grabbed Roger's arm. "My boy is no spy. He likes Brits and Yanks. We like Brits and Yanks."

The grandmother echoed those sentiments. "Yes, yes. They say Joey for our Guiseppe. He like Joey. We learn to say Joey to him."

The grandfather added, "Our Joey like planes, big planes."

"Lieutenant, you take over. Now's the time to get back to my duties." He tossed his cigarette and bade farewell to the family.

Roger noticed the severity in Giana's gaze and stammered, "Joey is a good boy… ah… not a spy." He lit another cigarette and offered one to Papa.

Papa gleamed with delight, rolled it under his nose and eased it into his shirt pocket.

Roger looked at his watch and started to leave. Nonna threw both hands up in the air, waving them back and forth, "Un momento, per favora."

Again, the threesome huddled in a conversation. A moment later, Nonna stepped to Roger, and said, "Soup and bread, mia casa."

Papa Puglia wiggled his hand up an imaginary stream. "Pesce, pesce."

Nonna demanded, "You come tonight." It sounded more like an order from his superior instead of an invitation from a grandmotherly figure. "Come hungry."

Roger understood he was to arrive at the Puglia's for dinner. Giana gave Roger directions using gestures to indicate the way. He repeated them and Giana added, "Go inside the alcove. You see my bike tied near our front door." She smiled. "Okay?"

She's very pretty ... lovely smile ... captivating eyes, he thought.

Papa broke the awkward silence. "Ahem." He walked toward Roger with an extended hand and said, "Grazie. Grazie."

"Grazie. Grazie," Nonna repeated. She held Roger's head between her hands and kissed him on both cheeks.

Roger waited for Giana to follow her mother's kind gesture. Instead, Giana waved her fingertips. "Ciao."

He sprinted down the busy hallway. He felt a tug of homesickness as he reflected on the young kid. He and his fiancée, Nancy, hadn't talked about children, but he was eager to start a family once he returned to the states. He would be proud to sire a curious son like Joey, drawn to airplanes.

The sun shone over the blue southern sky of Bari. He stopped and listened to birds chirp and tweet. His morning evolved into an unexpected, joyful experience. An Italian family invited him to a home-cooked meal.

He grabbed a ride back to the barracks, distracted.

I met a girl who thought of me as a hero. She's a sweetie and I'm her hero. All's well with the world except there's this damn   war.

Coming to Dinner

Chapter 3

Gossip spread quickly among the Puglia's neighborhood and grew in exaggeration from one person to the next. *A Lieutenant is coming to dinner,* quickly evolved into – *Yes, yes. A General, a U.S. American General is coming to dinner at the Puglia's home.*

Friends insisted on doing their share to show off their Italian hospitality. A block of Burrata cheese, carafe of red wine, and four Venice glasses were among the contributions.

A neighbor, with whom Nonna hadn't spoken to in years, knocked on her door. She handed Nonna a cloth-wrapped package and pleaded with her to use her silver forks and knives for the evening's dinner.

"Thank you. Your silverware will grace our table." With a long embrace, the women promised to renew their friendship and when she left, a tear came to Nonna's eyes.

Spreading out her Venetian lace tablecloth, Nonna could not remember the reason the two women had parted company in the first place. Joey followed and pestered his grandmother. "Let me sit here." He pointed to the guest of honor's place. "Next to the lieutenant."

"Yes, you can. Now, go comb your hair." She returned to the kitchen for last minute preparations.

After pedaling from work, Giana hurried from her bike. There was little time to style her long hair. She searched for her bright silk scarf, wide black border with various shades of peach, green, and blue flower petals set in the middle. A gift from her husband, she had not worn it since his death on the battlefield during the Italian-Ethiopian War. She had just given birth to Joey.

Despite those dark days, she was grateful for the Puglia family. Despite grieving their son's death, they took good care of her and Joey.

Giana pulled her hair into a ponytail, securing it with the scarf. She stared in the mirror, taking several moments to discern the person looking back at her. A big smile ran across her face.

Nonna stirred the pot of broth as Giana eased into the kitchen. "Is that you, Giana?" With no response, she turned. The spoon fell from her hands as she recognized the scarf. Squeezing her eyes shut, she bowed her head.

Giana put her arms around her mother-in-law's shoulders. "In the past, we've suffered much pain and loss. Today, we have each other, and our Joey is healthy. Let us hope for happier times."

§ § §

In the tent, Roger watched the crew assemble a makeshift card table. He finished buttoning his shirt. He was troubled. *It's not a good idea to tell my crew I'm dressing for a special meal and for another chance to be in the company of a lovely Italian nurse.*

Roger downplayed the invitation, explaining that the kid's grandparents invited him to their home. He didn't mention Giana, or an Italian supper. It quieted the men's curiosity as they prepared for a gin rummy game.

Billy Gibbons was a down-home farm boy from Texas. He looked over the crew. "We do form a 'right neighborly' group of men." He was a navigator, and enlisted right after he graduated from high school. "But, I do miss my lady friend."

Bruno Losasto hailed from New Orleans French Quarter. Although a bombardier, with a sense of style. He had more pride for his heritage and Yat accent. "Let's just keep 'em safe at home." He shuffled the cards. "Dammit! No room for dos mamas in our Air Force."

"You know them pistol packin' mamas?" Fred Clark was a co-pilot from Chicago. He inhaled sharply on his cigarette and slowly exhaled a band of smoke. "How do you think any of those gals got a pilot's license?"

Roger ran a comb through his hair and listened halfheartedly to their banter. The Women Air Force Service Pilot, or WASP, recently became part of military service. Roger knew where the exchange headed. He heard it many times, maybe not the same words, but same intent. If they kept their chit chat relatively clean, he went along with it.

Bruno tossed his cards on the table, grabbed a towel and wrapped it around his chest in the shape of a bra. "Bet I know how dem dames got licensed." With hands on his hips, he sashayed around the tent as if squeezed into a tight girdle. Looking over his shoulder, he added, "She just blinked 'em eye lashes and strutted 'round her dumbass commander."

Fred shot back, "Jesus Christ! Skirts don't belong in a bomber." He grabbed Bruno's towel, rolled it up, and smacked him on the butt.

"Wouldn't catch me dead in a cockpit with one of those dumbass lady pilots!" Billy declared.

"Probably where you'd end up." Fred blurted out.

Bruno interrupted. "Dead, along with da rest of our crew." He sat and fanned out the dealt cards.

They chuckled.

Fred tossed down his half-smoked cigarette and stamped it out. "It's damn nonsense! Who expects a member of the fairer sex to control a lumbering B-17, high-flying-engine aircraft? We need to keep our ladies at home where they belong."

"All I know," Billy said as he made the sign of the cross. "I can't wait to get back to the States and my sweet Marie." He kissed his fingertips and tossed his hand into the air.

Bruno turned to Roger. "I smelled a rat. You never spent time on looks. You got a shave, creases, and polished shoes." He gave a wolf whistle as Roger adjusted his officer's cap.

"Putting on your look-good-for-civilians, Lieutenant?" queried Fred.

"Find out if da kid has soeur ainee," Bruno instructed. "That means if she has an older sister. And, remember, my Jewish friend," clasping arm around Roger's shoulder. "I'm a good Catholic boy."

"And just watch when the Italian family finds out you, a good Catholic boy, have a lady and future mother-in-law waiting for you back home," teased Fred.

"Mayday, Mayday!" exclaimed Billy.

Puglia's Hospitality

Chapter 4

Roger strolled passed and lingered in front of the Mess hall. In the background, he heard the record, "At Last," by Glenn Miller's orchestra, playing on the company's phonograph. He hummed on the way to meet the Puglias.

He passed the impressive Basilica de San Nicolas containing the remains of the saint. He reached the old part of the city with its worn, narrow, and curved cobblestone pathways and laced together homes.

Some were whitewashed, some painted in muted colors of geranium red, and yellow. Some second-floor homes had wooden shutters and small balconies.

Roger stopped and studied his surroundings. He took the wrong turn daydreaming about the young Italian nurse's small warm body, her gentle smile, and dark eyes.

He retraced his steps to the correct alcove. The front entrance faced a circular patio illuminated by the moon. A woman's bike leaned against a door.

The two-wheeler reminded him of the fitness routine of the high school cycling team. After classes, they went on a long training ride up and down hills. Then, he took a quick shower and went to work, a night job bagging groceries.

Under the bike's metal frame a dark wad of cloth caught his attention. He picked up a hair net, a snood. Brushing the woolen fabric, he pulled on several long strands of hair and recognized the color.

He straightened his jacket and cap before knocking. Joey swung the door open and ushered him in. In unison, Nonna, Papa, and Giana extended their rehearsed greeting. "Welcome to our home. God bless America."

"Well, what can I say but thank you. It's my privilege being with the Puglia family tonight." Roger couldn't break loose from Joey's tight clutch. The youngster sported a black eye and a shaved hairline with several stitches. The rest of his hair—thick, and combed—puffed out in all directions. Roger thought some of that Brylcreem pomade, popular with the Royal Air Force men, just might tame the kid's unruly mane.

Roger showed Giana the hair net he found.

She reached for it. "It's my snood." Their hands touched. The brief contact had her look away as the blood rushed to her face. "Grazie. Grazie." She hung it on a hat rack.

Giana became interpreter for the evening and Joey grasped Roger's hand. He pointed to an enormous, wreath-shape loaf of bread. He chuckled. "Heavy, heavy," and motioned for Roger to pick it up.

"Pane di Monte Sant' Angelo," Giana explained. "My countrymen think of the bread as a healthy source of nourishment and hangs in many bakeries."

Roger bounced the bread up and down in his hands, emphasizing its heft.

In a loud voice from the kitchen, Nonna added, "Good … how you say … on outside?"

"Nonna, it's called crust."

"Good crust and soft inside."

Giana broke off pieces, handed one to Roger and one to Joey.

Roger took in its sweet aroma and, after a bite, kissed his fingertips. They looked at each other with big smiles.

"Excuse me," said Giana. "I will see if Nonna needs help."

Joey squeezed Roger hand, gesturing for him to sit at the place of honor where he left a rough drawing of a B-17.

Roger examined it. "Nice job, Joey. I like how you penciled in the name of our plane, Forget Me Not."

"Seeing your bike, reminded me of the one I left at home."

"You peddle a bike and not drive a car?"

"Well, I couldn't afford a car and was on the cycling team. After classes, we joined the fitness team. It was good discipline. I was a bagger at our corner grocery store, saving for a car. I'm still saving."

Papa came in and opened a bottle of wine and served everyone. He then began dinner with a prayer. Roger observed his surroundings and felt a sense peace. The family welcomed him into their home and, just briefly, he held a woman's hand. He bowed his head with private thoughts. *For the sake of all mankind, this conflict must end soon.*

During dinner, questions flowed easily. Roger asked about the Basilica he passed on the way to their home.

"That is the Basilica of St. Nicolas," Giana answered, "We think of him as the true Santa Claus and celebrate every December sixth with exchange of gifts."

"Can I show the lieutenant the Basilica?" Joey eagerly asked his mother.

Before Giana responded, Roger answered, "I would like that."

The family had a thirst for stories about America. It was near Thanksgiving, so Roger offered his rendition of the pilgrims, the Native American Indians, and their first feast together.

"They ate fish, deer. Used their corn for bread or stuffing. Played games, danced, sang."

"Slower, please," smiled Giana. "A beautiful story and I don't want to miss a word for my family."

Every now and then, he looked in her direction and smiled as she caught up with the narrative. At the end, his eyes caught and held on Giana. He studied her face, high cheekbones, and full lips.

He forced himself to look away. It felt like a betrayal to Nancy.

With dinner complete, Papa waved his forefinger back and forth for everyone's attention. He filled the glasses again and toasted, "Happy Thanksgiving."

As Roger prepared to leave, Papa and Joey shook his hands. Nonna kissed him on both cheeks while Giana waved, "Ciao."

Emboldened, Roger reached for Giana's hand. He bowed, placed a gentle kiss on her fingertips. "Thank you for interpreting for me." She resisted slightly, then she quickly settled into a relaxed squeeze. He released her hand and spoke to the small group. "I must make it my mission to learn your beautiful language."

As he turned to leave, he heard, "Wait, wait, Lieutenant." Nonna returned from the table with large slices of bread wrapped in a clean dish cloth. "You take." She handed it to him and kissed him on both cheeks.

Roger thought about the young Italian nurse on the return to the base. He was infatuated with her accent and her looks. He noticed the quiet way she took charge of her family. Impressive.

He couldn't remember if he paid such attention to Nancy, before their engagement. It was arrangement of convenience - for his father, and Mr. Katz, his boss. As far back as pilot training at Randolph Field, he recalled sharing his apprehension with a buddy.

It was often mentioned that young ladies Nancy's age found it difficult meeting a proper mate. Roger ignored chitter-chatter. When the United States was drawn into the war conflict, an overwhelming number of young men enlisted. A void of eligible bachelors was apparent, and Roger become the man of the hour.

I can't believe I was taken in with that line of reasoning. And that's how it happened. It was like a blur. Time past so fast.

The Katz and Atkins families gave the couple their blessing before he left for flight school. They claimed the couple would become better acquainted through letters. They'd have a proper ceremony after he returned.

The bright lights from the base interrupted Roger's memories.

Slapping Incident

Chapter 5

In the barracks, Billy continued to be annoyed with the mail delivery system, and struggled to make sense of other military behaviors. "Every time I think about that General who slapped that young soldier, I get redder than a hot branding iron." He leaned over their makeshift card table.

Earlier that summer, General Dwight D. Eisenhower, Supreme Allied Commander of the Mediterranean Theatre Operations, demanded his hard-driving commander, General George Patton, offer apologies to all involved with what became known as the 'slapping incident.' Word of the episode spread throughout the military.

"Asshole. Sit down," admonished Fred. "There's a war going on. We need our men to beat our enemy or they beat us, period."

"Doesn't mean you can't show compassion," Billy countered.

"Shit," Bruno piped in. "Me, I want my leader to show leadership, someone width a bad, real bad reputation like dat *Blood-and-Guts* Patton, who's been on da front line himself. Needs his men to follow by his example and not to act like a hypocon . . .well, whatever, not a coward hidin' in a hospital ward."

Billy's face turned redder by the moment. He cut the deck of cards and slammed them on the table. "But the young soldier was sick, and every soldier has a breaking point!"

Bruno roared back. "Damn! Billy. How many times we looked 'round us in da air? Seen dat plane next to us shot down by German flak, knowing dem men, our men, are burned alive as da big bird blows up."

Fred dealt the cards and added, "Or watching them parachuting out the plane, not knowing if they'll land in enemy territory or the sea."

Bruno offered, "I want to kill da enemy, every damn Kraut, everyone of 'dem."

Billy threw his hand down and circled aimlessly inside the tent.

"Come on, goofus," Bruno said. "Ya can't do nothin' about it now."

"Yeah, but that General Patton called the soldier a gutless bastard. Just who does Patton think he is with his flashy style, having some private polishing his helmet and boots and carrying —"

Fred reacted in his authoritative style. "Sit down and listen to me. When you earn the rank of General, you have my permission to do whatever you want as long as you lead your men to victory."

"And then I hear all this talk about our tour of duty being increased," moaned Billy. "My sweet Marie expects me back soon, back as a whole man. We want to start our family."

§ § §

Roger entered the tent and saw Frank and Bruno at the card table. Billy paced the room. "Did I miss anything?"

"I'm trying to start a game of gin rummy, but again, Billy's afraid of losing." Fred turned to his young friend. "Right?"

"Guys." Roger unbuttoned his jacket. "Remember, Billy's saving for an engagement ring and if he keeps losing, we'll have to chip in for one."

Billy flopped on his bunk, swung his arm over his face and covered his eyes "Where's our mail?" He mumbled. "I just can't wait to hear from my Marie. I write to her every chance I get."

"Hey, brainless wonder! Maybe that's da problem. She's tired of reading all your damn, romantic letters," Bruno chided.

"Well, men," Roger unwrapped the bread. "If you behave yourselves, I'll give each of you a slice."

Mail Call

Chapter 6

One hundred and fifty thousand one-sided pieces inside a canvas mail bag caught up with the men and their spirits lifted. The system of V-mail handled the back-and-forth flow of news to the front line. Notes were written on one side of paper and photographed before sent across the ocean, and reprinted. Letters not only supplied soldiers with moral support, the process offered the government a way of monitoring information.

Roger expected one or two letters from his mother. Mrs. Atkins kept him abreast of rationed war items like canned goods, butter, and cheese. Recently, she wrote about her victory garden, an activity foreign to her prior to the war. Victory gardens popped up everywhere as part of the war effort.

She wrote that she has small flower boxes with beans and peas and even some tomatoes growing. She traded these for carrots, lettuce and squash from some of her neighbors. It was their way of helping one another through lean times.

She followed her favorite Old Testament verse: Proverb 3:27. *Do not withhold good from those to whom it is due, when it is in your power to act.* His mother's nature was to fill a need whenever it came to her attention. He figured she would keep busy long after the war ended.

Roger was puzzled by the spotty correspondence from Nancy. Her letters felt impersonal, never using the words *us* or *we*. The blame also lay with him. His interest with his fiancée faded, so he, too, avoided intimate references.

§ § §

When mail call rolled around, Roger made the excuse that he had to polish his boots. A British Royal Air Force officer handed him a container. "Chap, melted beeswax produces a brilliant shine. Try it."

Roger found an isolated spot. He dabbed a small amount of wax between his hands, rolled to warm it, then wrapped a small piece of cotton sock around his index finger. He applied a thin layer to his boot, spat on its toe, and continued brushing. Beeswax did the trick. He admired the work with a satisfied smile.

"Lookie! For the Lieutenant." Bruno rushed to him, waving a small parcel wrapped with a note attached to a string bow. He took liberty to read the card: *Thank you for saving my Joey. I pray you and your crew stay safe, Giana.*

Roger snatched the note and package, and grumbled. "Don't you have work to do?"

Reading the note penned in a lady's penmanship, a grin flickered across his face. He brought the small, wrapped package to his nose, imagined a whiff of sweet perfume, and kissed the paper covering.

Roger noticed Bruno astonished stare and threw the beeswax tin in his direction. "Get lost! Damn it, get lost!"

Bruno apologized. Roger yelled in a louder and more commanding voice, "I said get lost and I meant it."

Alone, Roger opened the package. The handkerchiefs discarded at the hospital lay inside. They were scrubbed clean, and folded. He rubbed them over his cheeks and brought them to his nose, taking in the fresh scent.

What a mood changer! Forget the beeswax. Polished boots could not be measured against the joy Giana's thoughtful surprise brought him. He pictured his new lady friend as her gentle hands massaged and worked over each fiber to bring the blood-soaked pieces of cloth back to life. The image served as an aphrodisiac.

He returned to the crew's tent. Immediately, Bruno pivoted from him. *Wouldn't my bombardier be stunned to learn my outrage involved military issued handkerchiefs.* Lying on his wooden cot, he thought about the nurse, smiled, and dreamed on.

The Grande Room

Chapter 7

Bad weather over German airspace cancelled their mission. Roger and his crew were forced to wait another day for a bombing run. The break in the day's routine gave Roger time to search for and thank Giana for refurbishing the handkerchiefs.

He wanted to repay the Puglia family for their hospitality. Remembering the story of the Basilica de San Nicolas, he considered playing Santa Claus. He could pull it off by gathering US Army rations and accessory items.

The winds brought in cold, rainy weather. Roger pulled up his collar, tilted his crushed cap over his forehead, and made his way to the clinic. He dodged puddles forming on the sidewalks and ducked in and out from under roof overhangs. Pausing at the clinic's entrance, the ieutenant took off his coat and shook the water off.

After weaving through the hallway's medical activities, Roger located Joey sweeping the floor. The kid spotted him, dropped the broom, and ran as if greeting a long-lost relative. Roger embraced the kid, still sporting the remnants of a colorful black eye.

"I told my friends an American pilot saved my life."

An orderly wheeled a patient down the corridor. Roger steered Joey way from hospital traffic. He looked directly into

Joey's eyes and saw himself as a youngster, full of hope and fearlessness.

"Do you understand what the word promise means?" he asked.

Joey nodded.

"Promise not to sneak around hangars. You may get hurt if I'm not there to help you."

"Promise, promise," Joey echoed.

"Joey, I'm serious. Just remember, when you make a promise, you must keep it," Roger said in a sharp voice with his hand over his heart. "Now say, I promise to stay away from hangars and other dangerous areas."

Joey stared at the floor. After a moment, he eyed the lieutenant and placed his hand over his heart. "I promise. I promise to stay away from hangars, uh..." He gave a mischievous grin and let his hand fall from his heart, "until I become a bomber pilot, like you."

Roger eyeballed him. "You're a little devil. Just stay safe. Now, where's your mom?"

Joey pointed down the corridor. "The Grande Room, but she is only one there."

Roger headed to the desired destination. The door was ajar, he glanced inside without knocking. There she was. Excitement percolated within him. He knew she was Catholic and he a Jew. The difference did not diminish the sensual attraction within him.

Resting his eyes on a real lady trumped staring at the static art pinups on the nose of bomber planes. Bruno designed the artwork for Roger's B-17 with the caption, "Forget-Me-Not," above a voluptuous girl. She floated on a white fluffy cloud in a revealing red swimsuit, puckering her bright red heart-shaped lips, and winking.

Giana stood in front of the mostly emptied medical cabinet, documenting, and rearranging the surgical supplies. Roger took a moment to study her clear, olive complexion, no makeup. She wore her brown hair tied in a ponytail with a colorful scarf the last time he saw her. It surprised him that he remembered the details.

Today, she appeared disheveled. Strands of hair reached out around her face and randomly poked from her bun. When she brushed her hair, Roger guessed it must be close to shoulder length. He wondered why he was so attracted to this woman.

He tapped on the door. Giana jerked and stood. They locked gazes and, for a few seconds, neither moved.

Awkwardly, he blurted, "Thanks for returning the clean handkerchiefs."

"Handkerchiefs like new, no?" She raised her eyebrows.

Roger feigned interest as she explained Nonna was active with the Women's Resistance Movement. She added that was part of the anti-Nazi resistance. "Some cooked, some washed clothes." Her pride was obvious. "She scrubbed blood stains from clothing. Made them good again."

"An impressive job."

"Please, please," Giana pulled a chair from under the table. "Put your coat here." Together, they gathered her materials, and when Roger handed her the medical dictionary, their hands touched. Her face grew red, like last time. Quickly, she walked to the bookcase and placed the materials on the shelf.

They spent a few moments in polite conversation, talked about Joey, the weather, her in-laws.

Roger sat across from Giana and wondered if she shared a similar tenderness toward him.

To break an uncomfortable moment, Roger glanced around the tiny room and chuckled, "So, this is what's called the Grande Room?"

"Yes, yes. We laugh. It is tiny, but Dr. Gadaleta named it."

When idle chatter slowed, Roger broke the silence. "Oh, by the way, I passed several shops. I saw loaves of Pane di Monte Sant' Angelo hanging from their windows."

"My countrymen say bread benefits them."

Roger cocked his head and smiled at Giana's choice of the word 'benefits.' *Why not? Bread offered sustenance to cultures throughout ages ... a benefit. A real benefit.*

Each attempted to break the unease that followed. And each time, they tripped over unfinished thoughts. They laughed at the silliness of the situation.

Roger recalled the reason for his visit. "May I play Santa Claus for your family this afternoon?"

Stunned, Giana quickly responded, "But, early for your Santa, no?"

"I'm not sure I'll be stationed here for the real day."

Swallowing hard, Giana dropped her eyes. "This war makes everything so..."

He patted her small, soft hands. "My family is Jewish. We do not observe the Christmas. But I appreciate the season's good-will-to-all closeness and would enjoy playing Santa."

Giana held tightly to Roger's hands. "Of course. It will be nice for my family. And for me, too."

So, now she knows I'm a Jew. I don't think it matters. He released her hands and grabbed his coat.

Giana invited him to dinner.

"Just like Santa," he said. "I only have time to drop off gifts." He drew her close and planted a soft kiss on her cheek.

"I pray for you and your crew. I pray you stay safe." With a gentle smile, she said, "Ciao."

Roger leaned against the Grande Room's closed door to quiet his racing heart. It took a few deep breaths. Putting on his serious Air Force pilot demeanor, he walked through the crowded corridor. A smile creeped over his face.

§ § §

Roger entered the bakery shop. Sparse offerings were on display. Several shelves remained empty. A few loaves of Pane di Monte Sant' Angelo hung in the window. He pointed and purchased two. At the base, he traded slices with his crew in exchange for an assortment of tokens to fill his modest Santa's bag.

When he arrived at the Puglia's home, Joey greeted him. He swung open the door. After the usual pleasantries, Roger dug into his bag and began his role as Santa.

First, he pulled out treats for the ladies, Wrigley's spearmint gum, peanut and fruit bars, and sweet chocolates. Papa received small packages of Lucky Strikes, Chesterfields, and Camels. A big smile stretched over his leathery face. He immediately offered one to Roger, who politely refused.

Joey opened several Air Crew boxes with hard candy packed inside. He shook the small pieces from the boxes and studied the emptied containers for a long time, turning them over and over. The Air Force insignia on the boxes meant as much to him as the sweet morsels.

A whimsical moment occurred when Roger prepared to leave. He shook hands and slipped Papa a small packet of toilet paper, a provision included in the servicemen's ration kits. He winked at Papa, thinking the item would be shown once he made his exit.

Papa threw his head back and laughed merrily. He handed the special gift to his wife. Nonna pulled out a single tissue and caressed it against her cheek. Giana translated as her mother spoke, "We show to our neighbors."

Nonna ran forward, kissing Roger's cheeks.

Giana fluttered her fingers in the air, "Ciao."

He thought about blowing her a kiss, but felt the eyes of her in-laws planted on him. In his dreams he would fantasize a more passionate, romantic ending for the evening.

He sauntered back to the barracks radiating confidence. Two nights with the Puglia family would serve as memorable moments. *I must learn Italian because after the war, I will return to Bari.*

Pray for Us

Chapter 8

Roger rolled out of the bunk ready to face the mission. In predawn darkness, he headed for the Mess tent. After breakfast, the crew jumped into the military truck hauling them to their Flying Fortress.

On board, each man ran through his preflight routine preparing for a long mission— wheels up, and away they went.

Their engagement against the enemy was intense. Approaching the target in tightly packed formation, a direct hit by German flak brought down the B-17 next to the Forget-Me-Not. The injured big bird burst into flames and headed into open fields.

Bruno caught sight of airmen clinging to their parachutes, floating in the sky. He counted to himself, *one, two, three, four men*. He murmured, "Dear Jesus, please watch over and keep 'em from enemy hands. And Baby Jesus, please lead us safely back to our base."

Mission completed, they headed home through a blanket of enemy shells and fragments. Much of it hit into the air as the lieutenant struggled to maintain his plane in a level and rigid formation. *My sweet Giana, I've almost forgotten how to pray, and, in fact right now, I'm too scared. Deadly flak is exploding all around us. I'm counting on you to get out your rosary beads. We need all the help we can get. And now!*

The crew returned safely, but the aircraft suffered heavy damages.

"Sonofabitch!" A member from the ground staff greeted them. "You guys took off in a beautiful cigar-shaped fuselage. What the hell happened? Never mind. I got the picture."

§ § §

After debriefing, and a couple swallows of scotch, the crew returned to their quarters. Roger pulled out a pack of cigarettes. Staring at it, he remarked, "Right now, I'd trade all my cigarettes for just one soft bialy. There's a shop down our block in Syracuse. They offer the best bialys. I'd fill the center with onions and poppy seeds and sometimes I'd go for a second one with lox and cream cheese."

The men picked up the theme of their favorite home-town foods.

Billy, homesick for his mother's cooking, extended an open invitation for his buddies to stop by and enjoy a slice of her buttermilk cornbread. "She bakes it from her grandmother's recipe and in that same old original cast iron skillet. Her cornbread perks up any dish on the table. I'll see to it she'll cook up a bowl of her original chuck wagon chili to go along with it. There's nothin' like it."

Frank added, "Shit! Come to Coney Island and I'll treat you guys to an overstuffed sandwich, a hero—stuffed with meats and smothered with oil and vinegar. I'll take you to Defante's where they make their own hero bun. In fact, I'd just gobble down the crisp bun by itself. It's that good."

Bruno worked in his family's New Orleans deli shop in the French Quarter. In front of the group, he assembled his imaginary epicurean delight, a muffuletta. "Start with bread and then da meat." He slapped a pretend slice onto his opened, left palm. Plopping one ingredient on top of the other, he instructed, "Den I lay down an assortment of cheeses, provolone, and mozzarella. Next goes da pepperoni and da salami."

He licked his lips. "And here's my olive oil mixture." He gripped an imaginary bottle and sprinkled the seasoning over the improvised pile. "Y'all want to know our secret ingredient?"

Looking side to side, he leaned into the group, answering his own question. "Our secret recipe passed down from generation to generation—da wide, round, crusty loaf of bread we bake daily on our premises." He nodded to Roger. "It looks sort of like dat Pane di Monte Sant' Angelo you got for us." Then with a nod to Frank. "Like dat hero sandwich of yours, if ya don't have good bread, you don't have a good sandwich, right Frank?"

The men plopped on their cots and enjoyed quiet moments remembering the neighborhood specialty waiting for them on their return.

The image of Giana lingered with Roger. Someone must have been watching over him and his crew during their recent encounter with German flak towers. He gave the credit to the Italian nurse's prayers. Inside his flight bag, he had tucked away a U.S. Army G.I.'s sewing kit, affectionately known as the 'housewife.' He grabbed it and left the barracks, humming, "At Last," and burst out in song, "*My love has come ...*"

A private saluted and raised an eyebrow when Roger cruised past him. The soldier shook his head.

Roger picked up his pace, almost running.

A Jeep eased beside him and Roger recognized the passenger, Edwin "Ted" Cleland, officer in charge of the surgical division. Ted hollered, "You look like you're in a hurry. I'm headed to The Polyclinic but need to stop off at the harbor first. Want to hop in the back?"

"Yep. I want to see a special lady at the clinic."

"Your *angioletto*?"

"How do you spell that?"

"Man, it's not how you spell it, but how you say it that counts. I'm hoping it means, my little angel. Been saying it to many Italian ladies and haven't been smacked yet."

"My angioletto … well, I'll try it and see where it gets me."

The driver merged into traffic headed to the harbor. A truck barreled past as they approached the bustling facility, dust and debris swirled around. The roar of engines made conversation difficult. Sporting dark circles under his eyes, Ted turn to the passenger and yelled, "We still lack medical supplies and equipment."

"Sounds serious." Roger offered his friend a smoke.

The medic tapped the cigarette on his thumb nail, fingernails bitten to their quick, cuticles cracked and dried. "Damn man, it is serious. We're short on everything from surgical instruments to dressings to blood plasma." Ted took a long inhale and then exhaled. "Shit. Did I mention cots, forceps, surgical masks, sponges … just name it..."

The driver inched ahead looking for a parking space. Impatient, Ted flicked his cigarette out the Jeep and shouted above the clatter. "Pull over. I can run to the main office from here." He hopped from the Jeep as the driver eased to a stop. "Won't take long." And he was off and running.

Roger looked over the harbor. Allied ships lined each pier, waiting to unload. Within minutes, Ted appeared, shoulders rounded, head down, a hand over his nose blocking dust, dirt, and foreign particles. He hopped back into the Jeep. "Get a move on it," he barked at the driver.

They drove in silence until Ted continued with his litany of supplies. "Dammit, where are my hospital beds, my surgical supplies, and my goddamned medicines? Time's running out.

I'm telling you. We all may be shot and dead before I get my supplies."

§ § §

Walking through the Polyclinic hallways, Ted's words, *Time's running out,* nagged at Roger. Military life was unpredictable. The possibility of death hovered over them all. Roger and his crew could be wiped out with one direct hit on the Forget-Me-Not.

Roger knocked on the Grande Room door and was cheered when Giana answered with a smile. He grabbed her by the wrist and twirled her. "Your prayers worked!" Then he sat her down, bending close to her. "You must promise to pray every day for me and my crew. Do you promise?"

"But I do already."

He planted a soft kiss on her forehead. "You are my *angioletto.*"

"Angioletto," the nurse smiled. "You learn Italian?"

"I'm learning I'm falling in love with you. That's what I'm learning." He presented her with the sewing kit. "I know it's not romantic, but it's the best I could get my hands on … a token thank you for your prayers and for watching over me and my crew."

Giana opened the small package, placing each item on the table, metal scissors, needles, safety pins, buttons, and a thimble.

Without knocking, a nurse flew into the room. She looked first to Giana, then to the Roger, and momentarily stared at the table. Each time Giana attempted an introduction, the intruder interrupted, shouting in Italian. She shoved the sewing tools into a pile and dumped a handful of files in its place. Finishing her monologue, the nurse directed a series of harsh-sounding Italian words at the lieutenant. She left as quickly as she entered.

41

Roger said, "I don't think she likes me." After that remark, he sensed something was wrong.

"She came to tell me to expect combat injured personnel. They're coming from the north and arriving by train. We need to prepare."

Still puzzled, Roger asked, "But she wasn't happy seeing me here."

Giana chuckled. "She looked at the thread and needles and told you to learn how to sew on your own buttons and, not to waste my time."

Their laughter lessened the seriousness of the situation.

Roger cast a playful grin in her direction. "Well, I have no plans to learn how to sew buttons. You hold onto that sewing kit as my excuse to keep visiting my angioletto." He grasped her shoulders and leaned her against the door. "One kiss and I'll leave you to your preparations." Bracing his boot against the door, he blocked visitors from sudden entry. He wrapped his arms around Giana, and both engaged in a long, romantic embrace, followed by a series of heartfelt kisses.

Roger sauntered back to the barracks. Reflecting on the randomness of the global military conflict, his euphoric mood was dampened. *Countries invaded one another. Generals discussed strategy. Opposing foes found new allegiances. Service men and women fought and died. Bombs continually hit or missed their targets. Civilians were caught in the middle. Doctors and nurses cared for battle casualties.*

Under his breath, he mumbled, "When will this hell ever end?"

A Tour with Joey

Chapter 9

Every unit faced shortages. Daylight strikes were cancelled, and not because of the weather. There was not enough fuel to reach targets and return to the airfield.

Taking advantage of the break, Roger rushed to The Polyclinic. His fondness for Giana escalated into a strong romantic attraction. He wondered if it was love at first sight. Regardless, he willingly embraced the powerful and emotional force consuming his entire being.

He stopped in front of the Grande Room to catch his breath, then peeked through the open door. Giana sat with a dictionary and medical books open, flipping from one page to the next. Roger walked in and gestured for her to stay seated. He stood behind her, massaging her shoulders. "Dr. Gadaleta is keeping you busy."

Giana glanced up and tenderly squeezed his fingers. "It is good. I learn more English." She motioned for him to join her.

Roger took off his leather jacket and straddled the chair across from her. "I couldn't wait to see you." Giana's eyes sparkled as Roger continued, "This afternoon our commander scheduled a radio conference. After that, I'm free. I would like to take Joey up on his offer to show me the Basilica."

Giana began, "Joey will like —"

Roger took his forefinger and held it on her lips. She stared straight into his eyes.

"Angioletto, I'm falling in love with you and I don't want to lose precious time. I'm hoping you share a similar attraction. Do you?"

"Yes, but it is quick. Joey does not know. Nonna and Papa do not know."

"I didn't know until I was walking … no … running here. I've never felt this way and I like the emotion, the sensation, the caring … all of it and I want to keep these feelings and keep them with you."

"I, too, want to keep all with you."

With a broad smile, he said, "And I want to talk with your family … ask them if I can see you, just be with you, just you and me, alone and not at the clinic."

A blush crept over Giana's face. Staring without speaking, her brown eyes grew wider and wider.

For a moment, Roger felt he stepped over the boundaries of polite society. "Isn't that the proper way things are done here?"

"But— but—"

Roger glanced at the desk and grabbed paper and a pen and handed them to her. "Giana, I want to do the right thing. I want to ask your family if I could speak with them right after I return from the cathedral with Joey. I want their permission to see you, have a date with you. Can you write them a note and get it to them?"

"Yes, I can do that."

Roger rubbed his chin. "Please ask if we can all meet right after the tour."

With a chuckle in her voice, Giana responded, "If Nonna and Papa do not like the idea of a meeting, they may not let you leave with Joey."

Instinctively, Roger reached for her hands and clasped them. "Uh, yes, well, you pray. I'm off to my meeting and then I'll pick up Joey. We'll see what happens."

Giana held his jacket and helped him wiggle his arms through the sleeves. Slowly, she zippered him in. Roger took her by the shoulders, and held her for a few extra seconds, covered her forehead with soft kisses.

Giana tiptoed closer, cupped his face between her hands, and planted a passionate kiss directly on his mouth.

Roger left with a big smile, humming "At last..."

Ships need to Unload

Chapter 10

The press sat in the reserved area and photographers readied their cameras. Roger and Bruno scanned the smoked-filled room for seats, found none, so they stood in the back squeezed between members of the Royal Air Force.

Small packets of cigarettes were handed out immediately after the radio conference. At first Bruno ignored the give-away, Roger reminded him, "take a pack and stop bumming mine."

Bruno lit up and said, "Can you believe the commander said he would consider it a insult if the enemy should send even one plane over our city."

"The port would be a mess with all the ships needing to unload."

"The movie starts in a few minutes," Bruno changed the subject. "Let's grab a soda. Don't like subtitles, but it's free."

"You go ahead. I'm going to tour the Basilica."

§ § §

Not knowing the kind of welcome he may receive, Roger stood tall as he knocked on the Puglia's door. Joey, at the ready, swung open the door. The lieutenant noticed Giana's note, in Italian, laid crumbled on the dining room table.

A powerful bear hug gripped him. Turning, he discovered it was Nonna wiping tears from her cheeks speaking in Italian.

Joey translated, "These are her happy tears. And she

wants us to be safe and come back soon.”

“Happy. Happy. Happy,” Papa Puglia nodded, supporting his wife’s sentiment.

Roger placed his hand over his heart and gave assurance to the grandparents. “I am happy, too, and I promise I will take good care of Joey.”

“Nonna, look!” Joey put his hand over his heart. “This means he made a promise.”

She reached inside her apron, drew out her rosary, and kissed the crucifix.

Joey grasped Roger’s arm and pulled him close. He whispered, “My Nonna always prays the rosary.”

Papa reached up, clasped his hands around the lieutenant’s shoulders. “Come after church mass. We talk.”

That, indeed, is a good sign.

Nonna cupped Roger’s cheeks, her rosary tapping against his face. “We see you later. Che dio la benedica.”

Joey translated, “Nonna says, *may God bless you.*” Squeezing Roger’s hand, the kid and lieutenant headed for the iconic Basilica San Nichola.

§ § §

Once inside, Roger stared at its massive granite columns and arcades with an impressive, gilded 17th century wooden ceiling. While the lieutenant paused in front of numerous statues to soak up the history of the sacred house of worship, Joey shifted from foot to foot.

“Lieutenant, you need to read everything?”

Finally, Joey dragged Roger from the first floor to the underground level where the crypt and remains of St. Nicholas were located. Joey yanked Roger’s hands, moving him from one artifact to the next. The lieutenant picked up the pace, planning to return on his own at another time.

"Hey, Joey, I have an idea. Let's grab a soda. How about it?"

§ § §

Giana left the hospital and tucked her ponytail, tied with her colorful scarf, inside her snood. If she pedaled at full speed, she'd have time to help with last minute arrangements and freshen up before dinner. The thought of being in Roger's presence energized her.

Why was she so attracted to this foreigner? Was it his good looks, bright smile, commanding mannerisms? When she thought of their relationship developing, she shook her head.

She remembered he had mentioned he was Jewish. The Italian Racial Manifesto, a law unpopular with her family and herself, stripped Jews of many rights, including marriage between Italians and Jews.

Giana prayed Nonna and Papa would approve the idea of their mutual attraction by allowing them time to develop a long-lasting commitment. And possibly, marriage? She was dumbfounded even thinking that thought … but the thought made her smile.

§ § §

Roger and Joey made good time heading toward the Puglia's' home. "Your Nonna will be relieved we get home on time."

"Lieutenant," Joey said, "Nonna always worries. And prays the rosary. Always."

Roger lit up a cigarette and took a long drag. "Your Nonna finds comfort with praying." He blew out the match. "Your grandparents, they've lived through dangerous times. They want you to grow up in a free society …"

Abruptly, he tuned in the sounds of aircraft. He stood confused. What began as a faint rumble of planes became increasingly louder. Roger and Joey looked to the skies.

Roger whispered, "Those aren't ours!"

Scores of German Ju-88 Luftwaffe bombers flew into Italian airspace in a direct course for the city.

Flicking a half-smoked cigarette onto the cobblestone street, he grabbed Joey. The hellish uproar of bombs made direct contact with a target—ships docked at Bay of Bari. The sky lit up like the fourth of July. Sirens wailed.

Joey's fear was reflected in his eyes and wide-open mouth. He looked upward, back to Roger, and again, to the sky.

The lieutenant dragged Joey under a staircase, shielding him from flying glass, debris, and shrapnel. Trembling, Joey hung tightly to Roger's leather jacket. Screams blended with the cacophony of noises from planes, bombs falling, and crumbling buildings.

Roger yelled, "We're under attack! Do you understand?"

"I'm scared."

"Get home. It's not far from here." Roger held up Joey's head and looked him in the eyes. "Be careful and stay low." The lieutenant wiped tears from the kid's cheeks. "You can do it. I need to return to my men. I promise, I will return for you. Tell your mom… tell your family, I love them."

Joey threw his arms around Roger. Streetlights flickered, and then went dark.

§ § §

Roger dashed in the direction of the airfield and met his crew running in the opposite direction. Billy, out of breath, yelled, "Commander, the German bombs took out our aircraft. All hands to the harbor. Everyone to aid in the rescue effort."

The lieutenant rushed to the sight of crewmen directing heavy fire hoses over burning cargo ships. Several explosions occurred. He waded out in the waters and pulled seamen from the oil slick bay.

Wobbling on his feet, he faltered. His eyes burned and his itching became pronounced. With slurred speech, he had difficulty signaling for help. He fell to the ground, gasping for breath.

§ § §

A short distance from home, Giana reversed directions, turned her bike, and followed the rising plume of black smoke spewing from the port. She gathered with residents on the promenade that circled the water and stared at the other end of the bay. They were frightened by the sound of bombs. Their city was under attack.

"Over here! Swimmers here and now!" a self-appointed leader barked as he balanced on a walking stick.

Giana advanced in that direction, he held her back. "Nurses," pointing his cane to the triage set up, "over there."

"I'm a nurse and a skilled swimmer. Many medical personnel are working that area. If you need a swimmer, here I am."

In the middle of the bay, a seaman, balancing on a slippery wooden beam, yelled at the top of his voice. "Help. I'm burning. Help me."

Untying her nurse's white shoes, Giana ignored the leader's concern. Seeing she was determined, he took off his jacket and said, "Here. Have him hold on the sleeve and you just pull him to shore. Be careful. He may grab and pull you under. We don't want to send a rescue group for you."

She jumped into the water nearing the seaman. He teetered, thrashed his arms, and landed next to Giana. Seconds were important and handing the victim the garment was impractical. Remembering a successful technique from years ago, she swam behind, grabbed his chin, and propelled him near the embankment.

A group of by-standers formed a human chain to assist with the rescue. They took over and inched the exhausted man to safety. After a few deep breathes, he shouted praise for his savior. "She's my hero. She's a real hero."

Giana's scarf drifted a few feet from her. Another blast from the cargo boats didn't deter her from retrieving her hair decoration. She felt a sharp object, a piece of shrapnel, the side of her neck. Blood splattered from the artery. Rapid inhaling and exhaling prevented her from shouting for help.

§ § §

Joey stumbled through the rummage of the Puglia's neighborhood to find his grandparents. Unfortunately, they were not among the residents returning home from Mass. They perished under tons of wreckage.

He rushed toward The Polyclinic searching for his mother, pushing through confused and disoriented crowds. Joey waded through the wounded pouring into the emergency entrance. He couldn't find her, and finally a nurse waved to him.

She pulled him into a small doorway. She told him that his mother was struck by shrapnel assisting in a rescue mission. She drowned before the crews could rescue her from the burning water.

Be proud. That's what the nurse told him. *Her final act was that of a true hero, saving the life of a Merchant Marine.*

Joey pushed her away,

"That's not true. She's a good swimmer." Choked up, he continued, "And I don't care if she is a hero. She's my mom and I want her here. Here, right next to me."

Dr. Gadaleta

Chapter 11

Dr. Gadaleta arranged for Joey to stay in the Grande Office and continue janitorial tasks. The youngster grabbed one more duty, caring for Roger recuperating on a hospital cot in a long, narrow ward crowded with injured men. A straight-back metal chair, next to the lieutenant's bed, was set up for him.

During the night, Joey wriggled and squirmed, unable to find a comfortable position. His neck, shoulders, and back all ached. Calls for nurses, traffic noise from orderlies rushing in and out of the area, moans, and coughs, added to the unpleasant circumstances. The fear of losing the lieutenant overwhelmed him. He curled himself under Roger's cot and found solace reciting the rosary.

Many patients exhibited common symptoms of blisters, eye irritation, burns, and respiratory issues. Originally, the medical teams were unsure of the condition. Finally, they announced their diagnosis. The men suffered from exposure to mustard gas.

Joey learned to clean and change Roger's dressing every three to four days. To avoid corneal damage to the eyes, as instructed, he applied petroleum jelly on his eyelids.

§ § §

Whenever Joey attempted to talk about the loss of his family, Roger shut him down. In his scratchy voice the lieutenant said, "It's over. We move on."

Obediently, the kid abided by these wishes. Confused, Joey shared his concern with Dr. Gadaleta. Hearing that account, the surgeon decided to meet with the lieutenant.

Roger came out of a drug-induced sleep and felt a strong, but boney hand smoothing his. He blinked his eyes and, with effort, held them open. He stared at a tall, thin-framed visitor in wrinkled white medical garb dotted with blood stains. Beneath his bloodshot eyes, dark bags sunk to his cheek bones.

"Lieutenant, excuse me for waking you," the man whispered. "I am Dr. Gadaleta."

Roger squeezed his hand, recalling the name, from conversations with Giana.

In broken English, he said, "Lieutenant, please do not strain your voice, but I tell you." He released one hand and pointed a forefinger to his chest. "She told me, say, 'Lieutenant fits in my heart.' Capisce?"

"How is she? Can I see her? Tell me, where is she?"

With the palm of his hand, the doctor wiped a tear from his eye.

"Doctor, tell me everything. I need to know."

Respecting the lieutenant's wishes, the surgeon continued with a short narrative covering most details about her last moments.

He painted the picture that she jumped into churning waters, grabbed, and saved the life of a U.S. soldier. The doctor swallowed to clear a lump in his throat.

"Go on, please. Please, go on."

"Before Giana swam to safety," he said as his grip on Roger's hand grew heavier. But he continued. "Shrapnel hit an artery." He pointed to his neck. "Her body floated to shore."

"But, doctor, why did they let her do that? Why did she jump into the bay? She never told me she could swim."

"Yes, yes, yes. Our little friend was beach lover and good in water."

"That's not right. I'm the warrior, not her. I should have died." Straining his voice as he attempted to sit, forced words through his windpipe. "Doctor, do you understand? I should be the one to die. Me, not her."

"Excuse me. You're needed in the surgical unit," announced an American orderly, hurrying to the doctor's side.

"Uno memento," the doctor refocused on the patient. Before he moved on, the surgeon wanted to ease the terrible thoughts that overcame Roger. "The Puglia family loved you. Now, you … Now, you keep memories of Giana and Nonna and Papa. Okay? Share your memories."

"It hurts so much to just think about what you told me. But, yes. I will try."

"Grazie." The doctor patted Roger's hands and hastened to the emergency.

A team of nurses began the morning routine, passing out breakfast items and medication to their charges. One stopped by Roger's bedside. She offered her troubled-looking patient comforting words. "Lieutenant, you are still a young man and have much to look forward to." She handed Roger his food along with an assortment of medicine. "One day this terror will be over. Your job is to get healthy." The nurse continued with her duties.

Roger looked toward the ceiling. Cupid's golden arrow struck his heart and left him emotionally wounded. *Angioletto, you were a beautiful lady who captured my heart.*

He uttered Angioletto again and again, not concerned if others heard him. The soldier next to his bed stopped eating.

"Hey, lieutenant, you keep talking to yourself about this angel. Is she your sweetheart?"

"She was my first true love. She really was." Roger looked at his unopened breakfast items. He handed them to his hospital mate. "Here. I'm not hungry."

When Joey returned from his janitorial duties and plopped in his bedside chair, Roger turned his tear-stained face from the kid.

§ § §

A modest service was held in the Basilica to honor those who lost their lives—military and civilians—during the bombing. The commemoration began with opening remarks, followed by a prayer, a bugler performed "Taps," and a ceremonial laying of a wreath. The ceremony ended with the national anthems of the Allies.

Joey stood next to Roger's wheelchair, each absorbed in thought. Roger did not shed a tear, so Joey attempted to hold back his, but with the first notes of "Taps," the youngster abandoned that noble idea. A nurse surreptitiously handed him a handkerchief.

§ § §

As he healed, the lieutenant thought about his future. His infatuation with Giana overwhelmed him, and he neglected his commitment to Nancy. Roger became obsessed with the last words he spoke to the Puglia family: *I promise to take care of Joey.*

He grew fond of the kid. He could adopt him and give meaning to his life, a touchstone to Nonna, Papa, and, especially, Giana.

After much thought, he developed a path to follow. Roger scribbled a note and asked an orderly to get it to Dr. Gadaleta. The message read:

I want to adopt Joey as my son. Will you help?

55

Dr. Gadaleta held the note and rushed through the hospital's hallway to Roger's bedside. He took a minute to catch his breath before he said, "Lieutenant, Giana looks down to you. She throws kisses on you."

They mapped out a plan. "I must contact the Puglia relatives," the doctor suggested. "If they okay, we move on."

Roger fought back his tears, tears of joy and hope.

§ § §

Once Dr. Gadaleta gathered the necessary information, he reported to Roger, who sat in his wheelchair twisting his hands. The doctor put on his eyeglasses and prepared notes:

Able-bodied members from the Puglia family are... He stumbles with the word. *dis...dispersed in areas around their damaged city. None have the means to take Joey or provide him with a proper education.* He brought the paper closer to his eyes and smiled. *His closest kin agree with Dr. Gadaleta that Joey should be adopted by Lieutenant Roger Atkins and educated in the USA, land of the free and home of opportunities.*

Roger erupted with gratitude. "Doctor, I couldn't ask for better news. I thank you and your associate."

"Wait, wait, my friend." He returned to his notes. "They demand a ..." looking closer to the word he practiced, "a caveat be included. Joey is to be brought up a Catholic."

Roger swallowed deeply and admitted, "I never thought about that." He stared blankly at the floor.

An uncomfortable moment followed while the doctor tapped his rolled-up notes on his opened hand. The longer the silence, the more rapid the thumping.

Finally, Roger hit the arm rest of the wheelchair. "Well then, I'll see to it that Joey continues his religion."

Dr. Gadaleta prayed for that decision. "Yes, yes, yes, Lieutenant. We can do it and I got good plan." He explained that years ago his young brother, Martino, immigrated to the United States and serves as pastor of St. Aloysius Catholic Church in Queens, New York. Members of his church work closely with Catholic Action, an organization to promote social justice. Finding a good home for an Italian orphan might be a cause they would support.

"You get better," the doctor instructed. "I contact my brother."

Buoyed by the doctor's enthusiasm, Roger relaxed. He requested that, out of respect for Giana, their relationship toward each other be kept a private matter.

Atkins Family

Chapter 12

In December1943, Roger's correspondence with his parents stopped. Their concern for his welfare grew intense. Questions filled agonizing hours—was their precious son injured or dead? Was his plane and crew shot down over a mountain range? Shot down behind enemy territory?

Winter welcomed Syracuse, New York, residents with another dump of fresh snow on top of the dirty, slushy accumulation. Herman Atkins pulled the Venetian blind cord and fixed his gaze out the front window. He parked himself on his leather armchair with old issues of *The Post Standard* and the *Syracuse-Herald Journal* newspapers stacked beside the coffee table.

Herman continued his daily vigil, staring out the front window. His wife replenished his coffee throughout the day and tried to chat with him. He found little relief with the surface conversation.

Herman waited for a Western Union messenger with a special delivery telegram: a death notification. Perhaps Rabbi Kohut with the Reform Congregation would be the one to soften their loss. Relatives and friends visited, tried to distract them, brought them food, listened to their concerns, and prayed.

Roger's fiancée did not join when her parents paid their respects. Mrs. Atkins confided in a close friend, "That's strange but maybe Nancy is too distraught thinking or fearing the worst happened to her intended."

The Atkins rejoiced when they received news that Roger was at The Polyclinic in Bari, Italy, recovering from injuries. They also learned a young Italian boy named Joey administered to his care. Their gratitude toward the boy, they never met, erupted into overwhelming appreciation. Their joy continued when they learned Roger would soon return home.

§ § §

The wounded pilot decided to be frank about his intentions to adopt Joey. Nancy needed time to comprehend the huge responsibility asked of her. His writing must be clear. A first draft, second, third, and finally, Roger was satisfied with his detailed letter. He ended with *Please take your time. I accept your decision. Best, Roger.*

Roger informed his parents of his letter to Nancy and his plan to adopt the Italian boy. He wrote it was not an idle wish and was determined to take charge of Joey either in the United States or, when peace declared, he would return and seek residency in Bari.

§ § §

Nancy immediately telephoned her friend. "Marian, I'm getting married. I said yes to Roger's idea of adopting a kid. Because of this terrible war and our men getting shot up, we don't have many opportunities."

Preparing for a wedding absorbed her activities. She busied herself trading dresses and accessories with girlfriends in readiness for the big event.

Mrs. Atkins was sympathetic to her son's wishes. One afternoon she rushed home, stomped snow from her boots, and hurried inside, abruptly waking her husband from a nap. "My volunteer wartime activities are paying off!" She yanked off her gloves and slipped the hatpin from her felt hat. "We must help Roger."

"Help Roger do what?" Herman fumbled for his eyeglasses.

"In their office, I saw pictures of orphans from Italy. Two young children were sleeping, no sheets or blankets, on a makeshift wooden bench right in the middle of a war-torn street." Mrs. Atkins hung her coat on the rack. "There was a skinny little girl waiting in a long line to be measured for a simple cotton uniform. Heartbreaking. Just heartbreaking."

"So?" Herman winced.

"We need to bring Joey to the United States. Then, we'll have both Roger and the little boy." With a spring in her step, she headed to the kitchen singing the popular war-time song, "Ma, I Miss Your Apple Pie."

Herman orchestrated a secret meeting with Nancy. He pointed out that his son would be discouraged with the required red tape and lose interest in an adoption. He continued, "And I assume this crazy idea of his will be denied for at least two reasons."

He was met with dead silence while he took off his spectacles, rubbed the lenses clean, and returned the end pieces behind his ears.

"Number one, that kid's not an infant." Then with a wide grin, Herman offered, "and number two, not even the same religion. Remember, he's a Catholic."

Nancy cried out, "I never believed Roger was serious. What was he thinking! He knows we're Jewish."

"Nancy, Nancy, now listen. There will not be an adoption of the little Wop. Let's get going with the wedding celebration." He winked, "In fact, I keep reminding my son that we want grandchildren, American grandchildren."

In the spring of 1945, Syracuse held a hometown parade in honor of their returning heroes. After the public event, Lieutenant Roger Atkins retreated from the limelight and started looking for a job. He landed one as a mechanic with the Bike Shop. Under his suggestion, the owner changed the name to Orangemen Bike Shop, in honor of the color of Syracuse's athletic teams.

Joey's pending adoption offered the lieutenant a sense of buoyancy and enthusiasm. He warded off frequent flashbacks of Giana by keeping busy. He filed paperwork required by the recently passed G.I. Bill of Rights. One of its provisions included educational benefits for those having served in the military. A college degree promised him better job opportunities.

§ § §

Mr. Atkins opened the August 1945 issue of *Life* magazine and stared at the picture taken in the middle of the crowded New York's Time Square. A navy sailor, celebrating the victory over Japan, V-J Day, landed a dramatic and spontaneous kiss on a stranger in her white nurse's uniform. Herman raised his voice, making sure his wife heard. "Why doesn't our son show romantic affections like that to Nancy. After all, she's his fiancée?"

Mrs. Atkins untied her apron and walked into the living room to examine the article. "Now, you know, Herman. He's readjusting to civilian life. And, you must admit, Nancy's a cold fish."

"Cold fish!" her husband shouted. "Nonsense, she's busy planning a wedding. We

should encourage them to get arrangements moving. I hope Roger remembers I want … I mean, he must know, we want grandchildren."

The following year, guests watched Roger slip a plain gold ring on his bride's finger. Roger was impressive in his military uniform. Nancy looked stunning in her long, white wedding dress with a high neck and puffy sleeves. The newlywed couple settled into a small house located between both sets of parents.

My Son

Chapter 13

Nancy sat in the kitchen sipping coffee and waited for Roger's return from university classes at Syracuse. She sorted through mail fanned out on the breakfast table. When her husband walked in, he gave Nancy a peck on the forehead.

She pulled two letters from the stack of mail and handed them to him. "Here. Those Gadaleta brothers are stirring up something."

Roger first opened Dr. Gadaleta's short note. "Nancy. Listen to this. He's set up tutoring sessions for Joey to improve his English."

Nancy stared at her husband. *Well, don't expect me to learn Italian.*

Roger ripped opened Father Martino's letter. "And listen to this. A member of Father's church worked for Fiorello La Guardia, former mayor of New York. This parishioner is a politician who knows how to short-circuit the immigration process." He pointed to a postscript. "And here. Father writes the mayor is the son of a mixed marriage. La Guardia's own father was baptized a Catholic who married a Jewish woman."

"So, what's that supposed to mean?"

"Nancy, there's a connection like our family's going to be. Joey's a Catholic and we're Jewish. That's all."

She stormed out of the room. "I just hope he doesn't embarrass us, or my family."

§ § §

When a follow-up letter from Father Martino arrived, Nancy and Mariam were on another window-shopping spree. Eager to share the contents of the correspondence, Roger telephoned his parents. "I just received some good news. Will you and dad be there in half an hour?" He hung up and ran to their home.

Herman paced his living room floor muttering, "Finally, a grandchild." The bell rang, and Roger's father jerked open the door. He stretched his neck around his son's broad shoulders. "But where's Nancy? Shouldn't she be the one to share in this good news?"

Mrs. Atkins welcomed her son. He waved the letter back and forth in front of her and sat to catch his breath. Moments later, he blurted out. "Red tape and legal documents are complete. Guardianship is granted, and Joey receives the same status as a child by birth. He's arriving next week. My *son*."

Herman retreated into the kitchen. "Oy vey! This is what you call good news.

Father Martino Gadaleta

Chapter 14

The week passed slowly for Roger. On the day he was to meet Father Gadaleta, he reviewed the file labeled JOEY. Inside contained all the legal paperwork assembled in chronological order. Because the priest's parishioners were active with the Catholic Action Organization, Roger added a postscript.

I promised his Italian relatives I will see to it that Joey is brought up in his faith, a Catholic.

He brewed coffee and, when Nancy entered, he offered her a cup. She sat at the table and pushed the file from her. "Sweetie, I'm planning to help Mariam with her bedspread, the one she's crocheting." She reached for the cream and poured some in her cup. Returning the pitcher, droplets leaked from its lip and landed on the file's cover. She rubbed the damp mark with her napkin, creating a larger smear.

"Nancy, why today?"

"Sweetie, you go on without me to your meeting with that churchperson … What's his name?"

"Nancy," scolded Roger. "He's a Jesuit priest and his name is Father Martino Gadaleta."

"That's right, but you don't need me there. You have my signature on all the papers." Taking another sip, she added, "Joey and I will have lots of time to get to know each other."

She stood and gave Roger a peck on his cheek. "Now, I

need to get ready for Mariam. Don't forget to take a few handkerchiefs for that stubborn cough of yours."

§ § §

Roger drove to Queens and parked in front of St. Aloysius Church. He switched off the engine and ambled past the group of men speaking with Italian-accented English, deep into their Bocce Ball game. In Bari, players introduced the fundamentals to him.

"Want to try?" one of them asked.

"I'd like to, but I have an appointment with Father Gadaleta."

Pointing to Roger, he yelled in Italian to a distinguished looking man in a navy-blue blazer accented with a light blue polka-dot pocket square matching the color of his French long-sleeve shirt held with gold cuff links. With a swagger, the stranger approached Roger extending his hand. "Lieutenant Roger Atkins. No?"

Roger smiled and nodded.

"Well, I'm Filiberto Cetane, known as 'The Captain' to my friends and ..." a gleam in his eyes, "to my political opponents, I'm known by, let's say, a host of other names."

"Happy to meet The Captain," replied Roger.

"I've been asked to entertain you while Father's in the confessional box." The Captain chuckled and took Roger's elbow, ushering him down the pathway toward the rectory's side entrance.

They entered the priest's private study. A variety of pictures hung on one wall. Roger instantly recognized St. Peter's Square in Rome and, in Venice, a gondolier in a blue and white striped shirt piloting the boat down the Grand Canal. On the desk a replica of Michelangelo's statue of David sat near the Pieta, Blessed Mother holding her lifeless son, Jesus.

"Please, please, take a seat." The Captain gestured to the overstuffed sofa, while he slumped in a brown leather chair and crossed his legs.

Father Martino burst into the room. "Welcome, Lieutenant Atkins, welcome."

"It's Roger. I'm pleased to meet you, Father."

Pleasantries completed, the priest added, "Hope you came hungry for an Italian dinner. And your wife?"

Roger made the excuse that Nancy wasn't feeling well. If either the priest or the captain were skeptical of his excuse, neither showed surprise.

They sat around the mahogany table while the housekeeper spread out a meal beginning with a Caprese salad, adding the main dish of lasagna Bolognese and sausage.

The Captain scooped a large serving of each dish while explaining the immigration process. "I assure you that under my direction, it will run smoothly. The three of us will drive to the airport in the morning, not too far from here, and serve as Joey's welcoming committee.

"Now for dessert." Father offered choices of Italian Cannoli and Tiramisu to his guest.

Roger endured another sleepless night as his thoughts drifted back to memories of Giana. A void in his life existed. *I'm hoping Joey's presence will substitute for my lost love.*

Pop

Chapter 15

While waiting at the airport, several men greeted The Captain. He was on familiar territory, asking each about their families, their health, their girlfriends. When Joey's plane landed, his welcoming committee stood together.

As soon as the boy made it through the immigration process, he dropped his cotton tote bag and ran to Roger. After exchanging a long embrace, Roger said, "Joey, you grew a few inches!"

"And, Lieutenant, you have a new pair of glasses."

Squeezing the boy so close to his chest, Joey's hat fell off his head. Roger ruffled Joey's bushy hair, stopping at his hair line. Stitches from the original wound were faint but recognizable.

After making introductions, Roger explained the scar. "A souvenir from our first meeting when I yelled and caused him to fall."

"Lieutenant, it's my badge of honor."

"Joey," interrupted The Captain. "You can now call him father, or dad, or how about just pop?"

"Pop! I like that. Pop." Joey glanced at Roger. "Lieutenant, mind if I call you, Pop?"

"I don't mind at all. Pop sounds good to my ears."

§ § §

On the return trip from Queens to Syracuse, Joey snuggled near his pop, dozing most of the time. When Roger pulled into the driveway, all the house lights were off. Nancy had retired, but left a handwritten note on their kitchen table.

Welcome. I plan to fix you a big breakfast. Sleep tight.

The next morning while mulling around the kitchen, Nancy sneaked a look toward Joey. She forced herself not to stare at the new person at the table. Minimizing the chatter, she busied herself preparing scrambled eggs, lox and bagels, and fried potatoes. She pulled out the pre-cooked crepe from the ice box and added sliced strawberries. Joey devoured everything on his plate.

"Now, Sweetie." Nancy began stacking dirty dishes next to the sink. "I'll handle the cleanup duties while you take our little friend on a shopping spree."

"Thank you. And do I call you mom, or would ..."

"It's Nancy. That's my name."

"Thank you, Nancy," a confused Joey said. "I enjoyed the breakfast." Pop looked as perplexed and patted his son on the back.

She turned on the water. "Now, hurry along. And Roger, don't forget to get him a haircut … and buy him some new clothes."

§ § §

Roger and Joey cruised through the boy's clothing aisles. With the assistance of a saleslady, they selected a variety of long, and short-sleeve shirts, pants, casual and dress wear, pajamas, a robe, and underwear. The saleslady tossed a leather belt in the collection. "I think this will do for a start."

Each toted two large sacks out of the store, exchanging pleasant smiles. They headed for the barber shop. Joey got his hair cut in Roger's classic style—longer on the top, shorter on the sides.

The barber hunted for his can of Brylceem and held it up. "Lieutenant, this will hold his hair down. Okay?"

"Sure," was Roger's quick response.

They left the shop and Joey asked, "Do I look American?"

Holding his son at arm's length, Roger took a long look. "You know, you're not a bad-looking fellow."

They laughed.

Blending In

Chapter 16

Joey faced many challenges blending in with his new family, school, and country. At times, he wondered if he should have stayed in Bari. No avenues were available for him to share his Italian memories. *Veterans, my heroes who freed my country, they don't even speak of their involvement in the war.*

One evening, Herman Atkins took Joey behind his shed. He held tightly on the kid's bony shoulders and stared into young, frightened eyes. "Your father, he has nightmares about your country. He still suffers from war injuries and keeps saying, 'It's over, Move on.' Don't make his life more miserable." He shook the kid. "If you do, I'll see that he sends you back to that wreck town of yours."

At Saint Gregory Middle School for Boys, Joey got needled about his accent and unmanageable hair. He was not interested in playing team sports, a reason some members from the athletic groups picked on him. Instead, he developed friendships with the more intellectually curious students. It was a good fit.

Joey's presence placed an additional burden on Roger's fragile marriage. The expense of a Catholic school education added to Nancy's list of irritations. In time, she took up activities that did not include her husband, or their *little friend.*

§ § §

Roger graduated from Syracuse with a broadcasting degree and was hired as staff liaison, assisting military personnel with their benefits under the G.I. bill. Roger created activities that brought father and son closer. During football and basketball seasons, they were regular fans rooting for the Orangemen.

Joey enthusiastically joined with the cheerleaders' chant, "Let's go Orange! Let's go, Orange!" When the teams lost, Joey mimicked loyal supporters, doubling up, holding his stomach. "I'm bleeding orange. I'm bleeding orange!" Roger laughed and laughed at his son's foolishness.

§ § §

Joey's presence provoked a growing and continual annoyance within the family unit. Roger's mother, ever the peacemaker, tried to maintain harmony. Slurs about Joey's accent, country, and religion slipped from family members on a regular basis, usually when Roger was at work.

Roger's father let it be known he expected his only child to present him with a natural born offspring, or two. All through his life and out of respect, Roger brushed aside his father's snide statements, until he started in on Joey. Roger defended his son as the distance between the men grew.

When Nancy's parents removed themselves from family gatherings, she presented Roger with an ultimatum: "As long as you have him around, you don't have me."

Joey was his son and Roger's lifeline to Giana, and he was not willingly to give this up. It was clear the marriage was over.

He wrote of the breakup to a Syracuse classmate, who moved out west and wrote for the Catholic Associated Press. Roger received an immediate response with an invitation. "Hey, come out to the golden state. I'd like to meet your kid."

The timing was perfect. Joey graduated from middle

school and said farewell to his buddies.

Determined to break the chokehold stifling the man he truly was, Roger piled their belongings inside his Silver Streak Packard sedan and headed west. He designed an itinerary to acquaint his son with American history and introduce him to the highlights of different cities.

Among the sights, he included Independence Hall in Philadelphia, Washington D.C., historic Charleston in South Carolina, and New Orleans, Louisiana.

"Sorry, Mr. Bruno was out of town," said Joey as they continued to Crescent City.

"I should have written to him about our travels. But just one night in New Orleans is not enough."

"You know, Pop. New Orleans is such a lively city. Let's plan to revisit it one day."

"Good idea, son. Good idea."

The long road trip from San Antonio, Texas brought them closer to California. After their stop at the Hoover Dam in Boulder City, they headed forty miles west to Las Vegas, Nevada. The city received a post war boom in activities and population.

PART II:

Roger
Las Vegas
valley, NV

Taproot Hotel and Casino

Chapter 17

"Cast an eyeball at that! It must be over fifty feet tall!" Joey exclaimed as he stared at the colorful neon sign flickering.

The Taproot Hotel and Casino

"Can we stop here?"

Joey settled in the hotel room with the western novel, *The Big Sky,* while Roger went downstairs to get directions for the morning trip, Las Vegas to Los Angeles. At the front desk, the receptionist spread out a map and drew a black line between the two cities.

Jake, owner of the establishment, overheard their conversation. He, a New Yorker himself, recognized Roger's accent and engaged him in a friendly conversation.

"I'm Mr. Jake and noticed your license plate when you drove up. From New York?"

Shaking hands, Roger replied, "Yes, I'm Roger Atkins from Syracuse."

"But, Syracuse? That's upstate. I mean the real New York," both men chuckled appreciating the subtle remark. "By the way, I know your city. I graduated many years ago from Syracuse University."

"We have something in common. I'm an Orangeman, as well. I went through with the G.I. bill. Most of us couldn't dream of a college education without the help from the government's program."

"Last time I visited the university, I saw those dam Quonset huts and trailers springing up all around the campus, an enormous increase in enrollment." Jake chuckled. "You returning vets created problems for my frat brothers."

"How's that?"

"They had to buckle down and crack the books."

"Well, let's just say, we came back from our military experience as men. The college boys had a little catching up to do."

Roger turned his head with a cough and then resumed. "Now, I'm moving on to see what employment opportunities are out west."

Jake monitored the casino floor, eyes shifting from casino hosts, to dealers, cage cashiers, cocktail waitresses.

"You do have a busy place," Roger remarked.

"Yeap ... getting busier all the time." Recognizing a regular customer heading for the blackjack table, Jake doffed his cowboy hat in that direction.

Roger folded the map and extended his hand. "I wish you continued success."

"Tell ya what. You call me Jake and I'll call you Roger. How about you and your son sticking around in the morning so we can continue our conversation and begin a job interview? I could use a fellow New Yorker working for me."

§ § §

Early the next morning, Roger and Joey took the elevator to the penthouse. "Jake, my son Joey."

"I like your place, Mr. Jake ... first time I've been in a casino."

"Let me tell ya. Just remember, the house always wins."

"And, Mr. Jake, I like your sign. It's big and an eye catcher."

"My art director, Emmanuel Sanchez, designed it. At first, I didn't go for it. But it's grown on me." Pointing to the assortment of food on the breakfast tray, he added, "I'm taking your dad into my study. He agrees I can interview him for a job."

§ § §

Earlier that morning, Jake made contacts with his New York friends and found out Roger was given a hero's welcome. Upon graduation, he was hired as staff liaison working with military personnel going through on the G.I. bill.

Beginning the interview, Jake expected the lieutenant to talk about the medals he won. "Tell me about your military experiences."

"The long and short of it is I was given an honorable discharge."

"Well put. Now, let's get down to business. I want to hire someone in the role of public relations." Jake took a cigar from a humidor, got out a clipper, and with quick cutting motions, he cut the jagged ends. "A few years ago, we weathered that monster Bugsy Siegel's incident. He was murdered shortly after his Flamingo Hotel opened. Let me tell ya, our city got a lot of free publicity with that and his mob connections."

Jake settled into a relaxed position. "Recently, Senator Estes Kefauver ended his investigation into organized crime within the gambling industry. The televised hearings attracted wide viewership."

"You're saying there's concerns about Las Vegas's ties with mafia bosses?" asked Roger.

"Let me tell ya. I not sure about that. I just want The TapRoot to press on with our solid reputation. Any interest?"

"Yes, but …," Roger nodded to the living room where Joey was deep into his book. "I need to think about him."

"If you can spare the time, drive around our town. Tourists are surprised to see we have schools, churches, libraries, movie theatres..." Jake rolled his ash on the tray and continued, "and just about everything any other town has."

"That's a good suggestion."

§ § §

Roger and Joey whizzed through different neighborhoods, making comments along their tour. When Roger decided it was break time, he parked in front of The Drugstore, an active and noisy establishment. They walked past a line of bikes resting on the wide front windowsill.

Roger placed his order with the soda jerk wearing a bow tie and rolled up broad brim cap. "We'll have one hot fudge sundae and one vanilla cone."

Joey whispered as they slid into the booth. "I sort of like this city. I saw a library and a skating rink."

They continued the tour and returned in time for a late lunch with Jake. "And so, Roger, what do you think?"

"It's easier to get around here than in Syracuse, and traffic's not as bad."

"And you, Joey?"

"We stopped at the Las Vegas High School, the one with the Art Deco architecture, and the principal was a nice guy. Said he'd be happy to have me as a student and I can start in the fall."

"Does this mean we may have a deal?" Jake looked to Roger.

Roger didn't need much persuasion. He made a telephone call to his buddy in California about this new job in Las Vegas. "We'll visit you later, or you come visit us."

Jake developed a fondness for both Roger and Joey as they did for him. Roger built a solid relationship with journalists and community leaders. They, in turn, respected him as a go-to guy for a straight story.

Joey, a good student, earned money as a gofer for his father and Jake. However, Roger realized his son was not interested in public relations. Joey tended to not suffer fools gladly. He was his own man.

The Hospital

Chapter 18

Seven miles from The Strip, at the small Daughters of Saint Brigid O'Farrell Hospital, a group of Catholic Sisters sat around the U-shape table in the Sisters Lounge. They gathered to accept annual mission orders. Sister Marie, administrator, sat at the head table with a stack of sealed envelopes next to her place setting.

When time came to move to the agenda at hand, Sr. Marie dug deep in her pocket and fished out a small frog-shaped tin clicker. She held it in her hand and squeezed the lever. The cricket's pop-noise signaled for quiet and demanded attention. On the second click, the sisters scraped their plates, stacked them together, and passed them to the table's end. With the third signal, each stood behind her place setting.

Sister Zita, the youngest member of the congregation and the only one still in black veils, oversaw the kitchen. Her job was to load the utility wagon with dirty dishes and transfer it to the kitchen crew waiting in the hallway.

She pinned back her black veil and rolled up her wide sleeves. While she went about her duty, Sr. Marie led with the first notes of the hymn, "Ave Maria." The sisters joined in, *Ave Maria Gratia plena, Maria Gratia plena...*

Angelic voices floated through the hospital. The cart's wheel caught on the rug's ragged fibers. Dinnerware clacked against each other.

A hush fell through the room and a red-faced Sr. Zita mouthed, "Oops. I'm sorry." With head bent low, the humiliated nun carried on.

The hymn ended with a solemn *Amen, Amen, Amen*. Once Sr. Zita completed the task and took her place at the table, the ceremony continued. The administrator passed envelopes to her right and to her left.

"We stand in communion to celebrate the Feast Day of our patroness, Saint Brigid O'Farrell. Grant us the grace and strength of spirit to embrace our assignment, and, in all humility, follow the example of our founder." Looking to her charges, she continued, "Obediently, we accept our orders. In prayerful silence, we now learn of them."

Time was allowed for each nun to reflect on her next mission. Upon reading hers, Sr. Marie lifted her hand in front of her mouth, concealing a satisfied smile. She then directed, "Those leaving for a new assignment, please advance to the middle."

Three nuns approached.

Candles were lit, and Saint Brigid's prayer was said in unison.

> *Our Lord grant me the strength to meet all that*
> *the coming day may bring. Teach me to act firmly*
> *and wisely as I serve the needs of the poor and*
> *those suffering in pain. I am your faithful servant.*
> *Amen.*

§ § §

Father Dooley, the community's spiritual director, was in his late forties. He sat in the administer office across from Sr. Marie. Outside, sirens wailed, and lights flashed as an ambulance approached the hospital. They paused for the high pitch sound to trail off.

Fr. Dooley asked, "And the new ones?"

"We pick them up at the train station next week." Sr. Marie fingered the silver cross hanging from a black cord around her neck. "There's a tradeoff. Three of our sisters will move on, and only two are assigned to us."

"Would be a right nuisance if Mother Superior assigned you to a new mission." He filled the bowl of his pipe with tobacco. "Your leadership is still needed here."

"The government hospital was transferred to us in nineteen forty-seven." She took off her glasses to rub her eyes. "We've struggled these few years. God willing, we'll continue, but it is a constant struggle."

Father added a tad more tobacco before taking a test draw. "Sister, one of your patients noticed your staff is overworked. He suggested you hire a communications assistant." He struck a match and, in a circular motion, lit the tobacco.

Returning her glasses behind her ears, Sr. Marie focused on the slanted picture hanging on the opposite wall. It was a rendering of Saint Brigid, circa 1850, in a white nurse's habit. The sainted woman held a small crucifix as she administered to patients. Sr. Marie walked to the lopsided frame, adjusted it and asked, "And just what does a communications assistant do?"

"Mind you, anything clerical you ask her to do."

"That would relieve our medical staff. We could use someone with those skills in the office and to answer the telephone."

"We're getting our church bulletin printed for tomorrow's Mass. Want to advertise in the Work Wanted column?"

"Funds are scarce. What salary should I offer?"

Father chuckled. "As little as possible."

§ § §

Sr. Marie and Fr. Dooley reviewed answers to the interview questions while the candidate waited in the reception room.

Flipping back and forth through the pages, Sr. Marie said, "Look at this. She doesn't have a parochial background and is a divorcee!" The last words was whispered as a scandal was implied.

"Maybe we can serve as a good influence. After all, she read our notice in the church bulletin."

"And look! She signed her name Miss Joan Crawford. Is she delusional taking the name of a famous movie star?"

"Mind you, she just may like the name," Fr. Dooley chuckled.

After a pause, Sr. Marie said, "And, under special achievements, she listed articles to her credit in *Good Life* magazine — 'From Housewife to Elegant Hostess, Etiquette With Introductions, Setting That Perfect Table.'" Sister slapped the material on her desk. "I don't have time to waste. Should we even interview her?"

"Let's extend her courtesy. After all, some of her experiences may prove helpful."

§ § §

Sr. Marie, with a forced smile, asked the candidate to sit. "We've reviewed your material. Is there additional information you wish to talk about?"

"A person like me, with a variety of life skills, is an excellent choice and can serve as an asset to your hospital."

Sr. Marie tried to maintain a neutral expression, but a dumbfounded look spread over her face. Fr. Dooley smiled broadly. He had a flare for entertaining and the applicant possessed social attributes that could benefit him.

"And about your name… How should we address you?" asked Sr. Marie.

"Oh, that. Well, it's never been a problem. But. Ah, most

people just call me Joan, or Miss Crawford."

After a few more questions, Fr. Dooley escorted the candidate to the reception room for a decision.

Joan Crawford

Chapter 19

Joan paced the floor, smashed a second cigarette butt in the standing ashtray, and looked at her watch. *Why the delay?*

"Miss Crawford. Miss Crawford." Startled, she turned. Father Dooley mumbled, "I appreciate your background and I think you offer the hospital some interesting qualities." He lowered his eyes to the floor. "But mind you, the salary is not in line with your sophistication."

She voiced no objections with the terms. "Please convey to Sister Marie how grateful I am. And she will not be disappointed."

Father Dooley opened the door for her exit, but Joan hesitated. For years she carried a secret, personal burden. "Father, I have a confession to make."

"Our confessional times are scheduled on Saturdays, and at the church."

"It's more like a white lie I told Sister Marie."

Father Dooley pointed to the chairs and offered a sympathetic ear.

"Father, I did not expect a question about my name." She offered an appropriate sniffle. "How could I explain to a lady of the cloth, that I grew up as Joan Flasher and, after I had a shotgun marriage, I legally became Joan Crawford."

Father Dooley patted her hands. "I think it's best just to explain your legal name is Joan Crawford."

"But there's more. I knew I was not pregnant, but I married the guy for his last name, Crawford, anything but Flasher."

"Ahem! That may be more information than Sister Marie needs to hear."

"You see, I tricked the captain of the football team, James Crawford III, and his socially prominent family … I'm talking the blueish of blue blood."

In the confines of the confessional box, Fr. Dooley was not concerned with his facial expressions. In the presence of Joan, he fought back his stunned look as she paused, took out a cigarette, and lit it.

"And Father, the union didn't work. I chuckle when I remember grabbing that wad of money from my former father-in-law saying, 'I do. I do promise. I will never set foot again in your lousy town.'"

"Well, well. That was misleading and a serious deception. I ..." Dooley quipped.

"When I landed in Reno, Nevada, for a quick divorce, the other ladies thought I should keep the last name. After all, many starlets from California maintained their stage name. To me, the name Joan Crawford has a nice ring to it."

"Um, best if we keep your story between ourselves. Sister Marie signed on to hiring you." Fr. Dooley stood and opened the door. "And I'll pray that you'll do fine. Just no more lies, please."

Jim Riley

Chapter 20

Joan settled into a small office, barely enough room for a desk
and chair. She waited for the telephone installation. Responding
to a heavy knock, she opened the door. "It's about time."

A tall man with a muscular build entered. In his baritone
voice, he replied, "Waiting long?"

"Well, as you can see, I don't have a telephone."

Leaning against the wall and giving her a once-over, the
stranger replied, "I wasn't looking for a telephone, but what I
can see, I do like."

"And what do you mean by that? And what does that have
to do with installing a telephone?"

With an unadulterated belly laugh, the man exposed
chipped front teeth. She responded with a cold stare. *If he kept
his mouth shut, I might consider him handsome, but I've
observed too many of his type in my past. They're nothing but
bad news.*

Another tap at the door and Joan quickly called out,
"Come in. Come in."

"Telephone company, ma'am. Is this Miss Crawford's
office?" A workman stood in the doorway wearing a khaki
uniform with a wide leather tool belt strapped to his hips.

"You're in the right place."

The mystery visitor explained "I was just leaving. As a

benefactor of the hospital, I wanted to welcome you into our family." Angling for the door in tight quarters, he intentionally bumped hips with Joan. He snatched her hand. "By the way, I'm Jim Riley." He kissed her hand. "We must continue our conversation, and soon."

§ § §

Several days later, Fr. Dooley entered Joan's office. "A hundred thousand welcomes to you," greeted the priest.

"I am so sorry, but I don't have a chair to offer you."

"You do have a cozy space, now don't you?"

They engaged in small talk before Joan worked Jim Riley's name into their conversation.

"Oh, Jim. He's the owner of Riley Gun Shop and a supporter of the hospital." The priest chuckled. "And I keep him on my good side. He sees to it that I get my chance to visit my dear mother back in Ireland." Leaning closer, he whispered, "Now mind you … about his chipped teeth. He's like Cyrano de Bergerac who took on anyone making fun of his long nose. That's Jim with his teeth."

Tapping her fingers on the edge of the desk, she snapped, "A dental procedure could fix that problem."

Fr. Dooley continued, "Jim's a wee bit mad at times. One night, he caught a thief sneaking out his store, hauling off a handful of his guns. There was a struggle. Jim ended up with two cracked front teeth, but that poor lad ended up much worse. You see, Jim has a reputation among the men of our parish … he always gets even. And, well, he usually gets the best in most situations."

"Thank you, Father. I must remember your story."

"Now, Miss Crawford. I may be calling on you. You see, I play host for the sisters on occasions, and I remember you wrote an article, 'Setting That Perfect Table.' Am I right?"

She brightened up, pleased he remembered. "Yes, I did write that article …"

"Do introduce yourself to Sr. Zita who's heads the kitchen. I rely on her a great deal with my parties. Your assistance will be invaluable. And, by the way, do introduce yourself to the sisters."

"They're always rushing about. Do they ever stop?"

"Miss Crawford, I have faith you'll catch up with each one. God be with you."

§ § §

Joan heard the rustling of skirts dashing past her door. With the clickity-clack of her high heels, she hurried through the hallway following a white habit. The nun escaped through swinging doors. Crawford tiptoed back toward her office when she encountered Sr. Marie.

"Good afternoon, Miss Crawford. Everything all right?"

She pointed to the operating room. "Yes, Sister. Father Dooley suggested I introduce myself to the sisters."

"Come into my office. I'll give you a rundown on our staff."

§ § §

Sr. Marie motioned Joan to sit. "You'll probably have a difficult time chatting with Sister Michael," nodding to the operating room. "She's our anesthetist." With tired eyes, Sr. Marie confessed, "And like most of us is accessible around the clock."

"If you need help, I can do more than respond to correspondence and answer the telephone. I'm good with numbers if you want to give me a try."

Recipe for bread

Chapter 21

Sr. Zita pulled a tray of fresh baked bread from the oven. She waited for it to cool before offering a slice to Miss Mo, her helper.

Miss Mo was a small Chinese woman. She took a bite and spat it out. "No, no. Too much salt. One time, too much flour. Last time, too much sugar."

Sr. Zita shook her head. "But these are the same ingredients we used on our farm. I have them in my mind."

"You good family cook. Now, you cook big batches and for bigger family, the hospital peoples." Miss Mo tossed the unfinished slice into the garbage bin. "Keep ingredients. But you write what you do, how you make change."

Head bowed and with a quiet voice, Sr. Zita asked, "Should I even keep trying?"

"Come. We have tea." Miss Mo filled the tea pot with water. "Must remember Chinese saying, 'One step at a time is good walking.' Keep walking. Keep taking steps."

Following Miss Mo's instructions, Sr. Zita recorded the amount of each ingredient. After four adjustments, she was satisfied with the finished product.

§ § §

Sr. Marie called Sr. Zita into her office. "Is everything all right? Are you well? Do you want to talk about anything?"

The young nun, hands clasped in her lap, looked confused. She shook her head after each question. "I'm fine. In fact, Sister Marie, I'm happy … so pleased."

"And why's that?"

"I finally got the recipe right for baking my bread. I made four big batches and they came out the same."

"Now, Sister, please slow down. Catch your breath."

Sr. Zita continued, "Miss Mo says it's the best bread she's ever tasted. It's just like my mother used to bake. I can offer slices to our hospital family. I know they'll enjoy my bread."

"Is that the reason you were dancing around the patio?"

"Oh, my! I don't know how to dance. I was excited and just … just jumping for joy."

"You called attention to yourself. Your pride got the better of you. Did you forget your humility?"

Sr. Zita tightened her lips.

"Now, I want you to recapture your humility. Remember Proverb 11:2, 'When pride comes, then comes disgrace, but with humility is wisdom.'"

Sr. Zita bowed and apologized.

Showgirls and Dancers

Chapter 22

Roger's Las Vegas Valley articles earned the respect among his fellow journalists. Representing The TapRoot at various community events provided him with a relaxing place to keep current with business peers. During a black-tie event, Roger stopped by the raffle table.

A gentleman directed his attention to their big-ticket item. "Here we have an Omega Seamaster Calendar men's wristwatch with a black leather strap. Notice the black dial with gold dagger hour markers. The winner will be a fortunate person."

Admiring the watch, Roger purchased a book of twelve tickets.

The evening ended with a drum roll for the final drawing. A hush ran through the audience. Roger and his peers stood in the back of the room enjoying conversation when shushing sounds were directed to them. Their chatter stopped and the winning numbers repeated. A buddy grabbed Roger's stubs. He examined them and yelled, "Hoorah! Roger's the winner!"

§ § §

Returning to his TapRoot's fourth floor apartment, Roger showed his prize to his son. Joey squinted his eyes while examining its finer points and then put the watch next to his ear." "Pop, are you sure it's not a fake. It's not ticking."

"Son, it's the real thing. If it ticked, then I would be concerned."

"I really dig this. Next time I want to go with you. Maybe your luck will rub off on me."

Days later, Roger opened the door to their apartment. He put the grocery bag on the kitchen table. "Joey, Joey. Home yet?"

Sleeping at any time of day was his son's avocation. "Joey?" No response so he knocked harder and louder on his bedroom door.

"Sorry, Pop." Pointing to a set of bulky headphones. "Got carried away. Want to try them?"

"Later. I've got news. Been promoted to a new position as publicist for The TapRoot."

"Congratulations. What does a publicist do?"

Roger began reading the job description when his son interrupted him. "Pop, you're excited. I mean, you sound excited."

"Jake wants showgirls and dancers to open and close for a headliner."

"Dancers! Pop, that's not the job for you. Have you forgotten? You've got two left feet."

"I got that solved. I posted an advertisement looking for a choreographer."

"Whew! That's a start." Joey wiped imaginary sweat from his forehead.

"I'll follow with this ad, Dancers at least five feet, eight and a half inches, proficiency in ballroom, jazz, tap, ballet. Costume dancing. No nudity."

"What! No nudity?"

Roger chortled. "And, you, my son, I spent all that money giving you a good Catholic education."

§ § §

Roger took the back elevator to his office. When it landed on the bottom floor, he began another coughing spell. Tiny spots of rust-color blood appeared on the handkerchief. He spotted a metal waste container. Rolling up the soiled cloth, he tossed it inside the bin and proceeded to the appointment with the choreographer.

In the large empty room adjacent to the publicist office, Roger stood with Monsieur Lorenzo LeBlanc. The younger man was a snappy dresser. He wore a long, blue sleeve shirt, white linen vest and pants, a purple paisley ascot peeped from under an open collar, and a fresh white carnation affixed to the boutonniere.

When Jake entered, his reaction was the same as an amused Roger. Jake automatically rolled back his shoulders, raised his chest, and held his head high, mirroring the stance of the newly hired choreographer.

"Well," said Jake. "Roger and I want to get started as soon as possible. When can you begin?"

"I can assist with the stage design, work with the in-house orchestra, have auditions and my girls will be ready to open our first Tappers Dancers Revue by this Christmas season."

"That soon?" asked Roger.

He twisted his French cuff links.

"I am that good."

Jake nodded to Roger and back to LeBlanc. "I like your style and attitude."

"Monsieur Jake, this is a good space for a rehearsal studio. But I do have one request." The choreographer walked around the bare room.

"Shoot."

"You see here." He stood in front of the wall adjacent to Roger's office, and with his long, silver cigarette holder, outlined a rectangular design. "It is good to have a two-way mirror installed. My last job, the ladies started a catfight. I got in the middle." He waved his smoking accessary back and forth. "Never, never again. If it happens here, I knock on the window to be rescued."

§ § §

In a short period of time, LeBlanc hired a full complement of dancers. By opening night, their hard work and perseverance produced a polished performance that brought cheers and applause from the audience.

§ § §

Sr. Marie was comforted when the annual mission order celebration ended. All the sisters maintained their current mission, and a new one will join them. The medical needs of the community continued to grow. An extra hand was a blessing.

It took Joan less than a year to prove she was up to tasks asked of her. The communications assistant moved into a bigger office with a large desk, several chairs and a file cabinet.

With the telephone balanced on her shoulder, she jotted notes from the caller. "Let me get this straight. You want to place an order for Sr. Zita's healthy bread? Please give me your telephone number and I'll get back with you." Joan doodled on her stenographer pad, circling the words *healthy bread*.

Sitting across from Sr. Marie, Joan reviewed her notes. She repeated the caller's request word for word. Sister placed her elbows on the desk, her fingers in a prayerful gesture. "The caller asked for Sister Zita's healthy bread?" She took a moment to consider a reply. "I believe she's talking about the bread from her family recipe. It does taste good. But, healthy bread?"

"Am I to tell the lady we're selling bread at the hospital?"

"No. Just tell her we'll have a few loaves set aside and a donation is appreciated." Sr. Marie continued, "Miss Crawford, find out why it was referred to as *healthy bread.*"

Foundress Celebration

Chapter 23

Joey entered his senior year in high school with thoughts of pursuing a college degree in chemistry. Zita and her helpers kept up with the growing demand for loaves of bread. Nightly, Sr. Marie counted donations and placed them in a container labeled: Healthy Bread. When the contributions reached over $150.00, she called the manager of the local bank, Spencer Taylor.

When Sr. Marie requested a meeting, the banker was flattered. He considered the hospital and the sisters' presence essential to the continued growth of the community and made several overtures to assist them even though he was a devout Mormon.

After an exchange of pleasantries, Sr. Marie explained the reason for the meeting. "You see, we got permission to celebrate our foundress, Saint Brigid O'Farrell." She pointed to the box. "We're collecting money for an engraved name plate to be placed in the middle of our garden." She handed Spencer a drawing with the inscription:

Saint Brigid O'Farrell
1801-1853

Spencer nodded in agreement. "That's a perfect idea." He walked to the donation box. "Have you kept count of the money?"

"Just this morning when I counted it. I came up with one-hundred, fifty-eight dollars and twenty-five cents. Here, I have it written down. If you want, you can count it also." She handed him the accounting on St. Brigid O'Farrell Hospital stationery.

He picked up the box. The sounds of metal coins hitting against each other rang in the room. *Doubt if many paper bills are tucked inside.*

His count matched the number on the paper. "I'll see what I can do. By the way, is there a deadline for its completion?"

"As long as it takes for us to save. That's our deadline."

"I do understand, and I'll set up an account for you." From his personal bank account, Spencer anted up the necessary funds to purchase the memorial Sr. Marie desired.

§ § §

The community turnout for Saint Brigid's celebration was impressive. Joan combed through the audience checking out the men. Once again, she was disappointed. After three failed marriages, she calculated a hospital setting operated by religious sisters would provide fertile territory for a lady out for a new, amorous venture.

Joan's list whittled down to zero. Candidates were too young, too old, too sick, too needy, too boring, too poor, or too religious.

Joan left before the celebration ended. She returned to her office in time to answer the ringing telephone.

"Yes. Oh yes, Mr. Jake." She perked up. "Of course, I'm familiar with The TapRoot Hotel and Casino."

Jake explained he wanted Roger Atkins, his employee, to have a thorough checkup. If the hospital could accommodate the request in a timely fashion, he would like to make the appointment.

Joan recognized the name and picture of Roger attached to newspaper articles covering The TapRoot's events. *That's a hell of a good-looking man!*

"I can make an appointment for this coming Monday afternoon with Dr. Eaton, our medical director. And I personally will see to it that your employee's stay is comfortable."

Joan took notes while Jake supplied medical in-take information. Cunningly she inquired, "So, did you mention his wife will bring him?" The answer proved useful. She twisted her pearl necklace as a satisfied smile crossed her face. Roger, single, made him the object of her new love interest.

After reviewing her notes, Joan asked Sr. Marie for permission to leave early for the weekend. Permission granted and in preparation for Monday afternoon, she launched into action. First stop was to the hairdresser for a touch-up and a manicure.

When she returned to the trailer, she matched her newly purchased suit with appropriate shoes. Next, she pulled out a sewing machine. A slight alteration around the shoulder line of the jacket would camouflage the onset of osteoporosis.

Roger and Check Up

Chapter 24

In front of The TapRoot Hotel and Casino, neon lights blinked "Out with '56; In with '57 Tappers Christmas Holiday Revue." Red and green lights festooned from the first to the top floor added to the season's gaiety.

Joey decorated the apartment. He trimmed the Christmas tree. Under it, he placed a small Santa doll sitting in a sleigh with wrapped packages.

Roger checked the Omega wristwatch. He was early, as his habit, punctual if not ahead of time for appointments. Joey, on the other hand, followed Joey's time, but managed to pull off commitments at the appropriate time.

When the telephone rang, he grabbed it after the first ring. "Yes, Jake. I'm just waiting for Joey." He added, "Yes, we'll meet you behind the stage."

Roger walked into his bedroom for last minute adjustments. A regular at the downstairs hotel barbershop, he got a hair trim with a simple side part every two weeks. He ran a brush through his hair. Grooming complete, Roger stared at his red eyes.

Pain followed him since his time in the service. He intended to have this the evening as pain free as possible. Over-the-counter medicine offered relief, but his conditions troubled him. Recently, Jake caught him tossing a blood-stained handkerchief into a waste basket. His boss didn't say anything, but Roger knew he was aware of something; something not good.

His drug cabinet provided a variety of over-the-counter medicines. Roger tilted his head back and squeezed drops into his eyes. He popped a pill for his cough, placed extra ones in an envelope and stuffed it in his shirt pocket.

With time to spare, Roger turned off the lights. He reclined in his easy chair and shut his eyes. Joey's little Santa Claus sleigh transported him back in time, resurrecting haunting memories.

Like a mosaic pattern, one by one, images melded together—*first time he met Giana at the clinic with her family, playing Santa at their home, the bombing, the fire . . .*

Reliving those moments, his heart pounded, beating hard and faster.

The sudden, loud shutting of doors announced Joey. "Pop. Pop. They've got a new dancer." He rushed into Roger's bedroom and switched on the lights. "I saw her. Her name's Lucia and she's beautiful."

"Damn it, Joey! Can't you shut doors quietly?" Roger coughed, rubbed his eyes, and adjusted to the light. "I thought someone was breaking in."

"Pop! The new dancer ... she's from Italy. Isn't that unreal?"

Roger composed himself and buttoned his dinner jacket. "Hurry. Get dressed. Jake wants us to meet him behind stage. We'll catch up on your good news later."

Under his son's urging, Roger switched from his after-the-war wardrobe of broad-shouldered, double-breasted suits to the slimmer, tapered fashion of the day.

"Well, don't you look hip!"

"Enough, Joey. Get dressed. That's an order." He quietly closed the door and left their apartment.

Walking to his room, Joey tossed shoes and socks on the unmade bed. The phone rang. He caught it on the second ring. He cradled the receiver between his ear and shoulder. "Yes, Mr. Jake, I plan to be there soon." With the phone cord at its full length, he plopped on the bed. "You want pop to go to a hospital?" He jumped up. "Yes, Mr. Jake. Yes, sir. But you better be the one to break that news to him. See you backstage." He stared at the phone. *Pop won't go for that idea.*

§ § §

Roger waited for the back elevator with thoughts of his son. He knew Joey was not a good fit for the public relations profession. His goal was to become a scientist, a long academic road ahead. When the elevator reached the fourth floor, Roger entered and smiled. *I'm so proud of that kid. He brings laughter and joy into my life.*

§ § §

A busboy carrying a tray stacked with dirty dishes climbed down the stairs from the Atrium Room and headed to the kitchen. He carried a tray stacked with dirty dishes. In the narrow hallway he paused, glued against the wall to allow the showgirls Tatyana and Rita to squeeze past him. One by one they slid into the dressing room, offering an eyeful of loveliness. He sneaked another look, then resumed his cleanup duties.

Inside the crowded dressing room, they maneuvered around each other and slipped into sleeveless red velvet Santa helper outfits with deep V-shaped necklines. Their billowing mini-length skirts allowed for high kicks and glimpses of white lacey panties. White fur trimmed both bodice and skirt hems.

Hoofers sat on the long bench staring into the vanity mirror outlined with a string of lights. They worked on last-minute costume adjustments and theatrical preparations.

Rita parked herself on a stool, leaned down, and unbuckled the black ankle strap of her dance shoe. She massaged her calf and inner sole. "Just one more year left in these old legs."

Tatyana elbowed in front of the brightly lit mirror, stared at her image, and added a black beauty mark near her exaggerated lined lips. She applied a final layer of red lipstick, blotted her lips, and stuffed the used tissue into her bodice, giving an added lift to her already full bosom. "You said that last year at this time."

"Pumpkin, this time I mean it," responded Rita, straightening the seam of her black fishnet stockings.

Dancers strapped on Christmas-tree headpieces with battery-powered strands of mini red and green lights. After wiggling into white elbow-length gloves, they exited one by one. Tatyana struggled to keep the string of lights lit. Once done, she flew up the stairs and took her place behind the stage in line with the other dancers.

§ § §

Roger, Jake, and Joey huddled together in the wings. Jake's cowboy hat rested over his thick eyebrows as he stood chomping on his unlit cigar. His head bobbed in all directions, watchful for last-minute activities. He saw the juggler and magician warming up. The man in a tuxedo rubbed a rag over his tap shoes for a last polish. Crew members busied themselves setting up scenery changes. Prop men dusted artificial plants while technicians worked on stage lights. Tappers awaited their cue.

Roger covered his mouth to stifle a raspy cough.

"Shh! Shh! Shh!" the stage manager uttered and gestured for him to move to the crossover area behind the stage. Joey followed and was stopped by Jake.

"Joey, we know about his shortness of breath and eye troubles. See to it that your pop stays in the hospital until he's better."

Onstage lights lit up as music from the in-house orchestra signaled The Tappers entrance. Cheers greeted as they danced on stage, beginning the Christmas Holiday Revue.

Roger could tell Jake had something important to discuss by the way he approached. He listened to Jake say, "Now, you know, and I know, you're not well. So, let me tell ya something. I need ya to get better. December's our slow time. Joey will pitch in until you return."

Roger began to protest when Jake put up his hand and turned to Joey. "I've made special arrangements at Daughters of Saint Brigid Hospital in Henderson. Joey, you know how to get there?"

"Yes, sir, between us and Boulder City. Straight down Boulder Highway."

Jake took notes from his pocket and read from them. "You're to meet Miss Crawford, communications assistant." He handed them to Joey. "She's expecting you."

He turned again to Roger. "I mean it. Stay until you get yourself well. Ya hear?"

The dancers tapped their way off the stage to an appreciative audience. As the lights dimmed, the stage manager motioned to the juggler to set up for his act.

Dancers

Chapter 25

"For God's sake, slow down," Roger yelled. "I'm not looking forward to going to the hospital, but I want to arrive in one piece." He pulled out another cigarette and glanced at Joey holding a firm grip on the steering wheel. "What are you thinking? Get your damn foot off the pedal! Just slow down," Roger insisted. "Road's known as a speed trap."

"But where's the signals and lights—even the traffic?"

Joey's mind returned to the previous night, auditions for new dancers. He caught sight of the Italian dancer he nicknamed Lovely Lucia. Thinking of her, brought back memories—both pleasant and sad—of his Bari family. The possibility of sharing his Italian memories energized him.

Once he settled his pop into the hospital, Joey planned to meet her and didn't care what she talked about. He was just eager to hear an Italian accent floating from the mouth of the beautiful young lady.

Joey snapped back to reality in time to swerve from the shoulder of the road, barely missing one of Henderson's finest, a motorcycle police officer. The cop, writing a ticket for the driver of an old pickup truck, stared at the speeding '56 T Bird, too occupied to chase it.

"Keep your eyes on the road." Roger tossed his cigarette out the window and began another coughing spell. His son followed instructions, loosened his grip, maintained a slower and a steady speed.

They approached a large road sign depicting a golfer in knickers and Tam O'Shanter, hitting a 3-D golf ball.

Gateway to Lake Mead/Fishing-Boating-Skiing

A short distance beyond, another sign was posted:

Entering the City of Henderson

Turning into a small, horseshoe-shaped parking lot, young oleander plants climbed the walls of the one-story, wing-shaped structure. A sign was erected on a dry patch of lawn:

Daughters of St. Brigid Hospital, 1947

Joey hopped from the car and let out a sigh. He suddenly felt relaxed. The tension seemed to resolve. He had a sudden sense of relief. His pop would receive medical help, the kind of attention he lacked and resisted since Italy. Patting his pop on the shoulder, he said "You'll be alright."

Dr. Eaton

Chapter 26

Joan arrived early for work and began a vigil for the new patient's arrival. She watched the T-Bird with two men turn into the parking lot and sighed. *He's here! At last.* She took out a vanity case to check her hair and makeup.

Joan greeted the men with a smile and an empty wheelchair. She reevaluated her original assessment of the patient in front of her. *Mr. Atkins is more handsome than his pictures.* Her seductive work began in earnest.

She noticed Roger frown at a wheelchair. He walked past her to the lobby. Baffled by the situation, Joey offered Joan an awkward smile, held the door open, then followed her into the hospital.

Black framed pictures of various hospital milestones hung behind the reception desk. An assortment of holiday materials cluttered the floor. Ladies, in pink smocks, worked alongside with a teenager in her candy-striped uniform.

"I found the box with the nativity scene," announced a volunteer.

"And here's one labeled 'decorations'," voiced another while she unwrapped a colorful glass ornament cradled in tissue paper.

Roger ignored their prattle. He spotted signs and directional arrows to administrative offices and headed that way. Joey nodded to the group and rushed to catch up with him. The ladies stopped their busy work and watched as the three paraded down the hall.

§ § §

Miss Crawford stopped in front of her office and left the chair in the hallway. She welcomed the men into the office.

Picking up a clipboard from her desk with preliminary paperwork clamped on it, Miss Crawford motioned for the men to sit. Joey obeyed, but Roger stood.

Stretching her authority as communication assistant, she cleared her throat. "Well, I, ah, we'll give you as much privacy as possible. Let's see now. You'll find your gown folded on your hospital bed."

Roger tapped Joey on the shoulder. "Get me a decent pajama and robe set before you return to the casino. And, son," continued Roger, ignoring Miss Crawford and unclasping his watch. "Here. Put it in a safe place."

Miss Crawford pressed on. "Now, for the forms."

"I'm sure Mr. Jake gave you the necessary information already. May I just get settled in?"

"Of course. Dr. Eaton will look in on you and …"

Roger opened the door and gestured for her to exit with him.

"I'll go for the robe now," Joey stood. "Where are you taking my pop, Miss Crawford?"

"Ward Four. Down the hallway and past the nurse's station. And by the way," she pointed to a sign pinned on the bulletin board, "there's no need for you to follow our visitor hours. I've arranged, especially for you, Joey, to assist Mr. Atkins with any of his needs and at any time." She turned to Roger. "And I'm here to help make your stay as comfortable as possible."

§ § §

When Roger entered the ward, he figured the older man must find it difficult relaxing in the skeletal traction pulley system. He was not sure about the younger patient. Not sure he cared, as long as neither was infectious. With only a nod to the men, he made his way around the privacy screen and sat on the edge of the hospital bed.

Missing the privacy and trappings of home, he glanced around the modest furnishings of the confined area. On one side of the bed, a glass of water sat on a table equipped with a lift mechanism for height adjustment. A small trash bin stood next to a straight arm vinyl chair. He stretched his head toward the opposite wall and spotted a small wooden cross hanging behind the bed. Roger longed for a cigarette, but there was no evidence of an ashtray.

A nurse entered. "Mr. Atkins, I'm here to take your vital signs."

"But I don't see any ash tray on the night table, or any place."

She pressed her fingertips firmly against his wrist and watched her wristwatch.

"But I'm a smoker."

After she made notations, she looked up. "To save his patients' lives, Dr. Eaton limited smoking to the cafeteria and back patio."

"Why would he do that?"

With a forced smile, she continued, "The doctor will visit with you shortly and you'll have the opportunity to engage in a conversation about the current research he's following."

"What's that about?"

She slid the blood pressure cuff around his left arm and inflated the blub. "Smoking causes cancer. Cancer kills."

§ § §

Roger, tried to catch a nap, when he heard the younger fellow let out a moan. A voice encouraged him. "Come on, Ryan, just one step in front of the next."

The older patient chided, "Get a move on it!"

Ryan responded with a shaky voice, "Ha! Look who's talking! Do you think for a minute," he let out a heavy breath with another step, "I want to stay here longer than I have to?"

"Nurse, he bellyached before surgery and now he's at it again. How much longer do I need to put up with him?"

The men stopped squabbling as someone made small talk with them. He praised Ryan for showing progress with his exercise regimen. Then asked George about his leg pain.

"Do me a favor, Doc," Ryan butted in, "discharge the old man and soon."

With a slight limp, the doctor rounded Roger's screen. "Mr. Atkins, I'm Doctor Eaton."

Roger stood and returned the tall physician's firm handshake. The doctor gestured for him to sit while he flipped back and forth through a thin medical chart. "I have notes from a conversation between Miss Crawford and your boss, but I'm waiting for more medical records." He laid down a folder and drew a stethoscope from his lab coat pocket. "Until then, let's see what's going on with you."

Roger froze when read the label on the folder:

U.S. Army Air Force

Expressing annoyance, Roger said, "That phase of my life I don't wish to relive. Once my records get here, if they do, my medical history will be covered."

Dr. Eaton continued, "Mr. Jake wants you to stay in the hospital until you're as good as new."

"He's my boss, not my doctor."

The doctor began the examination. "Well, as your doctor, I'll be the judge when you're going home." He made notes with each procedure, including notations of scars visible across his chest, back and legs.

Roger started wheezing. After the episode, the doctor asked, "How many cigarettes do you smoke a day?"

"Never without a cigarette."

"And when was your last medical check-up?"

"Not sure. I don't like hospitals and I've avoided doctors for years."

"Mr. Atkins, I'm here to help you. I'm not the enemy." Writing out prescriptions, he added, "I've ordered blood work and tests for your cough. And a special pair of glasses. In the meantime, Miss Crawford will wrap gauze around your eyes — a temporary fix to filter out light and give your eyes a rest."

The doctor stopped writing and looked directly at Roger. "While we wait for your missing records, I want you to rest and exercise, like walking around the hospital grounds." He leaned close to Roger. "And try to give up smoking."

"But —"

"I said *try*. Miss Crawford will make you an appointment with Dr. Clark at Mount Sinai in Los Angeles. His medical specialty is pulmonary medicine, diseases affecting the lungs."

Dr. Eaton stepped into the hallway as Joey came toward Ward Four. He gestured for the doctor to stop and whispered, "I'm Mr. Atkin's son, Doc. I need to talk with you, that is, if you have time."

"Continue," the doctor said.

"You see, my pop's a war hero. Records are classified, under lock and key in England. Sealed for something like seventy-five years ... under Winston Churchill's orders. You know, he was the Prime Minister of the United Kingdom during the war."

"Thank you for this information. I have Miss Crawford working on it. Knowing her, she'll find a way to get them. And, once your father returns home, encourage him to follow my instructions."

Joey approached Roger's bed, and, after an embrace, he helped him work into a set of pajamas.

"Tap, tap, tap," announced Miss Crawford, stepping around the privacy curtain. She asked Roger to sit up as she rolled the gauze around his head, covering his eyes. "Can you see through the netting?" she asked.

"I can distinguish between different sizes of figures. That's about it."

"Good. And the doctor also ordered a special diet for you."

"Don't waste hospital food on me," Roger snapped.

Before she left, Miss Crawford fluffed the pillows and assisted Roger to a comfortable position. "I'll see to it, personally, that you receive the best of care. You can bet on that." She wiggled her fingers as she left.

Smiling, Joey gave his father a hug. He whispered that he'd sneak in some casino food when he returned.

Mr. Jake

Chapter 27

Joey wanted to report to Mr. Jake, the man he considered as his crusty, lovable uncle. He also wanted an introduction to the new dancer, Lovely Lucia, and the sooner the better.

Joey pressed his foot on the gas pedal. It got heavier and heavier as he zoomed down Boulder Highway. Roger was not around to bother him about it.

Officer Hafen was. When the officer spotted a T-Bird in the opposite lane, he threw his motorcycle in full throttle and made a quick U-turn.

He gave chase as Joey sped from him. Looking into his rearview mirror, Joey smiled and took a deep breath. *That was a narrow escape.* He must remember what his pop said about that stretch---a speed trap.

§ § §

Joey stopped at Mr. Jake's office, knocked, and peeked in. He sat in a swivel chair, facing the door behind an oversized cherry pedestal desk. He gestured for Joey to sit.

"Now, tell me how your pop's doing."

Joey let out a sigh. "Pop has to go to Los Angeles for his lung condition and I told the doc he's going to have a tough time getting hold of his military medical records."

Jake cleaned ashes from his cigar. "Just keep him in there until he's better, ya hear?" He thumbed through a stack of correspondence, picked out a letter as if ignoring Joey's presence.

"Hmm." Joey stuttered. "Hmm ..."

Jake shot a look to Joey. "Well, now don't you think you've got work to do?"

"Well, Mr. Jake ..."

"Well, what?"

Joey stood and stammered. "Mr. Jake ... Lucia ... the Italian dancer?" He leaned over the leather inlay on top of the desk and pleaded for Mr. Jake's attention. "Lucia, from Italy. Can you introduce us?"

Mr. Jake chuckled. "Of course, I plan to. And let me tell ya, Joey. She's already homesick for Italy."

"So am I." He continued to the door, sighed, and paused. "Mr. Jake?"

Jake walked from his desk. "Your father insists talk about Bari is off limits. He says 'It's over. Move on.' But you want to, right?"

Joey nodded. "My memories ... I hold my mom, and Nonna and Papa close to my heart. I'm afraid if I bring up my family or talk about Bari, he'll get ... Well, I'm not sure what will happen."

"I want you to consider one thing," Jake began. "You're your own man now, ya hear. Your pop may come around, or he may not. Allow him that. But you must create your own life. Your pop's memories are his. You don't need to make them yours."

"Thanks. I needed to hear that."

Jake walked back to his desk. He fingered papers on his desk and looked across to Joey. "Here's another piece of advice. You can't arrange Roger's life, but you surely can put his desk in order. Go to it, ya hear?"

With his spirits lifted, Joey strolled confidently to the mail station imagining the first meeting with Lovely Lucia. He practiced questions he would ask. *How did you know I was waiting for you all these years? What angel sent you to me? How about trying some of my famous spaghetti sauce?*

He gathered Roger's mail and made his way to the office. A smile crossed his face as he passed the Rehearsal Room. He would get to see his Lovely Lucia as The Tappers rehearsed.

The telephone rang as Joey unlocked the office door and switched on the lights. He tossed the mail on Roger's desk and reached for the phone. The ringing stopped, too late to answer. Joey busied himself sorting the mail into appropriate piles. The phone rang again, and in his haste, he knocked over a tin can holding an assortment of pens and pencils.

"Yes, Mr. Bentley," Joey responded. "He's out of town." Gathering the writing utensils, he continued, "He'll get back after the holidays. I'll tell him you called."

Joey thumbed through the correspondence and arranged them according to agents who represented a variety of talent—comedians, jazz singers, pianists, dancers, ventriloquists. The phone rang again, and Joey just stared at it until it rang itself out. He lifted the receiver and instructed the hotel operator to hold further calls and take messages until his pop returned.

He walked to his desk and grabbed a clean sheet of paper. After doodling Lucia's name in various shapes and forms, he crumpled the page. *My lovely Lucia, my thoughts are stuck on you.* Joey switched off the lights and locked the office door.

§ § §

Joey walked through the hallway to the back elevator. When he entered the apartment, he quietly closed the door behind him and placed his keys on the side credenza. One by one, he slid his Stockman style western cowboy boot into the boot jack. With a slight struggle, each was released.

In stocking feet, he sauntered to his pop's bedroom. From his pocket, he took out the Omega watch, gave it a kiss, and placed it inside his father's jewelry box among a modest collection of tie tacks and cuff links.

A growling noise originated from the pit of Joey's stomach. His mouth salivated for spaghetti topped with his special Italian sauce, so he headed to the kitchen.

In the pantry, an assortment of dry cereals stood next to three boxes of pasta. He pulled out the spaghetti. On the side panel of the box, he kissed the trademark map of Italy. Five cans of tomatoes paste were stacked in pyramid fashion. He grabbed one and tossed it in the air, yelling, "Yippie Ki-yay, ki-yay, ki-yay!" Catching it, he kissed the picture of vine-ripened tomatoes on the side. "While we talk and talk about Italy, I'm going to squeeze you, my sweet Italian tomato."

Angel-of-the-Night

Chapter 28

Nurse Watson checked the clock above her desk: 8:45 p.m., break time. She looked down the halls. Everything appeared calm. Taking her coin purse from her jacket, she left her post.

Roger sat up, restless. He extended his arms, twisted left and then right. He felt his cloth eye wrap and smoothed the edges back in place. His craving was not for food but for a cigarette.

Swinging his legs over the side of the bed, he stood, bracing himself. Light filtered into his eyes at different angles. Staring hard, he felt his way around the area. Roger found his robe, managed to work each arm in its correct hole, and wrapped the sash around his waist.

He tapped his pockets, feeling the cigarette pack and matches. He smiled. *Joey remembered.*

He patted the air in front of him until he found the screen and quietly moved it to the side. More light filtered through and, after a few moments, he adjusted to this new environment. George and Ryan eyeballed Roger shuffling into the open ward.

"Need help?" George inquired. "I can ring for the nurse."

"No thanks. Just a little restless. Uh, where can a guy have a smoke around here?"

"Pass the nurses station and go straight down the hallway to the back patio. Wish I could guide you, but I'm a little tied up at the moment."

"Stitches keep me from moving about," added Ryan.

"Thanks. Just need to work out the kinks," assured Roger.

"Follow the moonlight through the hallway and you'll reach the patio," George instructed. "There're several lampposts and two benches. One is set under a big tree and another is near the kitchen's back entrance."

"Too bad it's closed," Ryan chuckled. "Must be hungry and …" An abdominal movement restricted him to a moan.

"Smoke's all I need." Roger began to leave and turned to his ward mates. "By the way, men, I'm Roger Atkins. Sorry for all the commotion."

"I'm George Palmer," one of them responded. "Don't worry about it."

Ryan introduced himself and added, "Understand you're a war hero. Had a hometown parade in your —"

"Let's just say, I served in the military." Roger entered the hospital hallway.

Roger heard George bark at Ryan. "What a jerk you are! Why do you think he requested a screen around his bed?"

"He's modest?" Ryan's answer sounded more like a question.

"Grow up," said George. "He piloted the Flying Fortress, one of those big birds. Sat in his cockpit bombing our enemies when you were popping pimples."

§ § §

Roger slowly walked making sense of the surroundings. Swiping his hands back and forth in front of him like a minesweeper, he shuffled past the nurse's station. With one hand on the wall, he inched toward the back door, counting his footsteps from the ward to the patio to make the return easier.

He pushed open the back door and felt the brisk outside air. The light emitted from the lampposts allowed him to make out the frame of large objects. He crunched over dropped tree leaves to a bench.

Roger sat quietly reflecting on the pleasant atmosphere, a different ambience from that on a casino floor—slot machine noises, ding and dong of coins hitting the metal tray, bells alerting the winner of a reward, and smoke irritating the eyes.

He pulled out a cigarette, fumbled for matches, successfully lit up, and exhaled.

A beam of light and a slight noise from the far side of the patio caught his attention. He rolled his head wrap above his eyes to follow the activity. He made out the image of a black veiled figure, a sister, he assumed. It looked like she came from the kitchen. With her back against the door, she held it open balancing items in her arms. She eased onto the patio, kicking the door closed with her shoe.

He stood as a cat jumped from a bare tree branch. Just as quickly, it righted itself, hightailing it in the kitchen's direction.

A soft voice scolded. "Ping Pong, now shoo! Go on. Get away." The cat circled the hemline of her habit, causing her to lose her balance and trip.

Roger tossed his cigarette to the ground and lunged to help, but was too slow to break her fall. The sister landed on the walkway, dropping loaves of bread from her arms.

"Oh my! My bread!" she cried out.

"Here, let me help." Roger bent down, holding the nun as she steadied herself to her feet.

"Get away, Ping Pong. Scram!" Nurse Watson said as she ran to the patio after the commotion. She spotted Roger with his arms around Sister Zita's waist. "Good God! What do you think you're up to, Mr. Atkins?"

Roger didn't respond, focusing his attention on the nun.

Officer Schultz, overweight from years lacking physical activity, huffed and puffed as he felt for the flashlight tucked between his belt and uniform. His sweaty hands fingered the housing tube and settled the light on the nun cupping her bloody nose, muffling a series of soft sobs.

Roger ignored the overweight officer. He grabbed his handkerchief and handed it to the nurse. She blotted droplets from Sister Zita's habit while he scooped up loaves of bread scattered on the ground. He handed them to the officer.

"Please, Schultz, escort Atkins back to his ward," the nurse demanded.

"Yes, ma'am. Good evening, Sister." Balancing the bread with one hand, with the other he grabbed hold of Roger's elbow, who in turn shrugged off the assistance.

As the men headed down the walkway, Roger paused. "What was that religious lady doing at this time of night?"

Schultz, employed since the arrival of the sisters, gladly assumed air as an historian. "It's her special annual *angel-of-the-night* ritual. You see, once the nuns get their new assignments, she bakes bread for those moving on to their new location. And then, you see, she heads for the locker room to place a loaf on top of each suitcase, like her goodbye gift." He stopped to catch his breath.

"You see, some will travel by train for many miles. The bread may be their only food before arriving at their next mission. So, you see, Sister was just sneaking around to finish what I call her self-imposed duty."

The cat scooted across their path.

"And what's with that cat?" An annoyed Roger kicked at it.

"Just a stray," the officer explained, "not allowed in the hospital, especially the kitchen. Got its name Ping Pong from popping up at different times. Smells from the kitchen always attracts her."

"Damn cat! I'm afraid Sister will be sporting a real shiner by tomorrow."

"God love the good religious women. You see, mirrors aren't allowed in their convent. She'll never see it."

Father Dooley

Chapter 29

Early the next morning Officer Hafen, rested under the city sign waiting for the first offender of the day. Joey raced past him. Hafen smiled, revved the engine, and gave chase, edging the T-bird onto the shoulder.

Joey waited inside the car, but made an Italian gesture. Under his breath he mumbled, "Porca miseria! Damn it."

Officer Hafen pulled out a police pad and slowly walked to the car's back fender. Joey climbed out of the driver's seat, slammed the door, and followed him eyeing the metal etching, *Piccolo Bastard*, above the license plate.

"Piccolo Bastard," Joey pronounced in his finest Italian and then added, "copied from James Dean's car. Familiar with him?"

"Yep," and to Joey's surprise, "called his car Little Bastard." Then, mimicking Joey's Italian, he added, "Piccolo Bastard."

"Fan of his?"

Hafen jotted down the license number. "Saw that Rebel movie of his." He looked to Joey. "Keep speeding, you may end up like him."

Joey ignored the admonition. "But officer, I'm going to see my pop in the hospital." Still no reaction from the stoic officer. The kid continued, "He's a war hero."

The officer asked for Joey's license. He inspected it, took down pertinent information, and returned it to the frown-faced Joey who reverted to his hot-blooded Italian roots. "But I'm not bothering anyone on this two-lane dusty road in Hicksville, except you."

"Excuse me? Hicksville?" The officer pressed hard on his pen and signed his name on the bottom of the ticket, making it an official citation. He handed it to Joey. "You've entered the city of Henderson."

Grabbing the ticket, Joey didn't bother reading it before he wrinkled and stuffed it in the back pocket of his jeans.

"Henderson, Smerderson. What kind of a welcome is this?" Joey kicked a pebble across the lane and continued, "and who lives in such a Godforsaken place as … Hen-der-son?"

"I do." Officer Hafen took out his pad again.

Immediately, Joey asked, "But why?" He shook his head, looked over the dry, arid stretch of desert. Tumbleweeds waited for the next gush of wind to push them to a new location.

"Why what?" the officer asked, writing out a second ticket.

"Why Henderson, of course."

Hafen raised his eyebrow and smiled, "Why not? It's a great place to live." Pressing hard against his pad, the cop penned his signature to the second citation of the day. "Here. For insubordination," and handed it to Joey whose mouth dropped. "If you plan to fight it, I'll see you in court."

The officer walked to his motorcycle and grabbed the handle grips. "Why do you live in Las Vegas?" Not waiting for a response, Hafen wished Joey a merry Christmas, waved, and zoomed off in full throttle.

§ § §

Brass hand bells rang out as the annual Christmas Mass came to an end. Father Dooley blessed the worshippers. Altar boys extinguished the burning incense and the aromatic smells flowed from its fragrant smoke.

Members of the community began singing, "Adeste Fideles." Their voices trailed from the chapel, down the halls, and into the wards.

Roger tossed in his bed pressing pillows over his ears. He inhaled, twitched his nose, and inhaled again. "It's that incense," he snapped out to anyone listening. "Bells! Latin! Incense! How's a patient to get any sleep in a Catholic hospital!"

The hymn ended on a robust, "Amen, Amen."

The priest, in a surplice over his cassock and white stole draped over his neck, darted into Ward Four. Mr. Atkins's name appeared frequently as a representative from The TapRoot Hotel and Casino, known for its endorsement and financial support of community activities. *Our new hospital patient deserves a special welcome.*

In an Irish brogue, he acknowledged the patients in Ward Four and moved Roger's privacy screen. "Top of the morning to you, Lieutenant Atkins. I'm Father Dooley," and returned the screen.

"It's Roger Atkins. Just Roger will do." Roger automatically extended his hand. The covering over his eyes made for a clumsy gesture.

The pastor inched closer. "Mr. Atkins … Roger, this morning we were a bit overzealous with our special Christmas Mass, now weren't we?"

Adjusting the netted head wrap, Roger replied, "No one warned me about your special zealous Mass." After a pause, Roger confessed, "Sorry, Father. I'm not a morning person."

"And you're not feeling quite like yourself, now are you?"

Roger positioned himself on the side of his bed. "And that religious woman? Is she alright? I'm sorry I couldn't get to her before she fell flat on her face. She must have a real black eye."

"It's colorful. Dr. Eaton ordered her a pair of dark glasses and suggested she apply a cold spoon over her eyes every fifteen minutes to reduce discoloration and swelling."

Roger felt for his robe. Father handed it to him just as the clanking of a cart's wheels announced a candy striper's presence.

"Looks like breakfast is on its way," the priest said. "You must be hungry."

"If beefsteaks were on her bill of fare, I …"

"My dear friend, now wouldn't you know, steaks are not in the sister's budget. Not even sure she'd know how to prepare them."

§ § §

Joey entered the hospital clutching file folders and several bags. He rushed past the nurse's station. "Morning, ladies."

"No running in this hospital," a nurse commanded.

He slowed after spotting a Chinese lady carrying a few items. He followed her into his pop's curtained area.

She nodded to Fr. Dooley and moved closer to Roger. She held out a cleaned, white handkerchief.

Roger didn't react.

"I'll take it for the lieutenant," Fr. Dooley intercepted.

She offered a wrapped loaf. "Here. You help up Sister."

Roger didn't respond.

"Take, Mr. Lieutenant. Healthy bread … for you … from Sister. She say thank you." Father accepted the gifts, pointing to Roger's eye wrap.

"Oh, you hurt. Get healthy. You eat sister's bread," she ordered. She pivoted to leave just as Miss Crawford entered carrying a breakfast tray. They ignored each other.

Joey greeted his pop with a hug and tossed files and bags to the end of the bed, correspondences scattered about.

"Son, I'm Father Dooley. And you be Joey." Father set the handkerchief on the bedside tray and shook Joey's hand.

"And who was that?" Roger queried.

"You just met Miss Mo." Miss Crawford added in a low voice, "kitchen help." She opened the lid over a plate of scrambled eggs. Applesauce, and a slice of bread and butter were set to the side of the tray. "You need nourishment. Let me help."

Roger shook his head. "No appetite."

Miss Crawford handed him a small piece of bread. "Here. At least try some of Sister Zita's bread. She bakes it fresh daily."

Father noticed Roger took a liking to it. He said that the nuns set up a small commercial enterprise on a table outside the cafeteria. "Former patients return for more. They like its taste and claim it holds some type of health benefits. They leave a donation, sometimes small, sometimes generous."

"Pittance, most of the time," Miss Crawford said as she tidied up the bedside tray, then fluffed the pillow. Bending low, she whispered in his ear, "We're down to the felt. But the good sisters keep praying God will provide somehow."

"The man upstairs not listening?" Roger questioned.

"No one knows our plight. I keep encouraging the administrator to collect patients outstanding debts." She smoothed the top sheet and pulled it over Roger. "And we're growing so fast, we do need a new wing."

Fr. Dooley interrupted. "Tell you what, Mr. Atkins, uh … Roger. I'll change from my vestments and later we'll go look for Sister Zita."

"That'll be nice." Roger yawned.

At the end of the bed, Joey sorted out material from the casino files while the nurse unwrapped Roger's head netting and tossed it in the trash basket. She handed him a pair of dark glasses. "Doctor's orders. And how are you feeling this morning?"

"Just a little weak. Don't have an appetite for hospital food, but you know, this bread is tasty."

"Well then, for lunch, if the doctor okays it, we'll add more slices along with fruits and vegetables." The nurse exited, carrying the tray.

"Miss Crawford, so, you're here every day?"

"Stopped by for the special Mass and wanted to see that my favorite patient was properly taken care of."

Joey's eyes shifted from Roger and back to Miss Crawford.

A flirty expression stretched across her face as she fluttered her fingers at Roger. "I'll check on you tomorrow." With a change of expression, "And Joey, if you need anything, you just let me know."

When the privacy screen was pulled shut, Joey declared. "Wow! You get special attention from the cook, and you have a personal pillow-fluffier-upper. Something going on here that I missed?"

"Joey, just go. Brief me later the casino business." Roger slipped farther down into the sheets. "And don't forget my newspapers."

Miss Mo

Chapter 30

Swinging her towel, Miss Mo returned to the kitchen's back area. She noticed the china, silverware, and crystal goblets laid out on the counters. She glanced at her fellow workers busily preparing for another one of Fr. Dooley's parties.

Miss Mo mumbled to herself, *Next time, Father, with his fancy Irish Talk, he shine silver and cook and clean up himself.*

She returned to the front serving area, wiping food splatters around the heated serving trays.

Sr. Zita applied polish and elbow grease to a stubborn smudge on the sterling silver footed-serving tray. She picked it up and examined the tarnished areas when she made out her image. Curious, the religious woman took off her special dark glasses and looked at the injured eye. She moved the tray back and forth to view it from different angles. She patted the blackened eye when Miss Mo returned from the serving area.

"Black eye, good? No?"

Sr. Zita dabbed her eye with her apron. She whispered that she was the youngest with four older brothers. Being the only girl, she grew up a tomboy.

Her startled helper listened intently as she reflected on growing up, a subject nuns seldom shared. Religious women spoke in depth about entering heaven or damned into everlasting hot flames of hell. Holy cards, small handouts depicting various saints and religious scenes, were reminders of these events.

One of Miss Mo's favorite image was of winged angels flying around heaven while saints in long white robes sat on puffy white clouds. She prayed she'd end up there. No one wore an apron. No one polished silver. No one cooked dinners for priests.

Mo looked at Sr. Zita. "Never know Sister have family. Never *family-talk*."

Absorbed with memories, Sr. Zita spoke, in a low voice of the day she shimmied up the old oak tree in the back yard of their farm. She was quicker than her oldest brother who struggled to the top.

Sister sighed and placed the polished tray on the countertop. She dug inside her deep pocket and pulled out a handkerchief. "I sat on the top tree limb waiting for him, swinging my legs." She paused and blew her nose. "Called him *chicken*."

"Not nice." Miss Mo shook her head.

"My foot hit him right here," tapping the bridge of her nose. "For almost a week, it was a sight." Sister smiled recalling earlier memories.

"You happy. That nice." Mo turned toward the food line, stopped, and strained her ears. She looked back and saw her wiping tears.

Between sobs, Sr. Zita blurted out, "Miss Mo, I am so sorry. I'm so embarrassed. Please excuse me. My family … I miss seeing them. I miss talking to them."

The small band of kitchen employees, eyes and ears focused on their work, learned to ignore, or at least pretend to take no notice of conversations between Sister Zita and Miss Mo. They respected the close relationship the two developed over the years.

The workers kept a distance. In fact, Miss Mo intimidated them more than Sr. Zita and each found herself, at one time or another, on the short end of Miss Mo's tirades. When she scolded them in Chinese, it was both hurtful to their egos and penetrating to their ears.

Sr. Zita sat and buried her head in her hands. Miss Mo caught a fellow worker looking in their direction, eavesdropping on their private conversation. She stared, put her hands on her hips, and frowned. Immediately, rules of the kitchen were restored—no looking or listening to Sr. Zita and Miss Mo. Period.

"No cry. No cry. Mo and Sister need family talk." Miss Mo tried to comfort Sr. Zita prancing back and forth behind her. "I miss my family-talk, too. I miss mother-talk. My mother, Irish, left Mo and Chinese father when Mo only three." Sr. Zita looked up. Miss Mo sniffled. "Good father, but never family-talk. Never mother-talk. I get sad."

Sr. Zita dug into her pocket for another handkerchief, and handed it to her friend. Putting her arm around her coworker's narrow shoulders, she ushered her into the large pantry, their inner sanctum.

"But I wait for Mother. Wait, wait, wait."

A Staple, a Benefit

Chapter 31

"You're a good prop for the padre. An Air Force glamour boy will get a sympathy vote from his parishioners," Ryan joked while Fr. Dooley eased Roger into a wheelchair.

"And why don't you learn to keep a lid on it? You're not funny," George replied.

Fr. Dooley rolled Roger past the nurse's station, acknowledging warm greetings from parishioners. A visitor offered pleasantries and opened the patio door for them. Embarrassed and uncomfortable in the position of an invalid, Roger hung his head low.

Stationing Roger under a lamppost, Fr. Dooley locked the brakes, and waved greetings to those on the patio as he walked to the kitchen's back door.

Ping Pong meowed. She tried to sneak inside, but the priest shooed her away.

Fr. Dooley wheeled Roger inside the kitchen's back area, past ovens, a refrigerator, a dishwasher, table, pots, and pans, and a group of workers wearing aprons and hair nets. Sr. Zita was not in the kitchen.

§ § §

Dooley retraced the route. He wheeled Roger through the hospital halls to the cafeteria. Slowing down, he matched his speed with an older couple in front him. "Coming up on the right."

In front of the cafeteria, Dooley anchored the wheelchair next to the table with brown paper bags lined up, a loaf of bread poking from each. A sign rested on a can: Bread Donations. "You can't help but be attracted to a whiff of fresh, homemade bread, hot from the ovens."

Roger raised his head, inhaled the alluring sweet and comforting aroma. A vivid memory filled his head.

Nonna, in her kitchen, apron around her waist, stirred a big pot of soup. In the dining area, Papa stood proudly at the foot of the table with young Joey squeezed between him and Giana. Images of Giana breaking off pieces of Pane du Monte Sant' Angelo bread drifted in his mind.

Roger struggled to recall those earlier times; back to the Puglia's home, a picture of the Sacred Heart with a rosary hanging from its frame, and lovely Giana translating for his benefit.

Rubbing his eyes, he tried to focus on what Giana said, "Pane du Monte Sant' Angelo, a staple, a benefit."

The vision blurred and faded. Background mumblings blended into the flashback.

He heard an Irish brogue. "Ah. Sure look it! Now mind you, a brilliant placement for donations."

What the hell was Father doing in Bari?

There were too many distractions. His memory played tricks on him. Voices of various people jolted him back to the cafeteria entrance. Father repeated. "Now don't you think it's a brilliant placement for donations?"

Roger humored him, agreed it was brilliant, then made the excuse that he felt sleepy. He asked to return to the ward.

"Well, it's just what I will do. We'll look for Sister Zita another time."

§ § §

"What's up, Pop?" Joey tossed newspapers with file folders on the chair. Roger nibbled at the hospital food. Looking at the tray, his son snatched an untouched bowl of lime fruit dessert and a cottage cheese salad.

Roger took another bite of bread and explained, Miss Crawford slipped extra slices of bread with butter, jam, and honey on his tray. "Tasty. By the way, buy a couple loaves for Mr. Jake and the girls. Leave a donation." He rubbed his eyes and yawned. "Father's telling me the sisters are hurting for funds. So, leave a generous donation."

"Betcha Father pegged you right from the start as a soft touch, someone with juice." Joey jotted down the new order on his to-do list, then finished the fruit dessert.

"Betcha Father pegged everyone from the start as a soft touch." They chuckled, recognizing a kernel of truth to the manipulative ways of some men of the cloth.

"Betcha the chaplain also shifts his Irish talk into high gear when he wants to," added Joey.

Roger ignored the last remark and leaned back on his pillows. "Dr. Eaton wants me to stroll around the hospital grounds. Nothing strenuous, but says walking keeps the lungs healthy. He's encouraging me to stop or try to limit smoking. Says I have chronic bronchitis, simpler way of saying, it's smoker's lung."

"That's serious. But you without a cigarette! Can't imagine." He reached for a slice of bread.

"I thought you said you already ate."

Backing off, Joey asked, "So, what's up with your medical records?"

"They're working on it." Roger chuckled. "Not surprised they're having trouble." He pushed the bed table to the side. "I need more sleep. And thanks for the newspapers."

Joey left the hospital with two bags of the bread, slipping a generous donation in the can.

Rita and Tatyana

Chapter 32

Rita and Tatyana relaxed with Jake in his penthouse waiting for Joey's return. Nat King Cole's "The Christmas Song" offered background music as Rita mixed drinks at a bar set up in front of a Chinese folding screen. Decorated boxes of all sizes piled under the Christmas tree.

The lady's choice in styles and accessories reflected their opposite tastes. Rita embellished her sporty selection with costume jewelry: a large, multi-colored chunky necklace, dangling earrings, and bangle bracelets. Tatyana preferred fine jewelry and fashions of the day.

Jake and Tatyana squeezed next to each on an antique, golden leather, tufted chesterfield sofa. Several months earlier, Jake presented her with an engagement ring, a round diamond flanked with smaller stones in a yellow gold setting.

Ever since Tatyana became the special person in his life, he changed many of his bachelor-day habits. Gone were stuffed and mounted animals. Gone were his curse words, but he didn't sacrifice his cigar-smoking habit.

Joey kissed his friends and placed the loaves on top the bar. He commented on Tatyana's sack outfit, new style that hid a woman's curves.

"Let me tell ya, my gal even makes a sack look interesting, especially with those spiked heels," Jake admitted.

"Pumpkin, take my motherly advice." Rita rubbed the calf of her right leg. "You're asking for double trouble walking in those stilettos."

Joey flopped on the red velvet loveseat and brought the group up to date with Roger's diagnoses. He informed them the doctor treated his pop's iritis condition with medication and dark glasses, and of an appointment with a pulmonologist in California.

The sweet aroma of bread drew Rita's attention to the brown bag. She pulled out a loaf, looked at its gorgeous brown top, sniffed and said, "Ooh, ooh, bready, bready." She cut a few slices and held one up for closer inspection. "Would you look! Just like my mom's homemade bread, a little coarse and no bubbles. That religious lady knows what she's doing."

Never shy, Joey grabbed a slice. He smiled as the bread triggered memories of the Pane di Monte Sant' Angelo. At first, Joey was tempted to share the memory, but only his pop would appreciate it. He stayed mute on such topics. Instead, Joey licked his fingers and walked over to the record player and put on, "Let It Snow, Let It Snow," by Vic Damone.

Tatyana handed a slice to Jake. He took a few bites. "Umm, good. Joey, tomorrow, get me more loaves."

"And," Rita added, "tell Roger we girls can't wait to see him."

"Will do," placing cheese on another slice.

"Joey, you got another message from that Miss Crawford. What's that all about?"

"Oh, from the hospital. She's made friends with Pop and plans to keep her eyes on him." Joey read over the message.

Rita took a knife and plunged it into a loaf. "Friends? I bet she does keep her eyes on him." She walked over and wiggled between Tatyana and Jake. Rita elbowed Tatyana, rolled her eyes and, in a stage whisper, added, "Bet she wants to keep more than eyes on him?" Both women laughed.

Joey scanned the note and announced, "Seems tomorrow I have a date with Miss Crawford. She wants to meet me at the Black Rock Cafe before I see Pop." Joey turned to the group. "Now, for my dinner date with Lovely Lucia. See you guys."

If Only

Chapter 33

After a restful sleep, Roger decided to follow doctor's order and go for a walk. He grabbed his robe and pulled the dark glasses from the pocket. A devilish smile stretched over his face when he felt a pack of cigarettes.

Just one more smoke, he promised himself.

He folded a blanket and threw it over his shoulder in case the weather turned colder.

Roger slid open the private screen and made small talk with his ward mates. He learned George enlisted in the Navy on December 8, 1941, day after the Japanese attacked Pearl Harbor.

George drew an imaginary square in the air with his forefinger. "That day lines to enlist twisted from the recruiter's desk to outside and 'round the building down to the next corner." He added, with a big smile, "I was on active duty right until the end, after Japan surrendered."

"I heard the doc tell you to quit smoking. Maybe you should follow this old man's example." Ryan looked up at Roger. "He said smoking was restricted to certain times, never on night-watch duty."

The younger patient related the trouble his ward mate had giving up his smoking habit. The embers from a cigarette butt might attract the enemy and disclose the shop's location.

Roger sensed George, glancing around the ward, did not want to be remembered by such a lackluster war story.

"You young whippersnapper. Maybe you should just shut your big mouth."

"And maybe you should learn how to ride a motorcycle. Then you wouldn't be wrapped up in that body cast."

Time to leave, Roger thought.

§ § §

"O Come All Ye Faithful," played from the radio in the reception area. He peeped around the hallway corner. Last minute touches to Christmas tree decorating held the attention of a small group. Boxes, stacked against each other, were identified:

BOYS CLOTHES, GIRLS CLOTHES, TOYS, MISC.

Volunteers wrapped and decorated gifts with colored paper, ribbons, and labels for the needy in the community. Roger watched one lady pull out a Santa costume and finger-comb the white beard. He smiled, picturing his own portrayal of the jolly man many years ago at the Puglia's home and chuckled remembering the toilet-paper gift exchange.

Atkins wanted to tell the ladies their decorated tree and gift boxes added a special touch to the Christmas spirit, but felt uncomfortable entering in pajamas. He resumed his original plan and headed for the patio. That was until he caught a whiff of Sr. Zita's freshly baked bread.

Exercise and smoke can wait a little longer.

§ § §

He turned toward the cafeteria, took off his glasses and merged with the breakfast crowd. Patients chatted over juice, hospital personnel read the paper, and visitors sipped coffee.

"Mind if I wish the kitchen crew a Merry Christmas?" he asked the cashier busy counting the morning's receipts."

She gave a nod and continued her count. "Seventy-three, seventy-four …"

Roger walked confidently behind the food station. Remnants of scrambled eggs, shriveled oily bacon strips, and cooled biscuits sat in separate hot-food pans. Women with hairnets and aprons busied themselves—washing plates, peeling potatoes, chopping vegetables. He recognized Sr. Zita, preoccupied with her duties.

Roger mused, *religious women, whether with white or black veil, with or without an education, serve as foot soldiers to the Church's all male hierarchy.*

"Sorry," a kitchen server, wearing bulky potholders and carrying hot mashed potatoes in a large metal pan, bumped against Roger's elbow. He offered to help as she headed to the front of the food line. Flashing a big smile with drops of sweat trickling down her face, she said, "No sir, but thank you," and expertly wiggled the container into an empty spot.

Roger shook his head thinking of Sr. Zita in her liturgical garment, a black veil and coif framing her face, a black cord holding a large silver cross around her neck and the long skirts. *How do nuns tolerate wearing all that garb during the desert summer heat?*

Roger waved, hoping to get Sr. Zita's attention. He watched her move from the dishwasher to the oven, stopping momentarily to pin her black veil back from her face.

The kitchen worker returned wiping perspiration from her forehead and side-stepped Roger.

"Oh, excuse me. I'm sorry I'm blocking your way. Just got lost in my memories."

Roger noted similarities between Sr. Zita and Giana. Both projected an energic, wholesome appearance. Whereas Giana was Italian, he guessed Sr. Zita must be Irish with her light-skinned complexion. Her hair was tucked inside the head covering, but Roger imagined it was light in color, perhaps with red highlights. She might be Irish, but certainly not Black Irish.

He, a Jewish person with black hair, hazel eyes with black eyebrows and lashes, grew up in an Irish neighborhood. One of his freckled-face Irish friends nicknamed him, *my Black Irish buddy*. Roger accepted the moniker as a compliment.

His thoughts were interrupted when he spied Miss Mo exiting the pantry, tomato sauce cans clasped in her hands. She kicked the door closed with her foot and caught sight of Roger. Stopping, she said in a loud voice, "Sister. Nice Mr. Lieutenant Atkins here."

Workers looked her way, smiled, but kept busy with their duties. Sr. Zita jerked around and when she saw Roger, wiped her hands on her apron and quickly unfastened her veil.

With a playful smile, Roger confessed to Miss Mo, "I particularly enjoyed the extra slices of that tasty bread," then pointed to the back patio, mumbling that he was headed out, but wanted to properly introduce himself.

Sr. Zita slowly walked toward Roger, averting her eyes to the floor. She said she was happy to meet him and apologized for all the commotion the previous evening.

"As I see it, Sister, we could lay the blame squarely at Ping Pong's feet … or paws."

"That Ping Pong, what to do?" She laid the cans of tomato sauce on a long kitchen worktable.

Politely, Roger inquired how she was feeling.

With a nervous laughter, she assured him she was fine. "And, I am pleased you enjoyed the bread, Mr. Atkins," she said and scurried back to her duties.

Just then Miss Crawford walked into the cafeteria and glanced in search of Roger. She spied him in the back chatting with Miss Mo. Moving to the duo, she leveled her gaze on Roger. "Well, look at you. I stopped by Ward Four but couldn't find you. I'm surprised to see you here," she said with a snooty look to Mo, and added, "with the kitchen help."

Mo ignored the woman's presence, and reproach. She returned her attention to Roger, who told her Frank Sinatra frequently visited The TapRoot, along with other headliners.

When he saw Miss Mo's face light up at the mention of Ol' Blue Eyes, he invited her as his guest once he was released from the hospital.

Looking at Joan, Roger realized her frosty expression needed thawing, so he also extended the invitation to her. It worked. Crawford appeared happy. Miss Mo was happy. Sr. Zita was back to baking and probably happy, too.

That settled, Roger took his leave and headed to the back patio with a pack of cigarettes safely tucked away in his pocket. That made him happy.

§ § §

Slipping on the dark glasses, Roger settled on a bench under the lamppost, draping the blanket across his knees. Noise of an ambulance siren whined through the air and drowned sounds of the chirping birds.

Patients, and their guests, enjoyed the cool temperatures and pleasant outdoor setting. Roger assumed the couple sitting across from him must be a wife visiting her husband, the patient. On another bench a man sat alone, newspaper spread open. A teenager, with his two-wheeler bike laying on the grass, performed yo-yo tricks.

Just one more cigarette and I'll toss out the entire package. He scanned the area and fixated on the teenager's bike, a powerful reminder of his youth, and the night the Germans bombed the Port of Bari. His mind drifted back to that chaotic event.

Eyes closed as different images floated around in his mind.

A bike … Giana's bike … on the ground a few feet from stairs leading to the water's edge. Sailors yelled in agony and dove from damaged ships into the flame-engulfed bay. Giana in the middle of the water alongside the rescue team.

He smelled and felt something burning. He yelled out, "Giana. Watch out, Giana! Watch out!"

A high-pitched voice snapped him back to the present. "Sir, wake up! Wake up! It's burning."

After a long moment, Roger opened his eyes and looked around at the startled faces on the patio. The youngster frantically pointed to Roger's lap; his cigarette had slipped from his fingers. A smoldering fire created a growing circular ring around his blanket. Roger took off his glasses, jumped, threw the blanket to the ground, and stomped on it again and again.

With each violent motion he recited the *if only* litany he held in his head all these years.

If only she didn't join with the rescue effort. She didn't have to. If only she didn't jump into the churning, flaming waters. She didn't have to do that, either. If only she had been the one recognized as the true hero. I didn't deserve that honor.

His *if only's* never altered the string of events. The fact remained. Giana, young, vital, and beautiful, ended up as a civilian wartime casualty. Roger's heart remained broken. His brief love story came to an abrupt and mournful end.

Roger painted a disturbing picture in front of the small patio group. The teenager rolled up his yoyo, grabbed his bike, and pedaled from the frightening scene. The man folded his newspaper and stared at Roger. The wife helped her elderly husband to stand and began their exit to the hospital.

He couldn't forget Giana. He didn't want to. *She was Joey's mother. She was the woman I wanted to share my life with.*

He craved a cigarette. *Just one more and tomorrow I'll give up this nasty habit.*

He lit up and inhaled, then exhaled, watching the smoke trail out into the desert air.

Black Rock Cafe

Chapter 34

The parking lot in front of Black Rock Café was packed. Joey found a space a few blocks away and jogged back to the restaurant. He entered, out of breath, and scanned the eatery.

The ceiling was low, noise level high. A smoky smell permeated the air. A Christmas tree next to a table, towered over ae Nativity scene. Gene Autry's recording, "Rudolph the Red-Nose Reindeer," competed with chatter from the patrons.

Joey sized up the crowd. Construction workers in overalls, businessmen in slacks, some with ties, ladies in dresses, and children in neatly ironed outfits. A few accessorized their clothing with Christmas pins—a Santa Claus, wreaths, snowflakes. Joey threaded his way between tables, barely enough for accommodating a server, a thin one at that.

Joan, a standout in a red outfit, sat at a table in the middle of the restaurant with a clear view of the entrance. Seeing Joey, she stood and waved.

Joey apologized for his late arrival and hung his red windbreaker on the back of the chair. He got the two tickets from his blue jeans and transferred them into his shirt's pocket.

"Not one, but two lousy tickets."

Wiggling her fingers, Joan gestured for Joey to let her see them. She cocked an eyebrow noting the officer's signature.

"I'll take care of these," she said and slipped them into her purse.

"What the heck! Thanks."

Miss Crawford handed him the menu. "Let's just say now you owe me one."

Joey took a quick moment to check the menu, concentrating on the right side. Reassured he could cover their bill, he announced, "Okay, then, it's my treat. Let's call it even."

Miss Crawford took a drag from her cigarette. *No, no, no. The kid doesn't get it.* She smashed the cigarette in the ashtray. *I'm playing for a bigger stake. I want you to get me into Roger's mind. I need your help.*

The waitress flipped open her pad. Joey put in his order for fresh orange juice, two fried eggs, bacon, biscuits with gravy, and a glass of milk. Miss Crawford stuck with her usual, black coffee, one poached egg, and dry toast.

Joey shared Roger's comment that Boulder Highway was a speed trap. But, he admitted, the officer was cool. Rerolling cigarettes back into the cuff of his t-shirt, he said, "The officer knew all about the actor James Dean."

"I get it now. James Dean, with your red windbreaker and those cigarettes … I didn't think you smoked."

"Cigarettes are just a prop, but Dean and I, we're sort of alike." He pulled a paper napkin from the dispenser and unfolded it in his lap. "Well, not really. Dean was more of the silent type, like my pop. Guess you notice, that's not me."

Discreetly, Joan waited while the waitress set down the coffee, juice, and milk before she continued. "So, like James Dean, you're a rebel without a cause?"

"More like a rebel with causes."

Doris Day's "Here Comes Santa Claus" played on the juke box as diners flowed into the cafe. A family of six claimed a booth against the wall. A cowboy, bow-legged and wearing weathered boots, swaggered in. His fleshy midriff protruded from under a leather vest, barely held together by four buttons. Handcrafted silver and turquoise jewelry covered chubby fingers. He had a bandana tied under his double chin.

A broad smile stretched across his ruddy complexion when he noticed Miss Crawford. Walking to her table, he tipped his cowboy hat. "Mornin, Miss Crawford. Entertainin' a young friend?" He threw a stare to Joey, cracked his knuckles, then smiled back at Joan. "Looking mighty lovely, as usual."

The cowpoke walked through the middle aisle and settled at a long counter with brass foot railings. He situated himself on the oak bar facing the mirrored wall framed with candy canes. Without turning, he monitored Joan's every move.

She gestured for Joey to lean closer. "That's Red. Silly, rich, old fool. More money than sense. He's like a little puppy dog, always around, but can't take the hint. Anyway, he's not my type."

Joey took a swallow of milk. "Miss Crawford, like that guy said, you do look really nice!"

Always at the ready to ease conversation to her favorite topic, herself, she asked, "Heard of the movie star, Joan Crawford?"

"Yep!" Joey declared after taking a swallow of milk. "Now I get it. You sort of dress like she does."

Miss Crawford chuckled kindly and blew smoke rings toward the ceiling.

"Anything else I can get?" asked the waitress.

"Yes, another glass of milk and you, Miss Crawford?"

Red watched Joan put her hand over her cup and the waitress moved on. *I wonder what story she's designed for this young man She is entertaining.*

"Do you have a favorite Crawford movie?" Joan tapped her cigarette into the ashtray and questioned Joey.

Joey looked down and fiddled with his napkin, folding it in many directions. Joan waited for an answer. He confessed he never thought about it, just knew the movie star was a good actress. "And you? Your favorite?"

"Well, for starters, she's brilliant as Lorna Forbes in 'The Damned Don't Cry,' a girl from a poor working-class family. That's me." Joan leaned back and exhaled, forming a smoky O. She stabbed at it, breaking it into small white clouds evaporating into the air. "Lorna needs to get out of her rut. That's me, too."

The waitress refreshed Joey's glass of milk and turned her attention to other patrons.

"It gets better," Joan continued. "She sets her sights on a gangster. I'm still looking for my next love," she admitted.

"For a gangster?"

"Maybe not a gangster, but someone who's exciting." She opened her purse and dropped her pack of cigarettes inside.

"Just be careful." Joey took a swallow of milk.

"You're right." She looked to her left, then her right, and whispered, "Someone like a casino publicist. Now that's more to my liking … safer, too."

Joey gagged, grabbed his napkin, and spat out a mouthful of milk. Miss Crawford paid no attention, searching inside her purse for a mirror and lipstick tube. She drew on a fresh layer and smacked her lips together.

Memories

Chapter 35

Joey returned to the hospital with a stack of newspapers and placed them neatly on the chair, then focused his attention on the food tray. He grabbed the dessert dish. "Before I met Miss Crawford for breakfast, I weaved in and out of Henderson's streets."

He finished the fruit dessert and set it on the tray. "Do you know the streets are named after chemical elements on the Periodic Chart? I drove around identifying symbols for each. First, I drove onto Gold Street. That was easy. It's the element, *Au*. Then I took a right turn onto Iron Street. Everyone knows that's *Fe*. Then onto Magnesium Street. Of course, *Mg*."

"Makes sense," Roger gave a big yawn. "The town's history is tied up with the war effort. Their Basic Magnesium Plant supplied our country with munition and airplane parts."

"Yep. Knew that," and Joey added. "They should add the symbol under the name of each street. That just might boost young students interest in studying chemistry."

Roger realized his son was on the brink of enumerating every element on the periodic table. He changed the subject. "I met Sister Zita," but stopped short of saying how much she reminded him of Joey's mother and pushed aside his tray table. "And by the way, I want you to find out about our headliners scheduled for January."

Joey jotted down the request on his to-do list and continued, "I entered Zinc Street. Bingo! That's *Zn*."

"Tomorrow. I'm too tired now." Roger yawned and settled in bed. "And get a couple of dozen filet mignons send to the sisters." He pulled the bed sheet over him. "Send them in care of Father Dooley. Add a note, for sisters ice box in case of another black eye. He should get a kick out of that."

§ § §

Roger busied himself with his health: taking his medication, having vital signs checked, and daily walks around the hospital grounds. He tried to give up smoking, but the best he could do was to limit the number of cigarettes per day.

On a walk to the back patio, winds created a dusty haze over the desert landscape. Roger shielded his eyes following a crumbled piece of paper bouncing down a well-worn lane toward the former magnesium plant.

During the war, an underground tunnel was constructed for security reasons that connected the hospital's grounds with the industrial facility. It was sealed after the war. The above ground path, overgrown with grasses and sagebrush, presented a visual reminder of those earlier years.

Roger tied the robe tightly around him and sat on the bench. Ping Pong ambled next to his leg, jumped, and curled herself on his lap. As Roger petted the cat, she closed her eyes with a soft purr.

A couple strolled by with a little girl who asked if she could pet the cat. After getting approval from her parents, the girl moved closer to the feline, who hightailed it toward the kitchen's back door.

"Her name is Ping Pong," Roger exclaimed. "Doesn't stay in one place for long."

They smiled and moved on with their daughter pouting, arms folded across her chest.

150

Watching the cat scratch at the door, Roger imagined Miss Mo inside busy with kitchen duties and Sr. Zita with the baking.

He reflected on one of his mother's favorite Old Testament proverb, "Do not withhold good from those to whom it is due, when it is your power to act." He knew he had the wherewithal to do good for the Daughters of Saint Brigid in their time of need.

He had not formulated a plan yet, but decided to take on the challenge. The hospital had two pressing needs - paying their bills was number one, and secondly, to enlarge their hospital. The sisters needed to keep their doors open to offer compassionate care for the medical demands of a growing community.

§ § §

When Roger's military medical records finally arrived, Father Dooley, with envelope in hand, wheeled him to the doctor's office. They made small talk as they waited for the medic to join them.

"Sorry I'm late," said Dr. Eaton. He shook hands with Roger and accepted the packet from the priest. Nodding in his direction, the doctor asked, "Roger, mind if he stays?" and received a thumbs-up. He flipped through the material.

"Copies of lab work and medical procedures," he paused. "Umm … just as I figured, respiratory tract infection, changes in the hematological system and lymph glands, and injuries related to flying shrapnel and mustard gas."

"Mercy! Mustard gas. Hard to believe the Germans used such inhumane tactics." Fr. Dooley made the sign of the cross.

Dr. Eaton corrected him. "It wasn't the German's poison. It was stored in one of our Liberty ships, a precautionary measure, a backup plan. During the war, rumors surfaced the enemy might be storing nerve gas in a large underground factory."

The medic inserted the material back into the envelope. "That data flamed the idea that chemical warfare might become a reality. In case the Germans were first to employ harmful chemicals, we came prepared."

"Lord, Lord. What a dreadful situation!" Fr. shuddered.

Roger raised his eyebrows. He welcomed the fact that the top-secret classification of the bombing and its aftermath was lifted. With a strong voice he found himself saying, "When the Germans bombed the port, they hit the jackpot—our own poison hidden inside our own ship. It was … it was …"

A serious look passed between the priest and the doctor. Neither could relate personally to the lieutenant wartime experiences. Father asked for, and received, a religious exemption. Dr. Eaton's impaired foot kept him from military service.

"Is there more to your story?" The doctor noted Roger fidgeting.

Roger pointed to his head and then his heart. "Thinking about it, it stays inside, holding tormenting memories." Aware of a rhythmic clicking noise, Roger searched for the source. Large wooden rosary beads hung from Fr. Dooley's sash and clanked together as he nervously fondled and fingered each one.

"By sharing your story, the burden you've carried all these years may be lifted, or at least lessened." Dr. Eaton said as he tapped Roger on the shoulder, assuring him that his story would be kept in confidence. The priest nodded in agreement.

At first, Roger hesitated to mention Giana then swallowed. "I was in love with Joey's mother, Giana."

"Joey's mother?" the medic responded.

Father echoed the same. "You mean Joey's mother?"

"Yes, Father, and I'm embarrassed by all the attention thrown my way. I received medical attention for my condition resulting from mustard gas, got better, and awarded with medals and a hometown parade. Uh…uh!"

"Go on," Dr. Eaton encouraged.

Roger, hanging his head in his hands between his knees, mumbled events as told by Dr. Gadaleta—swimming in oily poisonous water, sacrificing her life for one of ours, shrapnel tearing her aorta. "Giana deserved public honor, the attention she never received."

Between short sobs, Roger continued. "I barely got to know Giana. Those were precious moments, moments I've never been able to duplicate, never. I yearn to see her just once more. I wish to tell her I loved her."

Both Dr. Eaton and the priest froze in silent brotherhood. After several moments, Roger lifted his head and grabbed the end of his robe to wipe away tears. Father fished inside his pocket for a handkerchief and handed it to him.

Noise from a food tray wheeling down the hallway signaled it was time for food. Dr. Eaton left the room momentarily. When he returned, he informed Roger he ordered a special meal to be delivered a little later.

Roger gave Dr. Eaton a dazed look. "If only I… if only …"

"Hell comes in many forms. Dying instantly might be a blessing for those exposed to such high doses of mustard gas," offered the doctor.

An awkward silence followed until Fr. Dooley broke in. "You've been carrying an agonizing responsibility all these years. The good Lord took her quickly. I believe He wants you to remember the grand times, as brief as they were. You deserve that."

The doctor shared his personal story of losing his brother on Omaha Beach during the D-Day invasion. "I'm sure he would not want us to remember his actions by *if only's*. We, his family, solemnize and salute him for being so brave and doing his best under dangerous circumstances. He's our hero. Your lady friend, I think, wants you to forge ahead and pay tribute to her heroic actions."

"Your lady friend was brave. I wonder if I were tested, if God would grant me the strength to stand up to the enemy? She was a hero … a good person. That's what she was, a truly selfless person."

Roger said, "Your words … I need to hear them again and again. They offer some comfort. I hope to find a degree of solace remembering her as courageous, and my hero. But my heart still aches for Giana, my Angioletto."

AMEN, AMEN

Chapter 36

"**I** think I ended up with more red on my face, than you have left on your lips," Joey smiled at Lucia. They sat together on the sofa in the apartment.

She grabbed a soda can from the coffee table and handed it to him. "We need to take it slower." Extending her arms, she pushed Joey to the other side of the sofa. "I remember what the good sisters taught us."

"Blah, blah, blah. I remember, too, but just look where that got them—stuck in a convent."

"Joseph, you must be respectful!"

"Right now, I just feel like being bad."

"Joseph. No, no, no," she pleaded. "Let's just talk."

"After last night, I thought you heard enough about me and my family."

"Oh, Joseph. When you described your papa coming home from a morning's catch, cupping your face with his calloused hands and dirty fingernails, I could feel the love between the two of you."

"He was special to me."

"And Joseph, your Nonna always in an apron, carrying her rosary beads and praying. And her gray hair in a bun. She was so like my own grandma."

"I got my spaghetti sauce recipe by watching her … always in the kitchen cutting up garlic and onions."

"And your mother … I remember you said she was beautiful."

"But those memories are not so strong. She was gone a lot studying to be a nurse and then she was busy being a nurse." He chuckled. "She had a fresh scent about her fingernails and hands, always scrubbed clean. Nonna had a pungent odor that stayed on her fingers and Papa could not shed that fishy smell that followed him. It's sort of funny what things stuck in my mind."

"That is good. And I like your stories about you and the lieutenant."

"I'll tell you more if you let me move closer."

"Please, no." She brushed him away. "Now, Joseph. I am serious. Tell me, how did you locate the lieutenant after that fateful night?"

"I cried for my mom, my Nonna, and my papa since they were not with me. My family liked the lieutenant. I really liked him, too." Abruptly, he stood and walked to the tall windows looking over the Las Vegas valley. "You know, Pop went through a lot." Clearing his throat, he held back a sob. "I don't understand it, but he won't share those memories and it hurts me."

Lucia walked to him with her arms around his shoulders. "His own hurt inside must be very large."

Facing her, he gazed into her eyes. He planted a passionate kiss on her lips. She offered no resistance. When he picked her up, she swung her arms around his shoulders holding tight as he carried her to the sofa. "Now, time for talking is over."

§ § §

Roger scanned the newspapers and froze on a headline from West Virginia: *Sell Fresh Bread not the Old Abbey.* After reading the article, he used Miss Crawford's office telephone. He gave Joey an assignment—uncover what was behind the story.

After a series of long-distance calls and meticulous notes, Joey discovered the Blessed Spirit seminarians baked bread they called Amen, Amen. They turned the loaves into a successful fundraising opportunity to save their old Abbey in need of restorations and repairs.

Joey related his conversation with the Abbey's spokesman, Father Homer Ellis. "The seminarians pestered their cook from the Republic of Poland to bake a bread they remembered from their childhood days. Several watched their grandmothers and mothers go through the baking process, but none could offer a list of ingredients or a recipe. They used words like 'the bread tasted good,' or 'had a cheesy flavor.'"

Joey continued reading from his notes. "During his experimental stage, the cook threw many batches out the back door. Stray cats gobbled up each failed attempt. Finally, he settled on a recipe acceptable to the community. The seminarians rejoiced with a robust, 'Amen, Amen.' So, the name stuck."

"Amen, Amen. That's certainly a catchy name," Roger added.

"Here's the turning point," Joey responded. "At first, they offered free slices to their parishioners. The demand and popularity for their bread grew and afterwards a price tag accompanied each loaf. The church administrators evolved into astute businessmen, developing a unique advertising plan."

Roger listened intently.

"From there, they borrowed the Burma Shave highway advertisement technique. On each side of the country road leading to the Abbey's property, they anchored free standing road signs six feet apart that read, 'Verily, verily, I say to you—healthy bread—cheesy flavor—good when toasted—Amen, Amen.' Arrows directed the cars up the mountain's winding road to their sweet-smelling gift shop."

"That's clever," said Roger. "They had a product and they just needed to reach a greater audience."

Joey ended his report. "Within a short period of time, the popularity of Amen, Amen reached a large market and became a financial success. From the profits, they made necessary improvements to their Abbey and maintain their property."

Burma Shave signs did not have a presence in Nevada because of sparsely populated areas and insufficient road traffic. Roger announced an alternate. "We can follow the Abbey's plan and develop a broader consumer base for Sister Zita's bread, but we'll use the print medium. The sisters could make a profit, pay off debts, and add a new wing."

He told Joey to make copies of the Abbey story. Then he asked Miss Crawford to set up a meeting with Sr. Marie and Zita, and Fr. Dooley.

§ § §

"About the article," Sr. Marie began, looking at the small gathering in her office. "That's the reason for this meeting?"

Sitting next to Joey, Roger tapped his son on the leg. "He did the research on Amen, Amen bread and there's a connection with Sister Zita's bread."

Sr. Marie beamed. "Well, ours is considered good bread by all accounts. Some say it's healthy, too."

Sr. Zita bowed her head and bit her lip as embarrassment spread over her face.

"Now, now, my child," her administrator admonished. "You do bake a tasty loaf."

Roger added, "And remember, the seminarians' success began by word-of-mouth. Their sales grew as they developed a larger consumer base. We can do that. We start citywide, reach out to a regional base, and then go national."

Sr. Marie shuffled a pen around on her desk and cleared her throat. "Mr. Atkins, we accept donations. We do not —"

"Ah, now, 'tis hard to build a new wing with just a bit of money," Fr. Dooley interrupted with a small laugh, looking around to four sober faces.

"Our superior never has allowed us to go public with our problems." Sr. Marie's facial muscles tightened. "And we can't take on additional work."

"I can draw up a plan," Roger replied. "And I can spread the word through print media."

"If you don't let the superior know about your true financial situation …" Dooley pinched tobacco between his two fingers, "or need for a new wing …" He worked it into his pipe's bowl. "These doors could be closed, closed forever."

"Oh, no! Oh, no!" a soft plea came from Sr. Zita. "The good Lord will never let that happen." She made the sign of the cross. "He must listen to our prayers. He must."

Tapping the pipe's bowl on the ashtray, Dooley said, "Let us remember, God helps those who help themselves." He turned to Roger. "I think your idea is worth exploring, but this is far beyond my experience."

"It sounds overwhelming at first, but once your superior gives her permission, I can work on a preliminary plan. If we attack it step by step, we should achieve our goal. In fact, it will be interesting to first come up with the project's catchy name."

"Well, it does sound daunting," Sr. Marie said. "I see you've given a lot of thought. But we…" She shook her head back and forth, lost in her concerns. After a moment she smiled in earnest. "We can give it a try. Sister Zita's bread may be just the recipe we need to pull our hospital from its dire financial predicament."

"It's a winner! Just think. Citywide, regional, and then national attention to our little hospital here in the desert." With a shrill voice, Fr. Dooley added, "I say we work with Roger."

Sr. Marie agreed to relay the information to their superior and ended the meeting praying for a successful outcome.

Roger followed the priest into the hallway. "Father, thank you for your spirited support." Cupping the Irishman's hands, he added, "Your influence with the sisters goes a long way."

§ § §

Walking toward the parking lot, Fr. Dooley fumbled for his keys, his heart pounding at the prospect of nationwide attention. He greeted nurses with a slight bow and a wide grin. He engaged volunteers in small chatter, asked about the health of various family members.

The reception area was a small space with black framed pictures hanging on one wall. The photo of the Bishop of Reno held his attention.

The entire state of Nevada was under the guidance of one authoritative voice residing in the north, over 500 miles from the Las Vegas area. As more Catholics settled in the state, the church would need to appoint additional religious leaders to match the growth. The Irish cleric was hopeful.

If this fundraising venture is a success, this just may give me a step up the clerical ladder and, at last, a chance to get notice to move on.

Years ago, he wasn't sure he had a calling to the priesthood. However, he was sure he had a call to escape his hometown in Ireland, a small seaside village next to the Irish Sea. It boasted a variety of freshly caught seafood, lots of beaches, and abundant rainfall.

When young Dooley entered the seminary, his personal aspiration was to receive an assignment either to New York City or a parish in Boston. The Almighty had other plans. Upon completing religious studies, the newly ordained young man was sent to a small desert town, Henderson, Nevada.

Henderson was a small town located in a hot and dry region of the Mohave desert, on the outskirts of Las Vegas. It was scenic area with cactus and black rock dotting landscape. The town's attraction was its proximity to a manmade body of water, Lake Mead.

Teaming up with Roger might be the cleric's ticket to a different setting.

Dooley threw on an overcoat and ventured into the brisk December air. *Sweet Jesus, if it is Your will, help me hatch my plan. I do pray it is Your will.*

Signature Production

Chapter 37

Dr. Eaton held to his promise. Roger was released in time for the Christmas holidays with two prescriptions, a reminder card for a January appointment with Dr. Clark at Mount Sinai Hospital, and a bag full of Sr. Zita's bread.

Jake had a surprise for Roger.

"I go to the hospital and I get a promotion. Not bad." Roger declared as he opened and closed various drawers to his new desk. "And who's to take my job?"

Jake remarked, "I'm in no hurry, but we can start the interview process after the first of the year. That will give you time to break in on your new duties."

"Mr. Jake," Joey said. "He'll need more time to work out his new project for the sisters. Their superior gave them the green light and even Father Dooley is on board."

"Father's a zealous supporter. It's curious," Roger added.

"Joey mentioned the sisters are need a new ward," Jake said. "So, what's your plan?"

"To sell Sister Zita's tasty and healthy bread." Joey jumped in. "We found out during their inventories, they seldom had a piece of bread or even a piece of crust show up on the patient's returned tray. And this part is funny. When crust was returned, Father says that's usually from patients with false teeth."

"You've got an ambitious enterprise going," Jake responded, "but we're miles away from a flour mill. Won't you need that type of a facility if you're planning on baking batches of bread?" His marketing mind touched on additional important considerations. "And what about a royalty fee agreement, setting up a legal formation, establishing a network of bakeries? I know, I know. You're probably ahead of me with your planning."

"Jake, I think I can do it. I'm already in contact with a mill on the east coast. They seem interested. And currently a loaf of bread sells for nineteen cents. Sisters could sell citywide at that price and make a profit of three cents."

§ § §

Waiting for the men to return to Jakes's apartment, Rita, Tatyana, and Lucia looked over Monsieur LeBlanc's sketches for the new signature production.

On the coffee table, Tatyana combed through a variety of pictures. She paused. "Well, look at this one with blue sequins and a jeweled Egyptian bra."

"Sure, fancier than what I'm used to wearing," Rita peeped down her own blouse.

"Do we know what his theme is?" Lucia asked, holding up a sketch with, "red and black satin" handwritten on the side of the page. "If it's burlesque, look at this one with a boned-corset laced up in the back."

"I like it. With fluffy, black feathers attached to our *dare-ree-air*." Tatyana wiggled her fanny. "We'll look terrific."

"Honey, save that for the guys," Rita joked.

Tatyana added, "And a tall black hat with a big red satin bow and hint of a black veil … oh, so sexy … so, oh, la, la."

"Add black fishnet stockings and a boa, something to hold with my hands while on stage," voiced Lucia.

"But monsieur mentioned he wants us to wear costumes with rhinestones and beads, so we shine on stage," reminded Rita.

"He wants us to jingle and jangle," Tatyana mused.

"To sparkle and spangle as we shimmy and shake, shake, shake on stage," Lucia added as each circled around the room jiggling hips and shoulders.

The ladies laughter peaked when the men entered.

"What did we miss?" asked Roger, as the girls ran to give him a big welcoming hug and embrace.

"What we missed was you, my sweet friend." Rita pinched Roger's cheeks.

"Coming up the elevator, I smelled the sweet scent of your perfumes. Quite different from the hospital's smells. And I'm happy to be home."

"I brought some bread for our roast beef lunch." Joey tossed a couple of brown bags to Rita who grabbed, but missed one. A loaf slipped out the bag and dropped on to the floor. Rita brushed the bread with her hand and placed it on a tray.

"Roger," Jake patted him on the shoulder. "Another consideration, a suitable wrapper to travel those miles, don't you think?"

"Right about that."

"Well, time for me to get room service up here and welcome you back into our fold."

Catchy Name

Chapter 38

"Top of the morning to you," greeted Father Dooley dashing into Crawford's office. "Grand news."

"If you're talking about that Amen, Amen enterprise, yes. I heard their superior gave approval."

"And, if she wants a catchy name, I'll fancy one for her. She also wants a financial committee to be set up to oversee its operation." Dooley beamed with excitement. "If that's needed, I'll host an Epiphany dinner, invite influential men of the congregation, and get them to sign on."

The priest slowly circled Miss Crawford's chair, then bent over the desk. "I need you to inform Roger about my Epiphany dinner plans. Dr. Eaton made an appointment for him to be in California right after the new year, so he'll miss it. A telephone call from me might be awkward."

"And why not wait until he returns?" Joan doodled on a yellow steno pad.

"Well, we must move quickly as the superior advised and, if you handle it, he may buy into it."

"That will be difficult for me."

"Tell him I plan to warm up the men with establishing a financial committee. When Roger returns, he'll have time to meet and work with them."

Dooley stood and turned to leave. "You know, we'll have to have the dinner in the Sisters Lounge." He looked downcast. "But with your help, I think we can transform it into a welcoming setting."

"Of course, we can."

"Thank you. I knew I could count on you. And now when I leave, you say, 'top of the rest of the afternoon yourself.'"

"I don't do an Irish accent well."

"Even without an Irish accent. Just, 'top of the rest of the afternoon yourself' will do."

§ § §

After Dooley left, Crawford sat in her office tapping her legal pad. *It's easy for him with his fancy Irish talk to get others do his unpleasant work.* Taking a deep breath, she dialed Roger's telephone number.

"Well, hello Joey. May I please speak with Roger?"

"Well, then," Joan breathed a sigh of relief. "I have three short messages. Can you deliver them to him?" She waited while Joey got a pen and pencil.

"Thank you and here's number one. Dr. Eaton spoke with Dr. Clark and made an appointment in California for Friday, January 4th. He wants Roger to set aside additional days for tests. Will that work?"

Crawford heard Joey walk over, to what she assumed was a wall calendar, and flip to a new year. She grabbed a cigarette from her purse.

After a few moments she continued, "I'm happy you can make those arrangements. Okay, now, number two and three - their superior wants to move quickly on Roger's fund-raising idea - to design a catchy name for the campaign, and number three, to establish a financial committee. That's it."

She took out a match. "Yes, a catchy name and Sister Marie wants you, Joey, to join the committee. I'll set that up before you leave for California."

"Hold on for a minute." She lit her cigarette. "One more thing. The good nuns thank Roger for the steaks. Father Dooley plans to serve them at the financial meeting, his Epiphany dinner, and only sorry you will miss out on it."

Joey sounded agitated. She just didn't want to be the fall guy for that decision. "Joey, Joey. Sister Marie will explain it better at your catchy name meeting. Must run and thank you."

Miss Crawford hung up. *Well, that wasn't so bad after all.*

§ § §

A volunteer in the reception area greeted Joey and Roger. They looked for Miss Crawford, and not finding her, asked the volunteer to extend their greetings.

Turning into the hallway, Joey inhaled the distinctive aroma drifting from the kitchen. He faced the volunteer. "Something good is happening in the ovens?"

"Sisters never seem to tire of Sister Zita's turkey menu. They had it for Thanksgiving, and now again for their celebration dinner with stuffing, cranberry relish, sweet potato, the works."

"I thought, for a change, they would enjoy steaks for their special dinner," Roger said.

"Oh, they decided to offer those to Father Dooley for his Epiphany dinner, and serve as a special investment to their hospital," the volunteer offered.

Sr. Marie gestured for Roger and his son to sit opposite, indicating the chair between them was set up for Sr. Zita. "And, Joey, thank you for joining us."

Roger began, "So, Father, uh huh, the sisters enjoy turkey tonight while on the Epiphany your guests sit down to a succulent steak dinner?"

Sr. Marie broke in. "We thank you, Mr. Atkins, for your generous gift of beef steaks. The sisters gladly offered them for a good cause—Father Dooley's dinner. You see, we sisters are not allowed to eat in public. Often Father Dooley takes our place and makes a fine host."

Joey, eyebrows winkled between his eyes, and tossed his pop an incredulous look.

"And," Sr. Marie added emphasis, "parishioners are loyal to him. If Father Dooley generates support to the fundraising idea—"

"Don't forget the men enjoy sampling my extensive wine collection," Dooley smiled.

A quick tap at the door and Sr. Zita breezed in, unfastening her black veils. Roger and Joey stood and offered her the empty chair between them. She smiled, declined, and wiped her hands on her apron.

"My turkeys … I'm sorry I'm late. My turkeys, they need basting every twenty minutes; every twenty minutes."

Irritated, Dooley tapped his pipe on the ashtray. "Sit down, child. Your turkeys can wait, but these busy men are in a hurry to drive to California."

"Father, we're not in that much of a hurry," Roger responded.

Sr. Marie nodded and began the meeting with a short prayer. She eyed the names on her note pad. "We should be able to agree on one of these."

Dooley rapidly dismissed the first two submissions as dull, reminding the group the superior expected a *catchy* name.

"Well then," said Sr. Marie. "The next is *Manna from Heaven*."

Immediately, Dooley reacted. "Not bad. Sounds like spiritual nourishment. But I'll save that idea for one of my sermons, and not saddle a loaf of bread with it. Let's move on."

With no further explanation, Sr. Marie moved to the next entry. "I eliminated *Heavenly Bread*. Name's already taken." She faced Joey. "And Joey, your *Yum, Yum Bread* …."

"Honestly, Joey, *Yum, Yum Bread* sounds like baby talk to me." Dooley grunted and shook his head ignoring Sr. Marie's raised eyebrows. "Let's move on." When he caught Joey's eyes, he shrugged his shoulders.

"Next is *Bread, Good Bread.*"

Instantly, Roger revisited the time Giana used similar words, 'bread, good bread' when she introduced Pane di Monte Sant' Angelo to him. He stayed with that pleasant memory until he heard Fr. Dooley voicing his objection.

"*Bread, Good Bread.* Sounds like foreigner's talk to me. Must be Miss Mo's idea. Let's move on."

Joey reacted, "But—"

"Now, now," injected Sr. Marie looking over the list. "Your suggestion, Father Dooley, *Leprechaun Bread.*"

"Honestly?" Meeting Dooley's icy stare, Joey shrugged his shoulders. "Sounds like Irish talk to me. Let's move on."

Father choked on inhaled smoke.

Sr. Marie, amused by the exchange, struggled to maintain a straight face. She continued, "Sister Zita, yesterday you mentioned your loaf as being healthy and patients return for more. Did you have time to work that into a catchy title?"

Sr. Zita stammered, "Well, well, ah …"

"Come, child. Has Ping Pong got your tongue?" The priest laughed, paused, and looked to the others. No one appreciated the humor.

"Ah, I suggest, if all agree, to name the bread *Cherub Loaf.*" Bowing her head, she awaited comments.

"*Cherub Loaf.* Why Cherub Loaf?" Dooley asked.

Sr. Zita began an enthused, rapid explanation. "Cherubs are protective spirits. They stand for goodness and love. They have a tradition among most religions." She threw Roger a quick glance.

"You're right, sister. My Jewish friends are familiar with cherubs."

Father Dooley said, "Go on. Go on now. Have you more to say?"

"They're winged creatures … protective spirits. They travel over the universe. With God's help, our bread will travel far and wide." She looked nervously at Sister Marie. "So, Cherub Loaf is a protector of our health. That's all I have to say."

"Indeed, Cherub Loaf is a catchy name," voiced Joey. "How about it, Pop? I mean, how about it, Sister and Father?"

With support from the group, Sr. Marie indicated she would forward the suggestion to the superior. The meeting ended with prayers for the acceptance of Cherub Loaf as the name for their project, and success for Dooley's Epiphany dinner.

Altar Boy

Chapter 39

Miss Crawford hoped Roger and Joey planned to stop at the cafeteria. Eager to learn more about the meeting, she positioned herself inside the ladies' room, the perfect location for eavesdropping on hallway activities. She kept the door slightly ajar.

She heard Dooley remark, "Dear child, Sister Zita is. First time I've heard her voice an idea of her own."

Joey chimed in, "Cherub Loaf. Cool idea. Cool." He added, "In fact, she's kind of a cool lady."

Inside the restroom, Miss Crawford kneaded her brows. *Sister is a religious lady of the Church. Sisters can't be thought of as cool.* She dried her hands on a towel and tossed it in the bin, inching closer to the door.

Continuing to the cafeteria, Roger took a jab at the priest. "Oops! Sisters aren't cool … just obedient. Right, Father?"

"Mr. Atkins, our Heavenly Father, I think, prefers an obedient sister over a cool one. Just remember, obedience and poverty are among vows each bride of Christ takes freely. Now, I must be leaving."

A visitor pushed open the bathroom door hitting Joan's elbow as she applied another layer of color to her lips. Time was ticking. She left the bathroom rubbing and making the red line smeared more noticeable.

§ § §

Joey and Roger paused in front of the bread donation table, a loaf poking from each brown bag. Joey selected one and took a big whiff. Speaking to the bread, he said, "Allow me to introduce you to your new name, Cherub Loaf." He selected two bags and dropped in a generous donation.

Roger patted Joey on the shoulder and ushered him inside the cafeteria. He went through the line, selected a piece of fried chicken, and chatted with the cashier before he settled on a table.

Slowing his pace, Roger spotted Sr. Zita in front of the oven, pinning back her veil. He entered the back area just as Miss Mo walked from the pantry, arms filled with sacks of sugar and flour.

"Special steak sauce from the casino," Roger held up a small package. "Thought Sister might be able to use it for Father's … ahem … steak dinner." They shared a laugh.

Miss Mo put her load on the table, took the bottle, unscrewed the top, and sniffed. She wiped the rim, covering her fingertip with sauce. "Yes. Good. Sauce good."

§ § §

Father took long strides as he scanned the parking lot for his car. Not finding it in its reserved spot, he remembered he had decided to walk. The morning had been warm, so he left his coat on a kitchen chair. As the day went on temperatures fell. Now, a late December breeze swept over his face. He squeezed his arms around his body looking forward to a spot of Tullamore Dew, his favorite Irish whiskey, waiting for him in a liquor cabinet.

He headed for the least traveled road, allowing him time to think and avoid any parishioners offering to drop him off.

I don't have to stand for this New Yorker's impudence, and to think his son had the nerve to reject my catchy name. He

172

was determined not to allow Roger or Joey to derail his plans for a different pastoral assignment.

This was not the first occasion John Dooley sought to cut loose from his home-town surroundings. The moment he served Mass as an altar boy, he planned to enter the priesthood, his ticket to leaving Ireland. The United States needed more clergy to fill their growing number of Catholics and he began preparing for a religious profession.

As little Johnny, he cherished the attention gleaned from the faithful waiting for liturgical services to begin. He smiled, recalling how he carefully set the stage entering from the sacristy with a solemn expression on his face.

Carefully, he walked up three marble stairs, approached the middle of the altar and with bowed head, genuflected. The young boy moved slowly, holding a long metal rod. The wick end lit the tapered candles sitting on each side of the tall, free standing solid brass crucifix. The altar boy tiptoed, extending it as high as necessary to reach the top of the altar candles. He milked the time he spent with the task.

As if on cue, his mother gushed in a stage whisper, "Tis my boy, Johnny Martin Dooley."

Many of the faithful whispered comments. "Ahh, now would you look at that Johnny Dooley. Nice little lad now isn't he!" Or, "My, hasn't he grown from a wee little one into a fine fellow!"

He smiled at favorable comments, put a deaf ear to offensive ones, and those about his father.

Most of the sharp comments rang out from Mrs. Sheehan's evil tongue. He remembered, and could not forget, the daily communicant in the front pew. A mean-spirited woman, she didn't mind spewing venom. She stretched her head searching up and down each pew, asking, "And now, where is that lazy plastered father of wee little Johnny Dooley?"

Parishioners anticipated these biting remarks. The woman nearest her took on the responsibility to force a violent coughing spell, drowning out Sheehan's irritating comment.

The position in Henderson allowed him an opportunity to reclaim his family's good name. An appointment to a more prestigious setting was his ultimate goal. He rested his aspirations on a successful Epiphany dinner, and, for the evening to flow as the priest intended, he needed to orchestrate the details himself.

§ § §

After the catchy name meeting ended, Sister Marie stayed in her office reviewing the names of men invited to Dooley's dinner. This would be the first occasion for the community to learn of the hospital's plight so care must be taken to select the right group.

The list began with a representative from the Diocese in Reno. The Church's hierarchy transferred Dooley's predecessor to a larger parish on the coast of North Carolina. The Epiphany dinner was Dooley's first opportunity to showcase his abilities. Sr. Marie feared that once her friend's fine qualities were on display, he, too, might be reassigned. However, that was a risk she had to take for the committee to succeed.

Looking down the list, she and Fr. Dooley agreed on Spencer Taylor, instrumental in arranging for Saint Bridit's name plate. The sisters appreciated he made up the necessary funds without any fanfare.

Then came Fred Downing, a small business owner. Fred owned the Goods and Hats Store. He was a no-nonsense man, weekly communicant, and sponsor of the Little Tot baseball team. Sister believed he would offer sound advice to the committee.

Others she included were Jim Riley and Patrick Watson. Patrick, an engineer with Titanium Metals Corporation, was from a large Catholic family. Both parents taught at a local school, Basic High School.

She twisted the sterling silver ring on her left hand, the bride of Christ ring. She stared at the next name, Jim Riley. As owner of a gun shop, he held sway and influence over men in the community. It troubled the administrator that Riley had the capacity for deflecting enthusiasm for projects he hadn't originated. She also disapproved of his calculated attacks on those who disagreed with him. Unfortunately, inviting Jim was a necessity if the committee were to get the project off the ground.

She said a quick prayer. "Dear Lord, for the sake of our hospital, kindly guide us as we enter into uncharted territory." She slipped the list into a newly labeled First Financial Committee folder and patted it closed.

§ § §

The four parishioners selected—Spencer, Jim, Patrick, and Fred—immediately accepted Fr. Dooley's invitation. Daily, the priest paced up and down the floors of his apartment, a worn pipe stem clenched between his teeth, waiting for the Bishop of Reno's response. When it arrived, Dooley ripped open the envelope.

The Bishop sent regrets, writing he had a previous engagement. Dooley held the letter closer to his eyes and beamed upon reading the following: Father Campbell, emissary from the bishop's office, would attend in his stead.

That's progress! I just hope Father Campbell knows his way to the southern part of the state.

Epiphany Dinner

Chapter 40

Members of the Women's Committee designed place cards for the occasion, and, on the afternoon of his Epiphany dinner, Dooley stopped by their office. He was greeted warmly as they proudly handed him their design for the meeting—a collection of drawings capturing the essence of the Epiphany—three Kings with gifts of gold, frankincense, and myrrh.

Dooley continued down the hallway to the sisters lounge. When he entered, his jaw dropped. He strolled around the well-dressed table and assumed the posture of a general reviewing his troops.

Ah! Beautiful! My fine Celtic furnishings add just enough style to impress the religious emissary from the north. Making a mental picture of the evening's seating arrangement, he placed Jim Riley, possible troublemaker, farthest from Father Campbell.

The priest took a long, last look. Pleased, he made the sign of the cross and offered a silent prayer, *Dear Lord, bless this dinner. And, if successful, I am Your humble servant willing to serve as a steward of Your Church in a larger city with a bigger parish, if You fancy, of course.*

He turned off the lights and returned to his apartment to freshen up for the evening's event.

§ § §

Clasping her rosary beads, Sr. Zita hastened from the kitchen and through the hallway. Preparations for the night's dinner were in place, allowing time to seek solace in the small chapel. A large, carved wooden statue of the crucifixion hung behind the main altar. She dipped her fingertips into the holy water font, genuflected, and made the sign of the cross.

Several individuals on kneelers remained in contemplative silence. Sr. Zita tiptoed to the side altar and settled into the pew directly in front of the Saint Brigid statue, known for feeding the poor and tending the sick.

For a few minutes, she sat. Her heart pounded. Speaking in public was a new experience. Her nervousness troubled her. She prayed, *Please, Dear Lord, give me the confidence I need to work successfully with Sister Marie, Father Dooley, Mr. Atkins, and Joey. I don't want to disappoint them, and we do need funds for our hospital. And please let me prepare the steaks according to Father Dooley's directions.*

She felt a layer of calmness as she returned to the kitchen.

§ § §

The Epiphany dinner began with small talk, after which Fr. Campbell led grace before the meal. The evening proceeded as planned, good wine, delicious steaks, tasty dessert, and pleasant interchanges. The kitchen staff stood by and performed their tasks, clearing the table and rolling out the carts, with minimum interference.

Fr. Dooley introduced the role played by the absent Lieutenant Roger Atkins. "He gifted these steaks and provided accommodations for Father Campbell at his hotel."

The men shrugged their shoulders, not recognizing the name, but clapped politely with the announcement of the donations.

Moving on to the importance of the dinner, the priest began, "Tis a great gift, it is, the fine dinner Sister Zita prepared, and let us not overlook the slices of her freshly baked bread."

With a bit of wine under his belt, Patrick called out, "Never, never …," he belched loudly, "tasted better."

Father Dooley swallowed hard, repressing his surprise as the parish men immediately directed their eyes to their guest. Fr. Campbell. He covered his mouth with his napkin, attempting, but failing, to stifle a laugh. To Dooley's relief, the men joined in, enjoying the humor of the moment.

"Uh, uh, well then," Dooley continued. He brought the men back to the seriousness of the meeting. "Saint Brigid's Hospital can be compared to a golden jewel nestled among black rocks, tumble weeds, and arid land. Its existence is a gift to our community as were the gifts of the magi to the baby Jesus." He had the men's attention. "Now, has every one of you received and read the story about the Abbey being financially saved by the baking and selling of their bread?"

"Yes, Father. But what does the Abbey have to do with us?" queried Spencer.

The priest carefully and deliberately rolled out a similar financial situation facing the congregation and their hospital. "Sister Marie took care of small bills on a regular basis." For larger ones, she paid just enough to allow for breathing room. Their suppliers were generous with I.O.U.'s and too sympathetic to demand full payment."

The men, each in their own way, expressed surprise to know nothing about the financial situation facing the hospital.

The priest credited Roger as the one who first learned the situation. "Roger is confident Sister Zita's bread could find the same success as did Amen, Amen loaves of bread."

"Their superior accepted the name Cherub Bread, Sister Zita's suggestion." The men expressed surprise. None remembered hearing the young nun saying more than "thank you." Yet, they all agreed, it was her bread so she should have the final say.

Fred offered encouragement. "Personally, I like the idea of setting up a financial committee. Anything to help the good sisters."

"And so, we will," said Spencer.

A loud clank rang through the room. Following the noise, heads turned to the end of the table. Jim continually flipped the top of his metal lighter open and then close. Getting the men's attention, he created a chance to throw a kink in the plans, or to act as the proverbial loudmouth. "Is this Atkins guy a parishioner, and let's say, one from our religious persuasions?"

Spencer, a member of the Church of Jesus Christ on the Latter-day Saints, looked around the table. "Am I one of you?"

Jim replied, "You know that's not what I meant."

"Spencer, we all know you're not a Catholic," Dooley quickly responded. "Our hospital staff and patients are Jewish, Catholic, Mormon, and Protestant, all beliefs."

"Of course, of course," Fred butted in. "We consider you as one of us."

"For now, at least," Spencer replied, "let's get the ball rolling and work with Mr. Atkins."

Dooley chimed in. "It's late. First thing in the morning, I'll report to the administrator with our positive support and set up a meeting with Mr. Atkins as soon as he returns from California."

Fr. Campbell ended the meeting with a short prayer. "God willing, the success of the Cherub Loaf Foundation is in Your hands and we pray for our Almighty's guidance."

§ § §

On his drive to The TapRoot Hotel for his night's stay, Fr. Campbell made mental notes. He reflected on the two incidents, one with Patrick and the other with Jim. Successful leaders of the church met and handled a variety of personalities. He evaluated Dooley as a competent minister exhibiting a sense of style and humor, sprinkled with a bit of Irish gab. In addition, he demonstrated an artistry for soliciting gifts from people in high places.

Fr. Campbell envisioned an ideal position for his fellow clergyman. Nevada experienced growing pains. Small unincorporated communities lacked Catholic clergy to attend to their members spiritual needs. The Latter-Day Saints marked out the Mormon Corridor, considered the eastern part of the state, as a target for prophesying and continued growth. The Catholic Church lacked a presence as strong as theirs. Upon his return to Reno, he planned to endorse Fr. Dooley as a candidate for the post in that sparsely populated part of the Silver State.

Femme Fatale

Chapter 41

In Los Angeles, a journalist with the Catholic Associated Press, extended a welcome to his friend and son. He planned a quiet New Year's Eve celebration at his apartment. Upon hearing of Roger's appointment with Dr. Clark, he said, "He's the best. You'll be in good hands."

At the hospital, Dr. Clark, swung his stethoscope around his shoulders. "Think of your wheezing like that of a train's horn. It's a warning that your lungs demand attention. Dr. Eaton asked you to try to stop smoking," a stern Dr. Clark said. "I strongly suggest you give up that habit completely. Smoking is associated with chronic bronchitis and emphysema, poor functioning of the lungs."

Roger grabbed his coat and dug into his pocket. "Here, take these," and handed over his cigarettes. "I did manage to cut back to just a couple a day."

"If you can stop altogether for the next few months," Dr. Clark explained. "I think you might be a good candidate for an operation called Lung Volume Reduction Surgery, or LVRS. It removes the affected lung tissue. You'll need to go through a protocol before acceptance for the operation."

"Tell me more about it," Roger said.

The physician gave a thorough account of the procedure with merits and potential risks. He assured Roger that he and Dr. Eaton would work with him throughout pre- and post-operative procedures.

Before Roger left, he told the doctor, "I know I can count on both of you to keep this information confidential. I don't want others to worry about me."

§ § §

On their ride through the Mohave Desert, road noise and wind gusts whipped through Joey's convertible making conversation difficult. Even with a few wheezing episodes, Roger wished he hadn't surrendered his pack of cigarettes to Dr. Clark.

To distract himself, he threw his burgundy leather briefcase over his lap, unzipped its main compartment, and took out a legal paper pad and pencil. He busied himself with a draft for the Cherub Loaf campaign.

Joey spent the quiet time with thoughts about Lovely Lucia.

§ § §

By the time they arrived at Jake's penthouse, Joey, late for his date with Lucia, gave a quick hello, tossed his hat on the love seat, and said good-bye. Roger claimed his favorite spot, on the walnut wood rocking chair. Leaning his head on the back pillow, he started a slow, relaxing rock.

Jake dialed for room service. "Yeah, Jake here. A plate full of sandwiches, chips, and what's for dessert? That's for two and, of course, asap." He replaced the phone in its cradle and faced Roger. "So, how's your health?"

"I'm not perfect, yet, but getting there."

Tatyana rapped on the door. "Heard you returned." She snuggled next to Jake.

There was another knock and Rita, blue and yellow roller curlers formed a halo around her head, hurried in without an invitation. "What's up? You okay?" She gave Roger a peck on the cheek.

Roger winked. "Told my doctor that one of your margaritas would be good medicine for me."

"Pumpkin, I'll be a good nurse and get it started."

Tapping his cigar against the ash tray, Jake got down to business. "And the religious nuns? How's that goin?"

"We're on a roll. Their superior approved the project's catchy name."

Tatyana twisted a strand of hair around her finger. "Joey's Yum, Yum Bread?"

"Didn't make the cut, but Sister Zita came up with Cherub Loaf. It took the prize."

"Cherub Loaf … religious and catchy," nodded Tatyana. "And with your contacts, I bet you can get it off the ground."

"Father Dooley, their spiritual adviser, contacted men of the parish and the bishop from Reno. While I was gone, he hosted a dinner to explain the situation, and if we get their support, I believe there will be a Cherub Loaf campaign."

Rita handed a martini to Jake and a margarita to Roger. "Have you begun with your typical, ten-point master plan?"

"Don't laugh. I worked on it during our drive back here, but it needs refinement."

"Let me ask ya," Jake raised his eyebrows. "How will these men take to having a … ahem … a—"

Roger interrupted, "You mean, having a Jewish person on their first financial committee?"

"Yeah, exactly."

"I haven't met the men, but Saint Brigid maintains a good relationship with all religions." Roger took a sip of his drink.

"And Sister Marie wants Joey on the committee. So, we'll cancel each other, adding one Jewish person with a Catholic."

"That's no guarantee."

"Jake," Rita encouraged. "Let's keep it on a happy note."

"Well, let me tell ya, if anyone can make it happen, Roger can." Jake raised his glass. "So, here's to the New Year and Roger's new project—Cherub Loaf."

"They've been good to me," Roger said.

"Is that femme fatale on the committee?" Rita chuckled.

"Who's that?" Roger stopped rocking.

Tatyana explained, "You know, Miss Fluffer-upper, the one who took care of your bed—your hospital bed, that is."

"Fluffer-upper?"

"Pumpkin, you know. That Joan Crawford stand-in."

"Oh, Miss Crawford. She wears many hats around the hospital."

"I bet she does." Rita started singing, "I'm Cha Chita Banana and I've come to say…" She danced toward Roger in a Latin box step, using the cocktail shaker as castanets.

Amused, Roger explained, "Miss Crawford is thankful for her job and is a darn good employee."

Circling Roger with her song and dance, Rita continued, "I've come to say ..." She stopped abruptly and looked directly into his eyes with a steady gaze. "I've come to say, be careful. *Miss* Crawford means she's single, right? Three words of advice to you, Pumpkin." She bent down, flickering her eyelashes, and said, "On the prowl."

"On the prowl?" Roger repeated.

Tatyana pointed her emery board at Roger. "Beware! They hunt for big game."

Rita returned to the bar, giving Roger an over-the-shoulder glance. "And in their mind, Pumpkin, you're a royal bull."

"At ease!" Roger insisted.

"Now, now, Roger." Tatyana cupped her hand and brushed her nails back and forth on her blouse. "You're a desirable trophy for any woman."

"Stop, you two. Stop."

"Let me tell ya. Roger's done a good job managing his personal life for a long time and without you two interfering."

"Pumpkin, don't allow yourself to get trapped," Rita said. "I may have falling arches, but I'm not too old to tear out the eyes of any woman who—"

"Thank you, Mother. I'll remember your words. Now, may I drink my margarita in peace?"

Ten Point Program

Chapter 42

Sr. Marie handed Fr. Dooley the ten-point program folder Joey dropped off. They were to review the documents before the meeting.

"Um, a ten-point program. That Roger's quick. Must have gotten on it right after his return from L.A." While Sr. Marie thumbed through each page, the priest took out a pipe. From previous experiences, he counted on the administrator to thoroughly read the material and come up with a prudent response. He concentrated on getting the pipe started.

Sr. Marie returned to point number two and read aloud, "Copyright, patent, trademark issues."

Dooley frowned. "I do believe that copyright commotion goes back to that English law."

Ignoring the comment, Sr. Marie continued reading.

After an uncomfortable silence, Dooley added, "Why don't the Englishmen stay out of our affairs. We're citizens of the United States of America, now are we not?"

Sr. Marie raised her eyes to meet his. "Are you suggesting we forget the copyright law?"

Sheepishly, he backed down. "Well, indeed, if it's our copyright law, too. I guess we do follow it."

Sr. Marie ran her index finger down to various other points. "Look at point seven: Organize a squad of women to visit local stores asking to buy Cherub Loaf."

Dooley said, "Now that's using your noggin. Praise the dear Lord! Put our ladies on notice and you may get your new addition after all."

Sister Marie closed the folder and exclaimed, "The Good Lord brought Mr. Atkins into our life. I believe he's the right man to spearhead this ambitious endeavor."

§ § §

As the members of the First Financial Committee entered the sister's lounge, Fr. Dooley, Sr. Marie, and Sr. Zita greeted each personally, introduced them to Roger and Joey and offered coffee and slices of bread. The Women's Committee designed snowflake name cards for the occasion. Patrick and Spencer sat at their designated places.

Nodding toward Joey, Patrick whispered, "I wouldn't allow my junior to attend in a red windbreaker. I'd have him in a long-sleeve shirt and tie."

"Doubt if this kid owns one."

Father opened the meeting with a prayer, restated the importance of their mission, and thanked the men for their support. They each acknowledged they had reviewed the ten-point-program Sr. Marie sent them. Father Dooley then turned over the meeting to the Administrator.

After a short prayer, Sr. Marie said, "We'll take one step at a time. There's enough work for all who wish to participate."

The enthusiasm shown at the Epiphany dinner remained with the men. Each voluntarily assumed a task. Spencer accepted the responsibility for working with his attorney friends to set up the committee's legal and financial aspects. He suggested accounting procedures be established so all profits remain with the Cherub Loaf Foundation.

Patrick's wife, a member of the Women's Auxiliary, took charge of the grocery brigade. Jim surprised the men when he offered to research the copyright, trademark, and patent items.

Having taken time to do some research, Roger offered his approach for production rollout. The bread market was fragmented, each locality with its own independent baker. "Initially, the plan is to introduce the production of Sister Zita's bread locally. I'll contact Snowflake Bakeries on Charleston Avenue here in Las Vegas. The next step is to develop a large distribution network of bakers in specific localities. As favorable relationships develop, we'll line up bakeries outside our area."

Roger advanced the idea that ultimately the goal was to convince over one hundred regional and national bakers to manufacture and distribute a new proprietary product, Cherub Loaf. He cited Los Angeles, Philadelphia, and St. Louis as possible locations.

Fred said, "I like your ambitious idea, and since I make business trips throughout the state, I'll offer to work on point nine, the promotion plan. First, I'll contact local places where the public gathers for meals: churches, casinos, and hotels. I can do the same statewide." He gave a side glance in the direction of the sisters. "I suggest we also contact Guest Houses in Reno."

An uncomfortable silence settled over the room. Reno, divorce capital of the world, accepted a practice the Catholic Church claimed to be a grave sin. Fred explained that while waiting the required six-months residency to get their divorce, guest houses offered temporary residents, mostly ladies, pleasurable activities, including bar-b-ques, horseback riding, shopping trips, and sit-down dinners.

"I sell a lot of my hats to these ladies. We could develop a lucrative arrangement serving Cherub Loaf at their many meals."

With downcast eyes, Sr. Marie took a few moments to digest Fred's suggestion. The men, respectful of her religious concern, maintained silence. Seconds, which felt like minutes, ticked by until finally she offered a sympathetic solution.

"Going through divorce, these gentlemen and ladies suffer painful scars in their hearts and souls. And I quote, 'We all fall short of God's glorious standards.' So, allow us to offer these poor souls some earthly, nourishing comfort."

"I could not have said it better," responded Fr. Dooley. Checking his wristwatch, he summarized the important points of the meeting.

Sr. Marie ended the meeting with a prayer that God watch over each man as he continues with his responsibility.

§ § §

Jim followed Spencer to the parking lot. They stopped at Jim's dented, dried mud-splattered '50 Ford pickup illegally parked in front of the hospital emergency drop-off entrance. Spencer mentioned surprise that his friend assumed responsibility for the copyright and trademark issues.

With his crook smile, Jim replied, "I know nothing about them damn laws. Could care less. Now that we know the hospital's financial situation, we don't need that outsider and his highfalutin ideas, his B.S. It's our hospital. We can do it without him." He slammed his fist against his fender. "Just watch me put a stop to this kike. Just watch me!"

Spencer, expressionless, walked to his blue-and-white hard top '56 Oldsmobile Super 88.

Invitation
to Atrium Showroom

Chapter 43

An outpouring of financial support appeared from a variety of places. Miss Crawford coordinated responses. She took every opportunity to report the activities directly to Roger in preparation for the March meeting.

Sr. Marie stopped by the Women's Auxiliary office to pick up three-leaf clover name cards. The candy-striper dashed in and handed her a long-distance message from Fred. Stranded with car trouble in a desert town between Reno and Henderson, he wanted the administrator to receive a positive report in time for the second meeting.

Fred developed a list of local entities offering support, including names of several properties on The Strip. While in Reno, he talked with management of the Guest Houses. They planned to add Cherub Loaf to their menu.

Sr. Marie opened the meeting with a short prayer and immediately announced Fred's successes. She then spoke for the timid nun. "Sister Zita expressed interest in designing an appropriate cover." The group looked in the young nun's direction, her head down, while Sr. Marie continued. "Instead of the brown bag, she plans to design a cellophane wrapper for effective transportation with a design that captures the essence of her bread."

Moving down the agenda, Miss Crawford handed Spencer a ledger pad with financial notations. He read from her notes and ended with, "Bottom line, all of it is good news." He returned the material to Miss Crawford for safe keeping.

Roger took papers from his briefcase and placed them on the table. On one sheet, he listed names of flour mills, mostly east of the Mississippi River. On another sheet, he wrote the names of large wholesale bakers he contacted. He highlighted the progress. "Once they heard of Saint Brigid's financial difficulties, they were willing to move on to the next step—bake a batch of Cherub Loaf bread and notify us of their results."

Patrick report was short. "The Women's Grocery Brigade is biting at the bit to start requesting loaves of Cherub Loaf at the local grocery stores."

"The demands of the coming hunting season have absorbed my time," Jim said. "But I'll have my copyright findings by the next meeting. Roger, you can bet on that."

The last item on the agenda, the Cherub Loaf article written by Roger, was approved by their superior. Joey handed each member a copy. Jim squirmed in his chair, grabbed Spencer's name card, quickly jotted a short message, and slipped it back to his friend.

This Hymie B.S. must stop.

Spencer, poker-faced, surreptitiously tore it in pieces and eased it into his coat pocket. The congenial spirit in the room stood a chance of being sabotaged by his friend's insistent ways.

Aware that Jim's lack of support could endanger the project, Sr. Marie decided to ignore his antics and focus on her agenda. She informed the men that Roger's friend, from the Catholic Associated Press in California, was instrumental in getting the article published.

Immediately, Jim spoke up. "Oh, Rog. You … you have a friend with the … the Catholic AP?"

Roger blocked the hint of discrimination before it had a chance to fester. He gave Jim a long lingering glance. "I make it my business to be acquainted with a variety of individuals from all religious backgrounds."

Jim scanned the article. It didn't take him long with another question. "But Rog," he said with a menacing smile, "why not tell the truth? It's Sister Zita's recipe. Why exaggerate saying it's over one hundred years old?"

"Jim, leave the PR to professionals. In our trade, it's called taking poetic license."

Sr. Zita stood up with all eyes in her direction. "Uh, yes," she began, "I learned from my mother who learned from her mother. Actually, the recipe may be older than one hundred years. Back then, the ladies didn't write it down. I … uh … I had problems. I went from a family cook to a service cook here at the hospital." Her eyes fell to the table. "It took time to get it right." She bit her lip. "But I wrote down the amount of each ingredient every time."

Dooley chirped in, "Now, let me tell you what happened when she perfected the recipe. She was dancing up and down and spinning around the patio. Sister Zita hit the jackpot!"

Sr. Zita, flushed with embarrassment, eased back into the chair.

Joey added, "We're moving on. A photo shoot is scheduled in a couple of weeks at J & E Bakery. We're aiming for the article and photos to appear the last part of March. I think we're playing our cards right. The Daughters of Saint Brigid will soon be known far and wide."

Jim tore his nametag into small pieces, piled them into a stack, and pushed it out to the middle of the table. "Should we bet on that?"

Holding his gaze, Roger replied, "Save your money. Leave betting to the professionals."

"Gentlemen. Gentlemen." Fr. Dooley tapped his pipe on the ashtray. "Let's not forget we have a good idea and a good product. We're making progress tying up legal points and publicity. By next meeting, Sister Zita will unveil her prototype for the bread's wrapper."

Sr. Marie ended the meeting with a prayer for continued guidance. Jim stood, pushed his chair under the table, and leaned to Spencer. "A little decorum with that young whippersnapper wouldn't hurt."

"At least he's not wearing spurs with his cowboy boots."

"I still think we can do without these outsiders."

§ § §

Miss Crawford sensed that Roger and Joey would stop in the cafeteria. She grabbed a table near the entrance and sat alone, dragging on a cigarette. As they entered, she smiled and gestured for them to join her.

Roger was looking for both her and Miss Mo. Hearing her name, Mo stepped from behind the food line and waved. Roger addressed them. "We have a good lineup of talent this coming weekend. I'd like you both to be my guests."

Miss Mo's expression changed from a smile to a frown. "How get there? No car."

Miss Crawford twisted her pearl necklace. "Well, then, I guess I can pick you up." She eased closer to Roger. "Anything to help you, Roger."

"Thank you, Miss Crawford. Mission accomplished."

"Roger, Roger, please call me Joan."

Roger smiled, and then he and Joey left.

Facing Crawford, Mo asked, "Where we meet?"

"In the back parking lot, 7:30 sharp." Miss Crawford turned to leave, paused, and stared at Miss Mo. "And don't even think about being late."

VIP Table

Chapter 44

Joan welcomed Roger's invitation to The TapRoot's nightclub, especially the opportunity to mingle with members of the opposite sex. The idea of making Roger jealous appealed to her. She had no idea why Miss Mo changed her mind about going, but she was relieved. She didn't want to spend the evening with her in tow.

Dressing for the evening, she carefully laid out her silk stockings with the butterfly design on its heel. *Why not! No reason to save them.* In her undergarments, she rolled the nylons up her legs and attached each to the garter belt. She zipped up her red satin scoop neck cocktail dress and slipped on her open-back high heels.

Back in the day, her walk snatched most men's attention, but she was out of practice. Looking at her full-length mirror, she rehearsed leading with her breasts and swaying her hips side to side. Age played tricks on the body. Seeing her dowager's hump concerned her. She squared her shoulders. *It just won't go away.*

In her closet, she reached for the large hat box. It held a fur inside. She patted the fox stole, complete with head, bright eyes, and a snapping clasp jaw. Draping it over her shoulders, she maneuvered its tail to camouflage her spinal curvature. Another swirl in front of the mirror, a stiff drink for luck, and she was on her way.

Before she inserted the key into her car's ignition, she took off her heels and wiggled a cotton sock over each foot, a precautionary measure to save her stockings from producing a run in her expensive accessory.

§ § §

Joan turned into the parking lot. With time to kill, she did not take the elevator to the Atrium Showroom. Instead, she walked through the downstairs entrance of the casino. The heavy odor of tobacco competed with the scent of overly perfumed ladies donned in their special attire—evening dresses, high heels, gloves, and carrying clutches.

Joan made her way through the gaming area. A barrage of sound effects from the large spinning roulette wheel and the ding-dong of coins falling into the metal pans of slot machines filled the room. Spectators crowded around the green felt craps table watching the shooter roll a set of dice. At the blackjack table, some sat, and some stood in front of their chips. Some fingered tall piles in various colors while others nervously tapped their fingers on the table.

"Cigars, cigarettes," girls called out. Each dressed in short circular red satin skirts, black leather vests, topped with red and black pill box hats. They roamed the aisles hawking wares displayed on oversized trays held by a wide neck strap.

Joan spotted waitresses in skimpy outfits navigating their way through tight quarters. They balanced alcoholic drinks on serving trays, and skillfully lifted the load slightly above their shoulders. Seeking additional fortification, she gestured for and paid for additional drinks.

Inside the Atrium showroom, comped guests partied at the VIP table. Roger, in a tux, approached the group. He introduced himself and sat between two empty chairs, one for

Joan, the other for Miss Mo.

Joan stood at the entrance, taking a pause to capture the interest of a man, any man—her strategy was to throw a flirtatious smile in his direction. Tonight, her game plan wasn't working, so she slowly petted the head of her fur and launched into her snakelike walk through the aisles. When she spotted Roger, she blew him a kiss. At the table, she unclasped her wrap and folded it in her lap.

"Would you like a drink?" asked Roger.

"Bourbon, straight," was her answer.

None in the party seemed particularly interested in the newcomer. The hungry guests stretched out their hands and waited for the waitress to pass out their long-awaited dinner plates filled with baked lobster tails and filet mignon.

With dinner completed, The Tappers danced onto stage with a loud blast from the orchestra. Roger moved his chair closer to Joan, discreetly pointing out Tatyana and Rita. "And here comes one of their most difficult numbers." He paused, then whispered, "Look, they aced it!"

Joan took a gulp of her drink and screwed her cigarette in the ash tray. *Well, isn't that what the overly made-up floozies supposed to do!* Noticing Roger concentrate on the show, she waved to the cocktail server. Pointing to her empty glass, she mouthed, "Another, please."

The Tappers exited the stage with cheers and whistles from the audience. The emcee took the mike. "What a nice crowd you are." He paused until the clapping tapered off. "Our headliners will soon make their appearance. Now's your time to grab more liquid refreshments and have a picture taken for lasting memories."

"I'll catch hell if my wife found a picture of me in a nightclub without her," an audience member yelled, fueling additional merriment.

Thirsty for Roger's attention, Joan inched closer to him. The drinks caught up with her when she eased to her favorite topic, the movie star, Joan Crawford. "She played Peggy Eaton O'Neal. Don't you just love the name of that film? 'The Gorgeous Hu… Husseeey.'" She dropped her jaw attempting to get her mouth and lips to work together. "Say it with me… The Gorgeous Hu—seeee."

Pulling the boutonniere from Roger's lapel, she kissed the flower. Laughing, she attempted to fit it back into the buttonhole and whispered, "Have I been naughty? I know how to be naughtier."

Roger snatched the carnation from her hand and smashed it in the ash tray.

A guest at the table winked to his friends and leapt to his feet. "Tell us more about that hu—seeee."

With her chance to capture the limelight, Joan tossed her wrap to Roger, staggered up, and leaned on the table to steady herself. "Let's see now. My favorite line of Peggy Eaton was, 'Don't look into a man's eyes… look to . . .'"

Laughter from nearby tables encouraged her. "She said, 'look . . .'" Miss Crawford, head bobbing, inched closer to Roger's left hand at his ring finger resting on his thigh. Her action was mistaken as a stare at Roger's crotch.

Another VIP at the table mimicked her. "Lady, I say, better waaa… watch whaat you're looking at."

Roger gathered Miss Crawford's fur wrap, gloves, and purse in one hand and grasped her elbow with the other. Sobering quickly, she said. "I meant to look at his ring finger. See if he's married. That's what I meant."

"Joan. Enough. Give me your keys."

"Now this sounds promising." Inside her purse, she sorted through an assortment of cosmetic items before locating and dangling the keys in front of Roger.

She protested as Roger made his excuses to the guests and escorted her from the showroom, maneuvered her through the casino, down the elevator, and to the exit.

Head wobbling, she asked, "Have I embarrassed you? But we haven't seen … we … I'm so sorry."

Waiting under the casino's canopy, Roger handed the keys to the valets and turned to Joan. "You'll be in good hands. They'll drive you and your car home."

Miss Crawford sniffled back tears. "Can we do this again? I need… we need to..."

When her car arrived, Roger helped her into the back seat, shut the door, and returned to the casino.

Apology

Chapter 45

During her lunch hour, Miss Crawford drove to The TapRoot. She mentally reviewed the list of excuses for her unacceptable behavior. After she parked and handed her keys to the valet, a security guard pointed out the Public Relations Office.

Standing in front of Roger's office door, Joan took a deep breath, package in hand, and tapped on the door.

Inside, Roger was on the phone. Joey watched rehearsals in the dance studio through the two-way mirror.

Choreographer LeBlanc stood with notebook in hand. The showgirls strapped on their sequined skull bases, securing the tall, beaded frames with fluffy ostrich feathers encircling their faces. Lucia, the novice, struggled to hook on and adjust her headpiece. She added hair pins for a more secure fit.

With a loud knock, Joey opened the door and invited her in. Roger quickly ended his conversation, stood, and gestured for her to take his chair.

Joan handed Roger two loaves of bread. "My peace offering. I am so..."

Roger accepted the bread. "It's over. We move on."

Lifting an eyebrow, Joan was stunned. No explanation required. Twisting her pearl necklace, she ambled around the office, pausing at several newspaper photos, Roger with various celebrities. Looking into the two-way window, she stopped. "My, how tall do you have to be for a burlesque dancer?"

The phone rang and Roger answered it. Joey whispered, "Miss Crawford, these ladies are showgirls, not burlesque dancers! Each has an intensive dance background in ballroom dancing, jazz, and classical ballet. And they come from all over."

"If you say so."

Calling attention to Tatyana, Joey continued. "She's Russian. Her grandmother was a member of the Bolshoi Ballet Company and her grandfather a member of the bourgeois social class. Under the leadership of Lenin, her family escaped to the states and settled in San Diego."

Joan rolled her eyes. *Joey, Joey, Joey. I have no interest in Russian history.*

Unaware of her disinterest, Joey advanced the story. "Her mother started a ballet school and, with instructions from both her grandmother and mother, Tatyana excelled as a ballet dancer."

"So, your job, Joey, is to act as their peeping Tom?"

"That's not right, Miss Crawford. We have a signal. You see the gentleman in the corner? He's conducting auditions. He wants us to monitor activities just in case something goes wrong. Two taps from his side means something is wrong. Three taps mean the rehearsal is over, or that he's got everything under control, so we close the curtain."

"What could go wrong?"

"Well, Mr. LeBlanc may need to cut one of the girls from the lineup. At his previous studio, a dancer didn't agree with his judgment and she went after him."

"How often does it happen?"

"Never here." Pointing, he continued, "That's Rita."

"You mean the one sitting on the bench, rubbing her

feet?"

"Yes, and she's a little older than the others. When it comes to dancing, she doesn't want to waste time, and is more of a disciplinarian than Mr. LeBlanc. And her background is interesting. You see, her parents worked for the San Francisco Opera Ballet. She received free dance instructions, and at a young age started dancing professionally in the Nutcracker Ballet."

Inching closer to Roger, Joan remarked, "Well, I remember seeing these … showgirls the other evening. Mind if I stick around just for a smoke?" She held tightly to Roger's hand as he lit her cigarette.

Joey continued, "The youngest dancer is Lucia, from Italy. She also has an interesting background. After the war, her family came to America, settled in Minneapolis." They watched as the young dancer added another hairpin to her headdress. Joey added, "Her parents took lessons at the local Arthur Murray Dance Studio. Lucia tagged along. She showed a natural talent and won dancing awards at an early age."

Joan walked over to Roger's desk and sat on the edge of it. "How did she end up in Las Vegas?"

The men ignored her question and watched the dancers line up for their new routine. Lucia's headdress wobbled but she managed to dance through the sequence of steps without missing a beat.

"Look," Roger patted his son on the shoulder. "She aced it!"

LeBlanc tapped three times on the window, his signal that the rehearsal ended. Roger returned with three taps and closed the curtain.

"But getting back to the young dancer, Lucia, she answered our ad for auditions. End of story." Roger smiled. "She's found a new home."

"I'm hoping Father Dooley is as successful." She wiggled off Roger's desk and flattened her cigarette into the ash tray. "He's looking for a new home, a new parish, hopefully, out of state."

"Is he under some pressure at the hospital?" Roger asked.

Avoiding eye contact, she said, "Well, any negative distraction surrounding the hospital could hurt his chances."

"Joan, I don't get it," Roger said.

"It doesn't matter who or what the gossip is about. Father is the hospital's spiritual leader. And I know I was a bad girl the other night."

"That's not what Pop said." Joey waited for him to echo a positive response.

Always prudent, Roger said, "I don't remember a thing … only that Miss Crawford looked lovely."

Stunned, Joan quickly reacted. "Thanks. I'm happy I can count on you. Got to get back to work."

Off she went.

"That was quick," reacted Roger. "I hope all goes well for him."

Joey returned to his desk and sat with his head lowered between his hands. After a few minutes, he looked to his father. "Pop, secretly I was hoping, if Lucia couldn't handle the headpiece, she would be cut from the lineup."

"Why would you want that?"

"Because when I ask her to marry me, she wouldn't have to make a choice—either me or a career with dancing."

"Son, she could do both for a while. But, it's easy to see you are both in love."

"We haven't known each other for long. Pop, she's really my first love. Do you think I'm going too fast?"

Roger hadn't prepared for this moment as the picture of his loved one, Giana, burst into his mind. How could he explain to him, after all these years, he still longed for his first love, Joey's mother.

After a long moment, Roger answered. "Love is a powerful emotion, not determined on a timetable. Love at first sight can be as enduring and dynamic as love that takes time to flourish."

The phone rang, and they both looked at it until it stopped.

"You and Lucia are young, but smart enough to tell the difference between infatuation and true love. I'm sure you'll be able to handle whatever decision you come up with."

"I don't want to spend my whole life looking for *Miss Right* when she's right here in front of me. I'm ready to make a commitment. Just hope she is, too."

Roger wanted to say, *Son, embrace love and when you find your Miss Right, welcome her into your heart,* but the phone rang again. He patted Joey on the shoulder and spoke over the noisy ring, said, "Let's grab lunch. This is no place for a serious conversation."

J & E Bakery

Chapter 46

"Look at that sifter! It's hanging from the ceiling by those flexible bands," blurted a wide-eyed Sr. Zita as she and Sr. Marie entered the J & E Bakery kitchen. "You sure know you're in a bakery with all these tantalizing smells."

Greetings were exchanged with Roger. He introduced them to Mrs. Down, scout leader, and girls in freshly washed and ironed green uniforms. Rounding out the group were Hank and Charlie, bakers, patiently awaiting directions from Nick, the photographer.

The sisters roamed around the area taking in the commercially supplied kitchen. Sr. Zita approached the huge mixer, wiping flour dust from the capacity plate. She turned to Sr. Marie. "It holds ninety-seven gallons. That's more than we need."

Nick instructed Hank and Charlie to maintain their station at the beginning of the baking process. Hank climbed a few steps up the ladder and steadied the sifter. Charlie moved the vat to catch the flow of flour once it was released through the screen.

Pointing to the nuns, Nick instructed, "Now get on either side of the ladder and looked to Hank." Sr. Zita moved to the left and Sr. Marie to the right. Nick checked the shot through his lens and gestured the sisters to inch closer to the ladder. He rechecked his shot and chuckled. "Remember, y'all are supposed to look pleased, not shocked seeing this huge, hygienically clean, steel mixer. The mills out east will be working with machinery twice this size, with greater quantities of flour."

Moving closer, Sr. Marie couldn't resist, "But we are amazed. There's nothing like this in our kitchen."

After another camera adjustment, Nick called out, "Now, Hank, I'll let you know when to let up on the sifter's handles. Charlie, just freeze and hold tight to the vat. And keep still till I let y'all know the photo shoot is done."

The talent was set and ready. "Perfect. On the count of three, let it flow. One. Two. Three." Flashes went off. Hank, momentarily blinded, misdirected the funnel. Charlie twisted the vat trying to catch the free-flowing powder showering down his side and on to Sr. Zita's black veil. Hank apologized as he grabbed a broom to cleanup.

The cameraman chuckled. "Now, that's a picture! Charlie a speckled man and Sister, 'ur veil looks like a Dalmatian. Get dusted off. After I get a picture with Mrs. Down and the girls, we'll do a Take Two."

Sr. Zita brushed flour from her face and looked up, spotting Roger smiling. She put her hand in front of her mouth and shifted her eyes to the floor, concealing her embarrassment.

Loading his camera, Nick noticed Mrs. Down and the scouts rehearsing their part. "No, no. No pinching up of y'alls noses. Keep 'ur nostrils wide open and then sniff." The little group laughed.

Sr. Zita felt Roger's eyes observing her. Her face warmed as she continued rubbing specks from her veil.

Nick reassured Mrs. Down and the scouts. ""Ah, that's it. Y'all savor the moment. Now, one. Two. Three."

§ § §

Fr. Dooley, Sr. Marie, and Roger sorted through contact sheets. Sr. Marie passed materials to the priest and sat back in her chair. "Sister Zita came from a family of four brothers and, being the only girl, helped their mother with kitchen duties. To survive among her siblings, she became her family's *little tomboy*."

Fr. Dooley mentioned Sister Zita was a handy mechanic who kept his car running.

"The car he won from the church's lottery," Sr. Marie added.

Roger looked from Sister Marie to Father Dooley. A brief, awkward silence ensued. "You won the church's lottery? Sounds like the fix was in."

Fr. Dooley gestured, with his hands up and palms open, facing Roger. "My hands are clean." The priest added, "And I don't tell them how to run their lottery." With a half-smile, he admitted, "I just mention to several parishioners when I'm in need a new vehicle."

"They also hold a lottery for his return visit to Ireland," Sr. Marie added to the intrigue.

"Father, that sounds more like a shakedown."

"Now, now, my dear friend, your New York attitude is showing." He handed the contact sheets back to Sister Marie. "What photos do you like?"

Sr. Marie shuffled through the prints, hesitating to make the final picks. "It's your article, Mr. Atkins. We trust your judgment and look forward to reading it." She handed him the stack. "We'll continue to pray for God's guidance. Our community can't thank you enough."

§ § §

Roger walked with Dooley to the emergency entrance and moved to the side allowing medical responders to roll in an injured man. Hearing the patient's moans and groans, Dooley

207

made the sign of the cross and whispered a short prayer.

Reaching the parking lot, Roger stopped at Fr. Dooley's 1952 station wagon. He gently rubbed the wood panel with chrome trim. "Designed after an old fighter plane instrument panel." With an inquiring look, he asked, "So, when's the next new car raffle?"

"I imagine, my dear friend, the next time Sister Zita is unable to repair this one." He nodded toward Joey's red convertible. "Nice car. A little sporty for me. By the way, how's your boy doing?"

Roger wiped dust from the fender. "He's busy applying for college. I'm proud of him. You know, he's my adopted son."

"Yes, indeed I do. Mind if I ask how your … your wife … your ex-wife, how did she feel about such an unusual arrangement?"

Roger picked up a pebble, rolled it between his fingers, and tossed it over the pavement, stirring up particles of sand and dirt. He swallowed hard before answering. "I have a war injury. In military terms, I'm shooting blanks."

"Friend, friend, there's glory in the fact you served your country. You're a war hero."

"Being a war hero doesn't make you a whole man." After an awkward pause between them, Roger opened Joey's car door and tossed the photo folder onto the back seat. He returned his gaze to Dooley, realizing he might be expecting a fuller explanation, so he put his cards on the table. "Well, we were unable to have a child of our own and, as you know, Joey's Catholic. In my … my ex-wife's word, a *goyim*."

Roger's eyes glanced away. "As time went on, it didn't sit well with her family and friends, and, especially, my own father. But since she originally agreed to adopt Joey, I refused to give him up."

"Your saintly act will be rewarded." Dooley reached over to pat Roger on the shoulder.

He shrugged off the intimate response and got into the car. "Father, I never signed up for sainthood. I signed up to fight a war. Things just happened after that."

Joan watched the men from the office window. She ignored the ringing telephone and grabbed her makeup purse. When it continued, she felt compelled to answer. "Yes, Sister. I'm very busy now. I'll return your call later." She took the rotary telephone, buried it between cushions on the chair, and continued with last-minute primping.

Almost breathless, she reached the parking lot in time to join Dooley and watch Roger slam on the gas pedal and speed away.

Dooley mumbled as he walked past her. "That man, indeed, is a rash, arrogant New Yorker."

§ § §

Driving back to the casino, Roger's spirits sank. Irritated with Dooley's inquiry into his marriage, he lit up a cigarette and tossed the match out the car window. He spotted Officer Hafen on his motorcycle on the opposite side of the highway. Both men slowed. Roger to avoid a ticket and Hafen to check the driver in the red convertible with the top down. He saluted Roger, who returned the gesture.

Reaction to Article

Chapter 47

In her office, Sr. Marie, on the telephone with the superior, scanned a newspaper article, "Cherub Loaf Warming Up for Local Grocery Stores."

"Yes, superior, a long article with many pictures." She selected the photo of the sisters looking up at Hank and Charlie. "The caption reads, 'Machine Designed to Mix Huge Batches of Dough' and … Yes, Yes. I'll send you several copies in tomorrow's mail and, yes, our prayers truly are being heard. God bless Mr. Atkins's efforts."

§ § §

Dooley spread the newspaper over the kitchen table. He braced the telephone against his ear with one shoulder and pinched bits of tobacco into the bowl of his pipe. "Yes, Your Excellency. Mostly men from our parish, men Father Campbell met at our dinner." As he continued listening to the bishop, he struck and lit a wooden match, and moved it in circular motion over the tobacco.

He took several puffs, coughed with the bishop's question, and responded, "Yes, excuse me. Yes, Mr. Atkins is Jewish. Maybe not the rosary, but I'm sure he does pray." Dooley put the pipe on the ash tray and searched for the paragraph that would offer clarity. When he found it, he did his best to explain that legal papers were drawn with funds earmarked for the benefit of the hospital.

The bishop referred to the paragraph that stated Jake, owner of The TapRoot Hotel and Casino, upped the ante to cover the organizational and promotional expenses, and planned to help with the advertising program. In addition, he generously donated thousands of dollars for the commercial production of the bread.

Holding the phone from his ear, Dooley listened as the bishop instructed him to make Jake mindful of various needs facing the Las Vegas Diocese.

Fr. Dooley bit his lip and meekly responded that the good sisters tapped Jake first. "But of course, I will try. And the good Lord willing, we'll succeed with the Cherub Loaf campaign and with your interests."

The conversation ended. Dooley felt rebuffed. With all the time and energy spent on the Cherub Loaf Fund, he gained little standing. He may have lost a chance for advancement to a larger parish. He tossed the newspaper into the trash.

§ § §

Different response came from the kitchen's back area with Sr. Zita reading to Miss Mo. "And it goes on. 'Then a sister in charge of the cafeteria offered him a slice of hot buttered bread.'" Moving to the next page, she continued. "'He requested more of Sister Zita's bread.'"

Miss Mo added, "More bread. Toast bread. Plain bread. Butter bread. Jam bread. Always more slice of bread."

Sr. Zita smiled and returned to the article. "Let me see now. 'He claimed the bread saved his life.'" Sister folded the newspaper. "Mr. Atkins may have exaggerated a bit. That's called taking poetic license." She took out her rosary beads. "Come. Let's continue to pray for Mr. Atkins and his health."

§ § §

In her trailer, Joan spread the newspaper over a sewing machine. She read and reread the article. Each time she saw Roger's name or picture, she pressed the page to her face. "I knew you were the right one for me the minute I met you." She kissed and caressed the paper. "In time, I will make you see I'm the right one for you."

Throughout the next weeks, the hospital was abuzz with excitement. On the phone with Fr. Dooley, Miss Crawford told him about the telegraph from Gateaux Limited. The priest remarked it was one of Ireland's largest bakeries and suggested she mail them a complimentary loaf.

"And just how do I send a loaf in a brown bag?" queried Miss Crawford.

Still bruised from the bishop's admonishment, the clergyman replied flippantly, "That's not my responsibility. I think Roger has a handle on that issue."

§ § §

Joey handed Mr. Jake his mail. After thumbing through the collection, he set it aside and asked, "Hey, Joey, after that article, how's the Cherub Loaf project going?"

"Moving along nicely, sir. Miss Crawford is receiving requests from all over. And Sister Zita is working on a packaging idea, but I think it's a real challenge for her."

"You know Emmanuel Sanchez, my art director who designed our TapRoot symbol?"

"Yeah, he's good. I remember the first time I saw it. I liked it."

"Tell Sister if she wants, I'm sure he would enjoy working with her."

"And I'll volunteer to be his chauffeur," Joey offered.

§ § §

Sr. Zita and Emmanuel began working together to create a central theme for the cellophane bread cover. He suggested the artwork should connect the product with the buyer and Sr. Zita took inspiration from the Bible.

After several meetings, they settled on a design. The art director weaved the approved text between two angels. He immediately dispatched the prototype for design development.

As Joey waited for their sessions to end, he read from the Book of Proverbs. In exchange for chauffeuring Emmanuel to the hospital, Sr. Zita presented him with a Bible.

§ § §

The sudden attention overtook Sr. Zita. She hurried down the hospital hall to the chapel, her habit swishing and the long wooden rosary attached from her belt rattling. She welcomed a few quiet moments before the April meeting.

Genuflecting as she entered and walked to the statue Saint Brigid, she cupped her hands over the Saint's feet mouthing a short prayer, *Please instill in me the courage to work with our committee. The Cherub Loaf must succeed. Our hospital needs the money.* Experiencing a sense of calm, she walked to the administrator's office.

Cellophane Cover

Chapter 48

Sr. Marie began the meeting by congratulating Roger on the success of the newspaper article. "It's sparked growing attention to the hospital's plight, and since Miss Crawford devotes much of her time to the Cherub Loaf project, I suggest she becomes a formal part of the committee as secretary/treasurer."

Patrick added, "She probably knows more about what's happening behind the scene than us men."

"Surely more about baking bread." Fred chimed in.

The door opened and Joey tiptoed in, apologizing. He sat at the end of the table. The group went through the process of formally accepting Miss Crawford as a board member with the responsibility of accounting for the sales of the bread.

She opened a black three-ring ledger. "Donations for loaves sold next to the cafeteria were up substantially and the —"

Patrick jumped in. "Just say the word. My ladies are eager to attack their job with great enthusiasm. I need —"

"Patrick, please." Sister Marie frowned at him. She returned to Miss Crawford. "Have you completed your report?"

Joan displayed a false smile. "Well, let me just say we continue to receive pleas to keep the hospital doors open." She eyeballed Spencer for an approving look. She did not receive one.

Next on the agenda, Jim claimed the copyright and trademark issues were more complicated than he first envisioned. "We've got a name for our product, but I'm still waiting for other elements." He read from an official government form. "Let's see. I need any symbol, writing, pictures, and etcetera," he slapped his checklist on the table. "That's before we move on to requesting a trademark plate. All of this takes time and I'm busy now."

"Jim," Roger responded. "I understand. And we've got good news for you." He turned to Joey. "Got them, right?"

His son nodded and held several prototypes completed by Sr. Zita. "We only have a few samples, so share with your neighbor." Sr. Zita, sitting near Roger, shared a wrapper. Looking over the colored layout, the script, and depiction of the angels, she beamed.

Spencer turned the wrapper around and read aloud from the text, "Baked with the homemade recipe used at Saint Brigid Hospital in Henderson, Nevada."

"Well done," said Fred.

Jim cleared his throat. "Joey, your angels, they seem so sober. I expected, well, I was hoping for angels smiling and flying around."

Roger, eyebrows knitted together, stood up on behalf of the young nun. "We can all learn a biblical lesson from the image of these angels."

"You, teaching me my Bible?" smirked Jim.

Silence prevailed. Sr. Zita dropped the wrapper onto the table and stared at Jim. She bowed her head and said a quick prayer, "Dear Lord, guide my thoughts and my tongue."

Suddenly, Sr. Zita sprang up next to Roger. "Excuse me, gentlemen. This is not Joey's selection, or Mr. Atkins. It is mine." Her chin quivered as she looked to Fr. Dooley for approval. Still bruised from the bishop's reprimand, he stared ahead. She turned to Sr. Marie who nodded for her to continue.

"Um. You'll notice the two standing cherubim are winged creatures." Her eyes darting from member to member. "In the Old Testament, Ezekiel describes them as angels having four faces and four wings."

Unintelligible murmurs came from several members. "Well, um," she continued, "I didn't use four faces. But I did keep the four wings on each of the angels." Energized by the men's smiles, she raised her arms. "Two of their wings face up to heaven." She then crossed two in front of her chest. "These wings hold the loaf of bread, protecting its freshness, aroma, and flavor. Sort of guarding it with love." She fidgeted with the silver cross hanging from her neck. "That … that's it."

Spencer remarked, "Brilliant." He felt Jim's kick from under the table ending further praise.

"Angels are watching over the Cherub Loaf with their wings," Fred said. "I like it."

"Jim," Roger looked to him. "This may be the material for the trademark plate. If it helps you, I can send it on to start the process."

"Why not," Jim replied with a blank expression.

Fr. Dooley remained mute while members accepted the cover design and discussed additional agenda items.

After Sr. Marie adjourned the meeting with a prayer for God's continued guidance, she and Sr. Zita left together. Dooley, Roger, and Joey headed to the cafeteria. Miss Crawford, clutching the financial ledger, walked with Jim and Spencer toward the parking lot.

When Jim thought the trio was a safe distance from the others, he whispered, "I still think that kid needs to dress like an adult."

Spencer laughed. "Get him on your gun range. Toughen him up. And, as long as I can afford leather shoes, I'd never allow my kid to wear tennis shoes or cowboy boots to a committee meeting." The men continued their babble about Joey's perceived shortcomings.

Neither mentioned Crawford's new position on the board, nor the professional way she handled the situation. When Spencer opened the door for her, she gave her excuse, "I need to secure the ledger in my office."

Returning to the hallway, Joan spotted Dooley, Joey, and Roger. She sneaked into the ladies room and cracked open the door just enough to listen to their conversation. She beamed hearing Roger say, "She's an impressive lady."

Dooley agreed. "We couldn't do without Miss Crawford, the way she's capable of handling so many issues at one time."

"I think Pop meant that about Sister Zita."

"Yes," said Roger. "Miss Crawford is impressive, but I think Sister Zita graduated from black to white veils today. Don't you, Father?"

"Aw, my friend, I'm not sure a white or black veil matters to Sister Zita. She obeys the dictates of her religious community." With a cold gaze, Dooley added, "And she does it freely." He took leave, failing to offer a handshake.

Miss Crawford bristled. *A Sister! Impressive lady! What is he thinking?*

Once the coast was cleared, she darted down the hall toward her office, ignoring the candy striper's greetings. She opened her office door, slammed it shut, and tossed the ledger on her desk.

This silly admiration must stop, needs to stop, one way or the other. And I'll see to it.

§ § §

As they reached the cafeteria, Roger lingered. "Meet me in the parking lot and don't order anything for me. Wrap up your food to take home." He grabbed a handkerchief to stifle deep coughs and held onto the wall to catch his breath. As he folded the handkerchief, he was taken aback seeing small drops of blood.

Dr. Eaton noticed Mr. Atkins. "Need assistance?"

"Who am I kidding? I think I'm due for another appointment with Dr. Clark and that special procedure he had mentioned."

"I can make arrangements," the doctor said, and held out his hand. "Mr. Atkins, want to hand me those cigarettes I see in your shirt pocket?"

§ § §

Returning to The TapRoot Hotel, Joey struggled to keep his mind on the road and within the speed limit. Concern for his pop's health shifted to thoughts about the dinner date plans with Lovely Lucia.

In the passenger seat, Roger studied the Cherub Loaf wrapper. He traced the wings on one of the angels. After repetitive coughs, he cleared his throat and said, "You know, she's very creative. She pulls you into her goodness with her simple mannerisms."

"And she's Italian, too," Joey grinned.

"No, no. Irish, I think."

"I thought you were talking about my lovely Lucia."

Roger stared out the window. A dust devil twirled around the hot desert floor picking up dust, debris, and sand. He reflected on the priest's reaction concerning Sr. Zita. "Father seemed bothered with me saying a nun is impressive."

"Well, Pop, it's okay to say it, but maybe just not in front of her pastoral minister."

"The sisters, they slip silently into your heart. They have a way of lifting your spirits."

Joey eyeballed the rotating column of dust and debris gathering volume. "Better get out of here, or we're in trouble. I mean real trouble." He floored the pedal as the swirling, vertical mass headed straight for the highway.

Grocery Shopping

Chapter 49

Sr. Zita and Sr. Evelyn sat in the middle section of Fr. Dooley's wood-paneled station wagon refining the grocery list.

Sr. Zita stared out the window at the dry, prickly landscape, a scene now familiar to her. Until ten years ago, she never ventured beyond the boundaries of Michigan, her home state and location of Saint Brigid's congregation community house. As a teenager, she conjured images of the west from lyrics on cowboy songs playing on the juke box and in matinee movies. One could expect to see boots, saddles, buckskins, spurs jingling and coyotes howling.

On orders to go west, she was the youngest of the small group of religious women in white habits, selected to carry out a new mission of a small desert hospital. Sister Zita had not completed her degree, so she still wore black veils.

The train from Michigan experienced mechanical trouble. Arrival into Nevada was delayed by many hours. It was 2:00 a.m. as the porter extended his hand, assisting each nun from the train. They stepped from the small ladder and into the Las Vegas party atmosphere.

Fr. Dooley greeted them at Union Station. Both luggage and sisters crammed inside his vehicle. "Look at that scene. In a few hours, you won't be seeing many people walking down these brightly lit streets."

He circled the grassy park in front of Main Street and headed south to their destination. Entering the pitch-dark Boulder Highway, he answered questions from the curious, but exhausted passengers.

After a restless sleep, Sr. Zita raised the blinds to check the surroundings on her first morning in Henderson. In her wildest imagination, she was not prepared for the setting. The scene was mind boggling. The religious woman, disciplined to keep her personal feelings to herself, gave a loud gasp that aroused her roommate.

The landscape was stark in contrast to Michigan, the Great Lakes state with trees, shrubs, and colorful flowers. She looked out to barren land, absent of trees, but instead filled with cacti, black rocks, and something that looked like dried up roots.

Sister thought, *if my superior made a mistake and would order me to return, I'd gladly walk all the way back.*

During the ten years since her arrival at the hospital, Sister Zita experienced many highs and lows. By the grace of God, support from her fellow sisters, and belief in their mission, she overcame one obstacle after another. She considered Henderson her home now.

§ § §

Dooley parked on Main Street and headed to the smoke shop. The nuns put on black capes, completing their full-dress habit. They proceeded to the market, passing the Connors Shoe Shop, Sears and Roebuck, and the Fremont Drug Company. Sr. Zita repeated to herself, "Yeast, oil, flour, sugar …"

Sr. Evelyn elbowed her companion to look at the person approaching them. The bleached blonde wore a scanty, two-piece sun outfit, high heel sandals, rings on several fingers, jewelry draped around her neck, and silver hoop earrings. Sr. Evelyn deliberately averted her eyes as the inelegantly dressed stranger politely greeted them. "Good afternoon, sisters."

Sr. Zita replied, "Good afternoon to you, too."

Advancing a few feet, Sr. Evelyn whispered, "Would you just look at that! Imagine! Wearing such an outfit in public and for all to see!"

"And what about us?" Sr. Zita responded. "We're wearing head-to-toe habits topped with sun-absorbing black capes walking down a main street in a desert."

Sr. Evelyn turned for a final stare. The bemused blonde glared back at the exact time. Their eyes locked. Embarrassed, Sr. Evelyn pretended she dropped an object on the pavement. She bent to pick up the imaginary item, and immediately double-timed to catch up with Sr. Zita.

Approaching the Valley Food Mart, they stood in front of its window with a large poster in black letters:

Cherub Loaf—Soon on Shelves

Sr. Zita smiled to herself. *God willing, we may get our addition after all.*

Apples to Apples

Chapter 50

Dr. Clark draped the stethoscope over his shoulders. "I'll need you for a few days for the procedure, a rigid bronchoscope. I'll look inside your respiratory system to see about airway obstruction."

News of Roger's hospital stay circulated like an unrestricted tumbleweed powered through the Mojave Desert by high winds. An orderly from Mt. Sinai casually mentioned it to another about their new patient, *that guy from The Strip whose picture always appeared next to celebrities*. Gossip spread at that point and arrived before Joey entered the Las Vegas city limits.

§ § §

Small baskets of apples, compliments from a former patient, sat in front of each member's place. Joey arrived early for the Cherub Loaf meeting and chatted with Sr. Marie and Zita. He assured them his pop was doing well.

With all assembled, Sr. Marie opened the meeting with a prayer for Roger's speedy recovery and for their committee's continued success. Joan handed the financial ledger to Spencer and pointed to her hand-written note. She was determined to throw negative distortions into Roger's efforts. Her plan began.

Spencer read the note word for word. "Hospital expenses continue to rise, but the mass production of Cherub Loaf bread has yet to be realized." He returned the material to Joan with a grin.

Patrick cleared his throat. "Tell Roger we need to get loaves on the shelf and soon. I can't hold back my Grocery Brigade ladies forever. They're eager and ready for action."

Jim tapped his name card on the table. "And, kid. How's those franchising contracts going with different mills and bakeries back east?"

"Slower than originally projected, sir," Joey admitted. "Once Roger's on his feet, I'm confident he can overcome these challenges. He's used to the ebb and flow of operating a business, faces them daily … part of doing business on The Strip."

Patrick stood, responding boldly, "Uh, Joey, it's admirable that you stick up for your pop. But we're talking about the business facing our hospital not … uh … a gambling den on The Strip."

Joey got to his feet and spoke slowly. "Sir, providing compassionate care is contingent upon the doors of Saint Brigid remaining open, employees and bills getting paid on time, attracting the best medical teams, and turning a profit for a new addition."

He grabbed an apple in front of him and one from Fred's stack next to him. Bouncing them up and down, he said, "Well, those are similar issues and challenges facing The TapRoot." He rubbed Fred's apple on his sleeve, took a bite, and chewed slowly while glaring at a wide-eyed Patrick. "So, we're comparing apples to apples or business challenges to business challenges."

Joey sat and continued taking bites from Fred's apple. "By the way, if anyone's interested, Roger's prognosis is good."

Sr. Marie fought off a smile as she called upon Fred and Jim for their reports. Neither was prepared. However, they promised to have one for the next meeting. She said, "When Roger returns, the committee will regroup."

Sr. Marie picked up a special basket with Roger's name on it and handed it to Joey. "Please tell him our prayers are for his speedy recovery and for God's guidance."

Joan jumped in. "Please tell him I miss … I mean, his presence is missed."

"Will do," replied Joey.

Dooley inquired, "So, how much longer will our good friend be incapacitated?"

Patrick and Jim did not wait for the answer and rushed from the meeting. Jim whispered, "That kid needs to learn respect."

Still smarting from Joey's reproach, Patrick opened the door for his friend, and headed to the parking lot. "Think we can go it alone?"

Jim chuckled. "The kid owes Fred a fresh apple."

"Didn't you hear me? Think we can go it alone without them?"

Jim took a moment. He slapped Patrick on the back. "Maybe we can. Let's meet for breakfast and discuss it."

§ § §

Joey dashed to the cafeteria for a quick bite before heading back to Los Angeles. He was just about to leave when Miss Crawford entered and hurried to his table. Joey stood and pulled the chair for her. She lit a cigarette and, after small talk, worked the conversation to Roger. "How's my friend? I do worry about him."

"Pop's doing okay. He flies out east early next week, a meeting with representatives from the Moore Brothers Mill."

Joan ground a cigarette butt in the ashtray. "Why wasn't that item included on our agenda?"

Joey wiped his mouth on a napkin, stacked the

dinnerware, and walked to the trash. As he returned, he said, "I just got the long-distance call this morning, and knowing my pop, he's all in. I confirmed the meeting date on his behalf."

Miss Mo approached the table holding two baskets filled with Sr. Zita's bread. She slid the baskets onto the table, hitting the ashtray, sending ashes, butts, and used matches onto Crawford's lap.

Joan jumped up, fanning the pleats of her full skirt. "How dare you! How could you?" *You little slant-eyed cook.*

Miss Mo winked to Joey and returned to the kitchen without an apology.

§ § §

Joey tiptoed into Roger's hospital room and stared at tubes connecting him to machines. A nurse, busy adjusting intravenous lines, nodded to Joey. When she turned to leave, Joey handed her a Cherub Loaf.

Flowers and cards graced the room. Joey walked to the shelf beneath the window and read notes attached to the various arrangements: the Las Vegas Convention Center, the Nevada Youth Council, the County Fair and Recreation Board, and the Las Vegas Chamber of Commerce. A large colorful display was signed by Jake and The TapRoot Hotel and Casino family. An array of a dozen long-stem red roses surrounded with greens and ferns caught Joey's attention. The note attached read:

Roger, I am here for you.
Call anytime, anytime.
Joan C.

Dr. Clark walked in and whispered, "Your pop's just resting. I'll have him unhooked and discharged tomorrow. His throat will be a little scratchy. By the way, he gave me his cigarettes. I hope you'll make a sweep of all his hiding places." They smiled and shook hands.

A nurse entered and took Roger's blood pressure. Before leaving, she asked if Joey needed anything.

"I'm fine, thank you," and he slid a chair closer to Roger's bedside. He returned to his personal thoughts. *I need you, Pop. I love you. And please, no more cigarettes.*

He recalled the lieutenant's words spoken to him many years ago in Bari. "Your Nonna finds comfort in praying."

Joey began to pray. And he, too, found comfort.

Lucia's Theory

Chapter 51

While Joey and Roger were in California, Jake invited Rita, Tatyana, and Lucia to his penthouse. He took the opportunity to get to know Lucia a little better.

"Young lady, do you know the word 'admiration?'"

Picking up marbles one by one with her bare toes, Rita said, "Of course she does. She speaks three languages and English is only one of them."

"Yes, Mr. Jake. It is a liking a lot," replied Lucia, sitting on the love seat, her legs pressed together with hands folded on her lap.

Tatyana pointed her metal nail file at Lucia. "Good definition."

"Oh, my achy feet!" Rita looked first to Tatyana and then Lucia. "As an old hoofer, see what you gals have to look forward to."

Jake shook his head back and forth, amused by Rita's antics. He continued his conversation with Lucia. "Let me tell ya. You've met two guys with 'a liking a lot' for each other. Call it love, or respect, or whatever word you use, in whatever language you choose, those two have it." He ran his cigar under his nose. "Been that way since they left Italy."

Lucia acknowledged Joey enjoyed sharing his memories of his times in Italy, but Mr. Atkins avoided the topic. She shrugged her shoulders.

Rita piped in. "We don't understand it either." She gathered the marbles one by one, tossing them inside a cotton sock. "We just go along with it."

"I think I am beginning to understand. I do not think for Mr. Atkins it is over," Lucia said with an innocent expression to three startled listeners.

"Continue, please." Tatyana moved the ottoman closer to Lucia.

"Do not think I am impudent; Mr. Atkins is suffering from an ache deep inside his heart, a broken heart."

"An ache deep inside his heart!" Rita and Tatyana echoed together.

Jake said, "But, let me tell ya. He's a war hero, scars all over his body. He never —"

"Sweetie, let's hear her out," Tatyana interrupted.

Lucia speculated Mr. Atkins fell in love, probably his first real love, while a young serviceman in Italy. Although reciprocal, circumstances prevented the young couple from acting upon their strong emotions.

"He found happiness in the middle of wartime horror and chaos. Those were his private, personal memories. He returned as a hometown hero. Headlines highlighted his bombing missions over enemy territory." Lucia paused.

"Go on," insisted Rita.

"Joey said he refused interviews. I think he was holding tight to remembrances of his special lady, the lost love he still longed for all these years. He would not permit anyone to tarnish the shine he wrapped around those memories. That patina grew with time. His silence is his refuge, his solace."

All eyes and ears stayed with her. "Do you think Joey knew this lady?" asked Tatyana.

"I do not know. Joseph was a baby when his father died, and he never knew him. And later, after the bombing of the Port of Bari, he lost his immediate family."

Rita provided intrigue to the ongoing story. "Maybe, maybe Roger's love lady died during that bombing." She swallowed hard and blurted out, "Maybe he witnessed her… How she died."

Quiet overtook the group until Jake summed it up. "Well, let me tell ya. That just might be the best explanation. He lost his love, but her memory is very much alive and one he keeps very private."

§ § §

Joey filled mugs with water and gassed up the car. When he arrived at the hospital, Dr. Clark and Roger waited. The doctor said, "Your pop expressed interest in the pottery sitting on one of our nurse's desk. Her husband owns the Honest Pot Pottery." He handed Joey directions. "It's one of the best in our area."

At the shop, the proprietor pointed out fine points of various pieces, and, after Roger made his selection, the owner carefully wrapped it. He decorated the package with three bells to ward off demons, his trademark, interwoven between bright bows.

§ § §

Joey entered the main highway and took stock of the long line of vehicles headed toward Las Vegas. A hot rod zoomed past him, but Joey curbed his instinct to lay on his horn or to swear. He shook his head, chuckling to himself. *Lucia would be proud to know she has a soothing influence on me.*

Roger followed doctor's orders, resting his vocal cords, sleeping most of the way home. Dr. Clark had warned him, *For the sake of your lungs, never pick up another cigarette.* Once again, Roger had good intentions to follow that advice.

San Pasqual

Chapter 52

Miss Crawford looked from her window and spied Joey lifting a package from his car. She grabbed a vanity from her purse to touch up her face and hairdo. She heard his footsteps down the hall, but they continued past her office. Annoyed, she threw down her makeup kit, picked up props—pencil and paper—and trailed after him.

She watched Joey turn into the cafeteria and run past the serving line into the kitchen's back area waving the package over his head. He called to Sr. Zita, but the grinding noise from the dishwasher prevented a response. Finally, he burst out, "Pop wanted you to have this."

Sr. Zita wiped her hands and accepted the decorated gift box, ringing the bells before slipping them into her pocket. She opened and read the short note loud enough for the benefit of the kitchen staff. "Stay safe."

"Hurry, Sister, hurry. I gotta get back to the casino."

Watching the drama unfold, Miss Crawford slammed the pencil and paper on top of the table.

Sr. Zita wiggled a large ceramic statue from the box as Miss Mo stood behind her collecting the paper wrap. Joey smiled as he explained that Roger got the statue of San Pasqual, patron saint of the kitchen, when he was in L.A. Sr. Zita raised it for all to admire and remarked it was a lovely and thoughtful gift.

"San Pasqual, saint of the kitchen and Sister's religious patron, Saint Zita, patron saint of domestic servants." Mo explained that two saints now watched over them.

Sr. Zita handed the statue to Miss Mo. "San Pasqual, a gift for our kitchen staff from Mr. Atkins and Joey."

Joey quickly corrected her. "No. From Pop and for you, his thanks for the bread while he was at Mt. Sinai. Now I must go. Later."

Miss Mo walked back to the food line and said to anyone listening, "Good man, Lieutenant Mr. Atkins, good man."

Joey scooted past Miss Crawford, declining her invitation to sit for a cup of coffee. His rejection, on top of presenting a gift to Sr. Zita, inflamed her. But, as she heard Joey reprimanded for running in the hospital's corridor, she found satisfaction somebody put him in his place. She lit a cigarette, calculating her next move.

She penciled the word *showgirls* on one side of the paper. On the other side, she wrote *Sister Zita*. Scratching over showgirls, she murmured, *if they haven't stolen Roger's heart by this time, my personal war is not with them.* She circled and circled Sr. Zita's name until the pencil point broke. *There's only one way to win this fight.*

Launching into her personal plot against Roger and Sr. Zita, she stubbed out her cigarette and stormed into the kitchen's back area. Stopping directly in front of Sr. Zita, she smiled. "A gift. How nice! May I?"

Sister returned the smile and handed it to her. "San Pasqual. Patron saint of the kitchen and ..."

Miss Crawford let the statue slip from her hands, hitting the floor with a loud thump. Sr. Zita immediately knelt, collected shards into her cupped apron.

"Oh! What a shame!" Miss Crawford leaned toward her, but did not help. "I thought nuns took vows of poverty, chastity, and obedience. Personal gifts should be off limits." She sneered at a stunned Sr. Zita. "Unless you encourage such earthly behavior." She stood and stormed out the kitchen.

Miss Mo knelt to help her. She spat out, "No good lady," and meticulously placed each piece of glass on top of the growing pile. "'Rotten wood cannot be carved.' She no good lady."

§ § §

Nostrils flared. Miss Crawford ignored staff greetings and searched for Dooley. He was not in his office, the chapel, or with Sr. Marie. She returned to her office, slammed the door, and grabbed the telephone. When Dooley answered, she cupped the receiver and whispered, "Things have gotten out of hand."

Dooley did not respond. Miss Crawford, after breathing deeply, said, "Allow me to remind you of your desire to be transferred from Henderson. And allow me to remind you that Roger has alienated certain board members. Then there's Joey's with his unacceptable antics." She carefully distorted the truth claiming that the relationship between Roger and Sr. Zita moved from one of esteem and respect to, what she noted, a more intimate exchange.

Dooley squeezed the earpiece and whispered, "I'll meet with you first thing in the morning."

"No need to meet just yet, but remember, this development could bring disgrace to you as the hospital's spiritual leader. Keep your eyes and ears opened to any suspicious behavior that might get you in trouble. I'll fix things so no one suspects your involvement. Just let me handle it."

Joan had mixed feelings about getting even with her most promising love interest. After failed marriages and old age getting the better of her, she felt compelled to block Roger's further contact with the Cherub Loaf project and, especially, Sr. Zita. *Revenge can be very satisfying.*

§ § §

Sr. Zita received the sample loaf from Mr. Moore, president of the mill contracted to bake the bread from her original recipe. She eagerly opened the package and found his note. "The mill is set up for production, and I await your response."

Sister drew out the bread, gently pressing slices together like an accordion. She set the loaf on a tray and selected a slice from the middle. She brought it to her nose. Something was lacking. Puzzled, she selected the heel slice and sniffed with greater robust. The bready fragrance was absent. She took a bite from several slices. Its flavor and taste troubled and disturbed her. It lacked characteristics familiar to her.

Sister grabbed pen and paper. She scribbled out several attempts to express her disappointment. Nothing sounded right. She struggled to find words to describe the taste and flavor she was accustomed to. Finally, after several prayers, she wrote a short note stating the sample bread did not match her expectations, but, in time and under God's guidance, success would be theirs.

In Negotiations

Chapter 53

Roger swung onto twenty acres of desert land adjacent to Maryland Parkway. He dropped Joey off for orientation at the Southern Regional Division of the University of Nevada campus. His son darted for the entrance of Maude Frazier Hall, the first building on the fledgling college campus. Joey turned with a thumbs-up.

Leaning on the steering wheel, Roger waved with a forced smile. He watched as Joey vanished through the doors.

He drove to the hospital and was greeted warmly by both sisters. Asian fan inspired name cards that offered a subtle reminder at summer had arrived.

Before the meeting, Miss Crawford agreed to throw a noose over Roger's neck and the men planned to pull it tight. She opened the bookkeeping journal and pointed to her amended handwritten report. Spencer, for the good of the group, reported that sales had been anything but brisk.

Patrick followed with a more disturbing announcement. Ladies from the grocery brigade barged into grocery stores requesting Cherub Loaf. With a devilish grin, he said, "The managers replied they had no idea if or when they would receive the bread."

Roger threw his briefcase on the table. "I suggest we hold off further grocery brigade activity until the time is right. We don't have a contract in place. That action could have produced negative publicity, something we don't need now."

Drawing out papers from the Cherub Loaf file, he read from his hand-written report. "Our project depends on manufacturing realities. On the positive side, we're making progress with several issues. We're negotiating with Moore Brothers mill, bakers and outlets, developing a uniform baking process, and getting ready to sell bread in large quantities."

"And where are we now?" Spencer asked. "The Moore Brothers mill, what are their terms?"

"Issues need to be worked out. We're in negotiations. Mr. Moore and I speak regularly on the phone and I'm flying out next week to meet with him. When I return, I'll present the committee with a proposal for our consideration."

Sr. Marie sensed the tense air that permeated the room. "We'll await that proposal. Now, let's continue with Old Business and New Business items."

Once done, she said, "It might be difficult for us to gather a quorum during the next months. I always marvel that tourists flock here when so many residents spend their hot summer days away from our desert heat." She noticed the men nodding in agreement.

Roger joked, "Summer is good for my industry. Each year we host more and more visitors. So, it looks like I'll hold down the fort until everyone returns."

Sr. Marie reminded the group that Miss Crawford would contact them about the next meeting. She ended with a prayer and all went their separate ways.

Roger looked at his watch. He had enough time to pick up Joey and return to the office before meeting with friends at Jake's penthouse. As he walked down the hallway, Miss Crawford tiptoed behind him, tickling the back of his neck.

Instinctively, he swatted at the sensation and hit her hand. Roger knitted his brows and met her with an annoyed stare.

"I plan to stay in the city," she said. "And just remember, I'm just a phone call away and willing to meet with you, any time, any place."

Roger led her to the side. "Joan, you have many talents, and the hospital appreciates everything you do for them. But about our relationship…"

"Roger, you must know I have feelings, strong feelings for you. I've tried to fight them, but—"

"If I've given you any suggestion that I have romantic feelings for you, I apologize. It was not my intention and I suggest you find another man to share your dreams. I'm just not the one for you."

Stunned, Joan mouthed, "Damn you!"

She turned on her heels and bolted down the hall to her office. She thought of the one person who rescued her on many occasions. Red, the timeworn cowboy and poor imitation of a knight-in-shining-armor, was always available for her. She picked up the receiver and dialed his number, and with a sugary voice, said "Hello, Red. I need your help."

Showcase Presentation

Chapter 54

At the college library, Joey sat behind a desk smiling. He summed up the meeting with the faculty advisor. "I get my basic college courses behind me here. In a year or so, I should transfer out of state to a university with an established scientific program."

Roger knew Joey was up to the challenge and should follow the professor's advice. He watched, with a tightening in his heart, while his son gathered his books. Soon, Joey will move on. *I'm beginning to miss him already.*

§ § §

Inside Jake's penthouse, Roger walked into the familiar gathering with friends he loved. He headed for the rocking chair. Joey sat next to Lucia. They spoke in low voices with intermittent laughter. Assuming the role of bartender, Rita measured ingredients for Jake's martini while Tatyana prepared an assortment of Cherub Loaf finger sandwiches.

Jake took a cigar from a humidor and went through his lighting ritual. He asked about the Cherub Loaf campaign.

"Well, I popped in my office before coming here. The phone rang." Roger paused, coughed, and caught his breath before he continued.

He explained how Moore followed their usual testing routine using industry standards. Sister Zita's bread received favorable marks and comments. In fact, once the process ended, many asked for another slice. He sent a few loaves to Sister Zita.

"Moore jokingly said he'd give Sister's bread an A-Plus."

Rita added, "That makes the two of us."

"But Sister's reaction was different. She hadn't expected the chemical change that affects the commercial baking of her bread. Moore gave me a brief rundown with the process. It seems like twenty percent of the flavor is lost when the loaf is sliced, and another ten percent is lost when the loaf is wrapped."

"Really!" exclaimed Rita. "What ever happened to the saying 'the best thing since sliced bread' if twenty percent of its flavor is lost when it's sliced?"

"When I contact Sister, I'm sure she'll consider those facts. But before that happened, an even more disturbing incident occurred during our Cherub Loaf meeting." Roger shook his head back and forth. "I can't understand it. I just can't understand it. One of our members jumped the gun. He sent a grocery brigade, ladies scouting grocery stores for Cherub Loaves, even before the first commercial one was on the market."

"I think I know what's happening," Joey responded. "I've been sitting in on some meetings and think some of the men want to hoodwink my pop. They …" Alarmed, he watched his father fish for a handkerchief to camouflage a wheezing sound as he inhaled.

The others diverted their eyes, allowing their friend to recover. As a distraction, Rita handed a drink to Jake, who raised his glass, "Here's to a well-made cigar and martini."

Roger regained his composure and walked to the oversized window facing The Strip and turned to his friends. "We're so close to tying things together. I just don't want to disappoint the sisters."

Jake drew in the smoke from his cigar, held it for a few seconds, then released it. "Do you think they'd come to our showroom, let's say, to accept a donation, a generous one? Good publicity for both the hospital and my place."

"I'm not sure they could get their superior's permission."

"Roger, see what you can do."

"Tell them it's not all sin in our city," Rita said. "We do have a heart."

§ § §

Their superior enclosed a short prayer to Sr. Marie.

Father, we give You thanks and praise for allowing us this special opportunity to continue with Your work. We pray for the wellbeing of our new friends as we accept their generous gift of behalf of Saint Brigid Hospital. Amen.

The presentation at the showroom was set for Labor Day weekend. Sr. Marie and Zita sat in the back seat of Dooley's station wagon as he sped down Boulder Highway. He looked forward to the event, an ideal time for a personal meeting with Jake. Such a contact could redeem his standing and impress the bishop. He zoomed passed Officer Hafen who ignored his speeding, always had. He just waved them on.

§ § §

In the casino locker room, Tatyana and Rita searched for appropriate costumes to wear on stage next to the religious ladies. Inside stored trunks, they selected red and white cheerleader outfits. A seamstress added a couple of modifications: a white lace handkerchief attached to the inside of the cotton blouse to minimize its low V-shaped neckline. A three-inch band of lace sown to the hemline brought the skirt to a more modest length.

Roger waited in front of the casino chatting with the valet. When the guests arrived, Roger introduced them to

Tatyana and Rita. In their four-inch red heels they towered over the nuns.

The dancers quickly followed Jake to the stage. In the wings, Roger informed the sisters that the press was present. "You may be asked to stay for a few photos." They looked at each other as Roger continued, "If you have any objections, just let me know now and I can run interference for you."

"The good Lord has brought us this far," replied Sr. Marie.

"And it's for a good cause," added Sr. Zita. Both agreed they were fine with the arrangements.

Dooley squeezed close to Roger and threw a glance to Jake. He was on stage preparing the audience for the occasion.

"Think I could meet Mr. Jake after the ceremony?"

Roger whispered, "I'm sure Mr. Jake would enjoy meeting with you, too." He held the stage curtains wide as the sisters prepared to take their places between Rita and Tatyana.

Sr. Marie looked at Roger, "My heart's pounding."

"That's the sign of a professional. Now go break a leg."

Behind the stage, Roger tried to muffle a cough. He moved to the outer wings of the stage. Fr. Dooley followed. "Roger, now mind you, don't forget to introduce me to Mr. Jake."

When the sisters returned backstage, Roger recovered from the episode, exchanged the poster-size check that Jake held onstage for the real one. Sr. Marie immediately kissed it and slipped it safely inside a deep pocket in the habit.

The sisters continued their conversations with the dancers. Sr. Zita chatted with Tatyana, learning about the difficulties her family suffered under the Russian dictatorship of Lenin. "After escaping to the United States, we settled in San Diego and continued as active Russian Orthodox Christians."

Sr. Marie encouraged Rita to speak more about the San

Francisco Opera Ballet. She stood fascinated as Rita talked about her mother, costume designer for the full-length productions of the Swan Lake and Nutcracker ballets.

Roger stayed busy with the photographers, seeing that the details and names of the sisters were correctly recorded. He answered further questions about the Cherub Loaf campaign. In the meantime, Fr. Dooley moved toward Jake. With a wavering voice, he attempted a conversation. "The bishop would like …"

"Tell your bishop my check is good. The sisters know it won't bounce." Jake moved closer to the activities surrounding the others. Dooley was left alone, disappointed.

Emergency Meeting

Chapter 55

A big spread appeared in the papers. Renewed interest in Cherub Loaf surged as did His Excellency's interest in future contacts with Jake. Dooley assured the bishop that he, personally, planned future contacts with the owner of The TapRoot Hotel and Casino, which should produce similar outcomes on behalf of the church.

Inside Roger's office, Joey read an article in the *Las Vegas Review Journal*, dated September 17, 1957. "Wow! This lady's got chutzpah!" He scanned a few more paragraphs. "Listen to this: 'We need to block the scheduled bomb test tomorrow.'" He looked at the calendar and declared, "Gotta run!" He grabbed his car keys and windbreaker. "Gotta do my part and help this lady. Later, Pop." He rushed out the door.

Roger called after him. "What about your … your classes?" But there was no sign of Joey.

A few days later, Joey sat at the dining room table covered with textbooks. Roger walked in holding the morning paper. He showed Joey the article with a photo of pedestrians approaching the Valley Food Mart with super large, red letters:

FOR SALE

"Sr. Marie called an emergency meeting, probably to discuss the closing of the store." He folded the paper. "Just another stumbling block. We're in the early stages. We can handle these difficulties as they pop up." He slipped the paper in his briefcase telling Joey to stay with his books. It wasn't necessary to attend the meeting.

§ § §

Sr. Marie began with a prayer and thanked the men for coming on such short notice. All eyes focused on Roger as he swung his briefcase on the table and took out the morning newspaper.

"Glad to see you're up to date with the news," Jim commented. "We got us one heck of a problem."

Roger agreed that the closing of the Valley Food Mart came as a surprise.

Fr. Dooley faced Roger. "I think you understand the real reason behind our hastily called meeting."

"The closing of one store shouldn't kill our overall plans. We'll rework our campaign, make—"

Jim interrupted, throwing a copy of a previous newspaper on the table. He pointed to the headline. "This trumps the closing of the grocery market."

Patrick held up a copy with the picture of Joey surrounded by uniformed men at the Nevada Test Site. He slammed the copy on the table.

Roger responded, "Let me reassure you, Joey's all right." Hearing that news, Sr. Zita let out a sigh of relief and made the sign of the cross. Roger smiled sweetly at her bowed head and folded arms inside the habit's sleeves.

Miss Crawford monitored the subtle interaction between the two, but maintained self-control. Her stomach churned. *Time to end these shenanigans.*

"Why was he at the test site in the first place?" Spencer asked.

Roger grabbed a cigarette. "I'll tell you why." He

continued, "Bombs destroyed Joey's home and killed his family in Italy during World War II. He's exercising his constitutional rights as an American." He stamped out the newly lit cigarette.

Jim noticed an emotional weak spot. "Rog, your son, he's starting to act like a commie!"

Roger jumped up. A glass of water spilled as he lunged for Jim. Patrick and Spencer pulled him back. The sisters looked horrified as Dooley mopped the spill. "Sisters, the men are only looking out for what's in the best interest of our hospital."

Roger sat down and took out another cigarette, shrugging off Miss Crawford's lit match and lighting his own.

What is he doing ignoring me in front of this group? Miss Crawford sat back, smoldering, determined to get even with him.

"We need to avoid scandal to our hospital, scandal to Father, and scandal to the good sisters," Patrick said.

Roger's clenched his jaw to check his anger. "Patrick, look at the article again. Read it out loud."

Patrick cleared his voice and reluctantly obeyed. "'College student joins protesters at main cattle-guard entrance …'" he paused and looked up. Roger stared him down so Patrick swallowed and continued. "'In protest for the health and welfare of all men, women, and children in the Western United States.'"

Roger looked each man in the eye. "In the first place, what did Joey do that was wrong? Was Joey's name ever mentioned? Is the hospital or Father or the good religious ladies ever mentioned?"

Jim said, "That's not the point, Rog."

"And you probably pulled strings to keep his name out," Patrick added.

Rocking back and forth in his chair, Spencer said, "We

just can't afford bad publicity, and unfortunately, your son can easily be associated with the Cherub Loaf effort and our hospital."

Calmly, Roger stacked his papers together and slipped them inside his briefcase. He stood and faced Jim. "My words have value. I refuse to waste an insult on you." He turned and faced the sisters. "We're in the middle of wrapping up important issues. I'm sure when the final contract is presented to the committee, it will meet everyone's expectations."

Quiet reigned. Roger snapped the brass latches closed. "Miss Crawford, please notify me when the next meeting is scheduled. Until then, good evening."

He bowed to the sisters and left.

Plan B

Chapter 56

Having completed her morning chores, Sr. Zita walked into the chapel for a spiritual lift and to sort out personal feelings. She dipped her fingertips into the holy water font, blessed herself, and genuflected. She positioned herself in the side pew in front of Saint Brigid's statue. She waited for other churchgoers to take their turns with the Sacrament of Penance.

Miss Crawford planted doubts in her thoughts. Sr. Zita did not imagine she treaded on a sinful experience and Mr. Atkins never acted inappropriately. But recently, she felt an awkwardness in his presence. She didn't have a name for the concern, but recalled from earlier catechism instructions that any thought, word, or deed can lead one to a sinful occasion. Sr. Zita wanted to express her feelings with another person and be reassured it wasn't a sin.

Fr. Dooley sat in darkness on the other side of the screen as Sister Zita entered the confessional box. She knelt and began with the sign of the cross. "Bless me, Father, for I have … no, I have not sinned. I just want to purge the uncomfortable stirring inside of me and I hope confession might help."

There was a long pause. The priest tapped on the lattice divider and instructed her to speak up. Sr. Zita cleared her throat. "Father, I have thoughts, not impure thoughts, but just thoughts about a man. He's a good man …"

"Now, child, are you doing anything to encourage this man you keep thinking about?"

"Oh, no. Father. No, Father. I would never do that."

"And your vows of poverty, chastity, and obedience?"

"Oh, I keep them next to my heart."

"And your service to the Lord?"

"I've dedicated my life to Him. I am a bride of Christ." Her quick response held back a nervous whimper.

"Then my child, don't you think He is the only one, the one you should keep in your thoughts?"

Attempting to keep Dooley from hearing her sob, she took a deep breath and said, "Yes, I do try. I do pray. I love My Lord."

Fr. Dooley gave absolution. "Keep your thoughts pure and follow the virtues of your patroness, Saint Brigid. For your penance, say three Hail Mary's."

Perplexed, Sr. Zita left with her head down. A troublesome guilt feeling swept over her. Gone was the usual spiritual closeness she experienced with her Savior after the Sacrament of Penance. She took out her rosary beads, hands trembling, and began her penance.

§ § §

October came and went without a call for a meeting. Roger needed to squeeze in a follow-up appointment with Dr. Clark before the end of the year. He telephoned Miss Crawford to avoid conflicts with any scheduled Cherub Loaf meetings. None were noted so in early November he made an appointment to go the California and, by telephone, continued ironing out details with mills and bakeries to produce Cherub Loaf.

§ § §

Winds ushered a thunderstorm into the Las Vegas valley, unusual for early November weather. Forecasters predicted rainfall later in the day. Two members from the committee,

Patrick and Jim, walked around the hospital grounds, followed by Mr. Dunkleberger, wearing a jacket with a Dunkleberger & Son, Contractors logo. Red and Fr. Dooley hurried to keep pace with the group.

Dooley resisted the force of the dust and sand stirring around him. He held tightly to his clerical black work cassock, keeping the front flap from blowing aside. Mr. Dunkleberger struggled to raise and keep the blueprints so all could see.

Fr. Dooley was not in earshot of his presentation. "I beg your pardon, but what are we doing here with Mr. Dunkleberger?" He asked when he caught up with Jim.

Mr. Dunkleberger rolled up the prints and slipped them in a storage tube. He capped it and handed it to Jim, who passed it on to Fr. Dooley. "Make sure the superior gets them as soon as possible."

Fr. Dooley stuttered, "But … but …"

Jim replied, "It's time we leave bread making and go for the real dough."

Patrick added, "We can't afford more delays if the sisters want to see their addition built in our lifetime." The men snickered. Their secret exposed.

Dooley held onto the tube with both hands against the force of the wind. "What about the Cherub Loaf Fund effort and Mr. Atkins? Does he know about this?"

Red cracked his knuckles and chimed in, "Father, can't you tell? They're moving on to Plan B."

Father ran to Jim, who pulled out a handkerchief and put it over his nose blocking dust and sand particles. Through his mask, Jim yelled, "Plan B doesn't include Rog." They hurried to the hospital door.

Red caught his breath and laughed. "Father, we thought you already agreed that this bread thing was getting a little stale."

Jim held the door open and ushered the men inside. He faced Father. "Just remember what side your bread is buttered on."

Patrick and Jim followed with a surprise visit to Miss Crawford's office. It was not a friendly meeting. They stood over her and demanded she follow their instructions.

§ § §

In early December, Joey parked his car near the hospital's entrance and unloaded boxes filled with stuffed animals and toys, donations from The TapRoot employees. He handed them to the women from the auxiliary and stayed to unpack Christmas decorations.

Joan and Dooley, walking down the hall, spotted Joey and abruptly turned in the opposite direction.

Idle Gossip

Chapter 57

Preparations for The TapRoot Christmas Holiday Revue were in progress. In the hallway between the Atrium and The Tappers dressing room, a busboy with a tray of dirty dishes snuggled against the wall allowing Tatyana, Rita, and Lucia to squeeze past and into their dressing room. The Tappers took their places before the rows of bare light bulbs.

Lucia found a large floral bouquet resting on the dressing table. She looked to the other dancers. "Someone's expecting flowers?"

All smiles, they urged her to read the note. When she recognized the penmanship on the envelope, her hands shook. "Joseph, it's from Joseph."

Tatyana encouraged her friend, "So, go on. Go on. What does he say?"

While Lucia read the message to herself, Rita counted, "Nine, ten, eleven long stem red roses. Where's number twelve?"

Lucia stuttered, "He's asking… he's asking… he's asking…"

"Go on, Pumpkin. We're in suspense," urged Rita.

Lucia waved the note back and forth in front of her face, tears streaking her rouge and powdered face.

Rita asked if she could read it to the group. Lucia nodded. When Rita looked at the note, she laughed. "It's in Italian."

Laughter continued, allowing Lucia time to regain her composure before she mumbled that Joseph asked her to marry him. Lots of hugs, tears, and joyful greetings filled the dressing room.

Alerted with the five-minute warning, The Tappers rushed to complete their makeup and costumes, including headdresses. Before heading backstage, each blew Lucia an air kiss. She tucked Joey's note inside her bodice and followed the group. When the lights went up, a blast of music began, and The Tappers danced onto stage. Joey, in the audience, sported a single red rose pinned to his pocket lapel.

§ § §

At Saint Brigid Hospital, the nuns gathered for their annual mission assignment. The dinner complete, Sr. Marie handed out letters from their superior. After a few moments, biting back tears, Sr. Marie announced for those receiving a new mission to move in the middle of the U-shaped table.

Sr. Maria and Zita walked to the middle of the table. Under the glow of hand-held candles, the two of them joined their fellow sisters singing, "Ave Maria."

The next day, in obedience to their religious tradition, they left for new and different assigned missions.

§ § §

Roger twisted the telephone cord as he paced up and down in front of his desk. "Joan, tell me. What's the real purpose of your call?"

With a sugary voice, she replied, "I know you're having trouble reaching Sister Regis, but as our new adminis—"

"Sister has many pressing concerns. But I can't understand the real reason she won't return any of my calls."

Miss Crawford purred, "I'd answer your call anytime, Roger."

Roger sat and rubbed his head. "Joan. Stop. It's over." He cleared his throat. "No, no. It never started."

"Roger, give me another chance. I can make amends. I'm willing to start over if—"

"Excuse me. I have a busy day ahead of me." Roger slammed the receiver in its cradle.

He lit a cigarette, inhaled, then exhaled. Abruptly he screwed the cigarette into the ash tray, jotted a note to Joey and grabbed his hat and coat. He slammed the door behind him. Eager to get to the root of the problem, he drove directly to the hospital.

Without acknowledging greetings from members of the women's auxiliary or the candy stripers, he marched directly to Sr. Marie's office and stared at the newly brushed metal door sign:

Sister Regis, Administrator

Roger straightened his tie, knocked, but didn't wait for a response. "Good morning, Sister. I know you are busy but allow me to introduce myself. I'm …"

Sr. Regis abruptly stood from behind her desk, arms crossed, and cut him off. "I am aware who you are, Mr. Atkins. You are correct. I am very busy. May I make an appointment for some other time so—"

Roger interrupted. "Sister, stop playing games with me." His facial muscles tightened. "You know I have been trying for weeks to introduce myself properly and …"

Sr. Regis picked up a folder from her desk. "Must I remind you that I have a hospital to run? That requires both my time and attention."

Roger assumed a military posture, hands clasped behind his back, chin up and out. He focused on her. "Must I remind you the only reason you have a hospital to run is because of Sister Zita and her Cherub Loaf."

Sister fanned out the assortment of file folders on her desk, selected the one with the tab Cherub Loaf, and nonchalantly thumbed through it. She stopped on the last financial page. "As I read it, very few funds went into our new addition. The results were," looking up with an evil smile, "shall we say, ahem, negligible."

"Kindly allow me to clarify your misunderstanding about the results. Your superior was made aware of the financial severity of the local situation. The AP publicity was invaluable. The Cherub Loaf campaign, with the financial help of The TapRoot Hotel and Casino, got things moving. The community supported the sisters and their dream to keep the doors of this hospital open."

Sr. Regis shut the folder and tossed it back on her desk. "Dreams? Our hospital can't exist on dreams." With a cold stare, she added, "I'm not going to allow you to become a distraction in my life as you did with Sister Marie and Sister Zita."

"A distraction? I don't understand."

"You are not to worry. Both have been assigned to new missions. There were some concerns, but..." She broke her stare and crossed over to the wall calendar marked with crowded activities throughout the month. "Allow me to make an appointment so we may continue our conversation."

"No appointment needed. Just tell me. Has Cherub Loaf been scrapped?"

"Wasn't it dead on arrival before I was sent here? Wings from the Cherub Loaf campaign have been clipped. We're planning a more professional and successful fundraising effort this time around."

Sr. Regis returned to her desk, sat down, and shuffled papers until she found the precise one. Looking it over, she grinned. "In any case, we've moved to the Saint Brigid's Fundraising Committee. Father Dooley has been transferred, so Mr. Jim Riley has taken over."

"Who?"

Sr. Regis put her index finger to her lips. "Please. Please. Just a minute." She continued to shuffle papers, then picked up a page. Running her finger down the list, she stopped and with a flat voice, said, "I can't seem to find your name as a trustee on the list."

Roger bowed and moved for the door. "Thank you for your time. I wish the hospital continued success with … their new fundraising committee. Good day."

Roger rested against the closed door, caught his breath, and cooled off. He reviewed the exchange and shook his head. The meeting didn't go as he planned or expected. He hoped Sr. Marie and Zita would not be casualties of his blunt encounter with the new administrator.

He heard footsteps and noticed Joan walking down the hall toward Sr. Regis's door, holding a stack of files. She spotted Roger, and like a carved ice sculpture, froze in place.

Roger planted his eyes directly on her and walked to her. She backed away a few feet, clasping the files closer to her chest. He said, "So. I hear Father Dooley moves on, with your assistance, I presume."

"Well, uh …"

"Is sainthood your next move for him? And how do you plan to pull that one off?"

"Roger," she bit her bottom lip. "He's a spiritual adviser. That's a big responsibility."

Roger stood sure-footed and didn't respond.

She swallowed deeply. "He steers his flock away — away from occasions of sin, and, uh … he …"

A puzzled look spread over Roger's face. "And this is accomplished by creating idle gossip?"

Rolling a tray of medicines down the hall, a nurse nodded in their direction and continued with her mission.

Joan stepped closer to Roger and whispered, "And just where were you leading…" She looked down to the floor and then directly to Roger's eyes. "… leading us?"

"Leading who? Or what?" Roger's voice became louder. "Leading a project, a project where Catholics, Jews, Christians, and Mormons worked together for a common goal."

Miss Crawford grabbed his elbow and attempted to usher him down the hall away from other ears. Roger shook loose. "Getting the whole community aware of the financial need of the hospital and for their support."

Sr. Regis abruptly opened her office door. "Please. This is a hospital."

Ignoring her presence, Roger continued, "We witnessed leadership qualities quickly developing in a young, timid, and of course, an obedient sister." Roger's lower lip quivered. He looked down, shook his head, then faced Miss Crawford. "I think you know the true picture." He looked from Sr. Regis to Miss Crawford. "And not the manufactured one."

Sr. Regis commanded, "Miss Crawford, if you must carry on with this conversation, please conduct yourself accordingly," and slammed the door.

Roger dismissed the reprimand. "I don't know what you told people, but you know I never made any improper overture to any of the sisters. I hold nothing but admiration for Sister Marie and Sister Zita."

Joan grabbed Roger's coat. "I didn't think it would …" Roger yanked away as she awkwardly rebalanced the files in her arms. "Please. Please give me another chance. I don't know what I was thinking."

"I'm sure, in time, you'll fabricate an answer or invent a good excuse." Roger turned from her, stomped down the hallway, and out into the parking lot.

Joan turned quickly, sliding out one of her strapped heels. She wobbled after him and, between sobs pleaded not caring who heard her cried out. "Roger, wait. Please wait."

He did not wait or turn back. She ducked into her office and dumped the files on her desk. From the office window, she watched Roger slam the car door and accelerate from the driveway. She wiped her cheek, catching some of the tears streaming from her eyes. She buried her head in her hands mumbling, "What have I done? Why did I do this? I've lost him." She erupted into uncontrollable sobbing. "Lost everything."

§ § §

In front of the filing cabinet, Joey sorted material when Roger burst into the office, slamming the door behind him.

Startled, papers flew from Joey's hands. He bent down to gather them while carefully monitoring his pop's frenetic movements. He tossed his hat on the desk, unbuttoned his jacket, and swung it onto the back of his chair in haste.

"Religious life runs like the military." Roger flopped in the chair and rummaged through various stacks of letters and magazines in search of a cigarette. "You follow orders, follow orders filtered from the top of the chain of command to the bottom."

Joey spied a pack, but it was too late.

Roger shook one out, lit the wrong end, crushed it in the ash tray. He banged his fists on the desk looking to Joey. "What's more to say?" He lowered his head, resting on his elbows, and mumbled, "A bad beat ... bad beat."

"But, Pop, I knew they were after you and it's just not fair."

"Son, it's over. We move on."

"Pop, I can take care of this. I'll call Sister Marie—"

"I said it's over. Both Sister Marie and Sister Zita have been moved to different missions." He fumbled for another cigarette, lit up, took a drag, exhaled.

"Let me try. I'll get to the root of this injustice."

Roger barked back. "Didn't you hear me? It's over. Time to move on." He stood and circled the perimeter of the room. "But I just wonder about the sisters. How must they feel about how this ended."

PART III:

JOEY

Grandpop

Chapter 58

Sitting on the love seat next to Lucia, Joey got up and paced around his pop's apartment. "I don't get it. I just don't get it. He says it's over and we move on … like he always says. But it's not over for me."

"Joseph, he's hurt and that may be his way of handling his feelings. Allow him time."

Joey walked to the bookshelf and pulled out the bible Sister Zita gave him. He turned to the dog-eared page, Proverb 12:17-27. "Listen to this, 'An honest witness tells the truth, but a false witness tells lies.'"

Staring down at the page, in a muted voice, Joey continued, "But those were twisted facts about Pop's effort." He closed the bible. "I know that and, I promise, I will be his honest witness."

Life's daily events caught him in a whirl of activities. As a full-time college student, he maintained solid grades, continued work for his pop and courted his Lovely Lucia. During a college semester break, he and Lucia exchanged I do's.

Roger, Jake, Tatyana, and Rita attended the private ceremony held at the Little Church of the West on The Strip. They teamed up and surprised the newlyweds with a honeymoon to New Orleans, each picking up the tab for various activities.

Taking time from exploring the city, Joey wrote a

postcard to Jake:

Hotel has a great location. Lots to do. Fishy smells from the open French Market followed us while strolling stalls next to the banks on the Mississippi River. Enjoyed watching port's activities—tugboats, barges, cargo ships, steamers, and hearing the fog horns, bells, and whistles. The suite is luxurious. Thank you.

To Tatyana and Rita, Joey penned:

Bought umbrellas. Rain every day. Lucia heard rumors the above-ground tombs are haunted, and ghosts come out at night. She's relieved you got us day tours. Fascinating. Thank you.

Roger arranged for his son and daughter-in-law to eat at famous establishments—brunch at Brennan's, lunch at Galatoire's, and dinner at Antoine's. As a special addition, or *lagniappe,* the word used by Orleanians, he contacted Bruno. His former co-pilot was the new owner of Bruno Grocery Store. Roger arranged for him to fix the honeymooners one of his never-stopped-talking-about-Italian sandwiches, a muffuletta.

Joey wrote a letter.

Pop, we've put on some pounds. Also, met Mr. Bruno. He reminisced about your crew's time in Bari. Tears came to my eyes as he recalled the kind words you used speaking about my Nonna, papa, and mother. He never met them but said you held them dear to your heart. He showed us how to make a muffuletta, then directed us to Jackson Square with instructions to sit, take time eating, listen to jazz, and people watch. A special treat. A gift to remember. Thank you.

He slipped it inside the hotel's envelope and mailed it.

On their last day, Lucia and Joey stopped at Café du Monde for beignets, the iconic deep-fried pastry sprinkled with powdered sugar. While drinking a cup of café au lait and wiping the sweat from their brows, they joked about the city's high humidity compared to the dry heat of Las Vegas.

It took the couple several days to settle back into their routines and stop talking about their experience in The City That Time Forgot. Lucia continued with her dancing and Joey with his undergraduate studies.

Time came for Joey to prepare for the next step in his academic pursuits. After sending copies of his transcripts, letters of recommendation, and additional requirements to select universities, the long-awaited acceptance letter arrived. Joey burst into Roger's office, waving the envelope. "Hey, Pop, look! I got accepted into Syracuse University, your old stomping grounds."

Roger helped his son pack the '56 T-Bird. He gave him a tight hug, then watched as the couple rounded the corner and drove out of sight on their way to their new home. Rita slipped her friend a handkerchief and wrapped her arm around Roger's shoulder. Both stood quietly wiping away tears.

§ § §

Late one evening, Joey's faculty advisor noticed him at a library table buried in books. "You've found your niche. Your enthusiasm for research is infectious."

Joey completed a master's degree, which led to a doctoral degree. He concentrated his research and writings on the effects of biological and chemical warfare. In the recesses of his mind, he still thought of being that witness for his father's good name, but time and opportunity slipped by him.

Roger finally gave up smoking and developed a daily exercise routine, but his health continued to be problematic. When he retired from The TapRoot, he joined Lucia and Joey in his new role as grandpop to their growing family.

The roles as wife, mother, daughter-in-law, and the home's chief financial officer worked for Lucia. She shared her new passion, refinishing old furniture with her children and father-in-law.

Together they traveled to auctions in small upstate New York towns. On one excursion, a vintage, rounded-top, wooden steamer trunk grabbed her attention. She continued bidding as Roger's eyes grew wider and wider until the activity stopped.

Lucia justified her emotional response to her prized object. "Mr. Atkins, it is like the one my family used when we sailed from Italy to America. Do you think Joseph will understand?"

Roger kissed his daughter-in-law on the forehead, "I'm sure he will." His personal thoughts drifted back to Bari. *My sweet Angioletto, you would be so proud of your son and his lovely family. I am.*

§ § §

Through the years, regular long-distance telephone calls kept the Syracuse family in touch with their Las Vegas friends. Good news or bad news, the conversations served as the glue maintaining their tight friendships.

After dinner, when long-distance rates were cheaper, Lucia gathered her husband and father-in-law around the kitchen table facing their black rotary telephone.

Roger held the receiver inches from his ear so all could listen in on the conversation; after he sent his greetings and news, he passed the receiver to Joey, who then passed it to Lucia. Their conversations centered around the weather, their children's activities, and health issues.

On the other end, Jake, Tatyana, and Rita followed a similar routine, allowing each to enjoy the give-and-take and hear the voices of their loved friends. Their news included current activities at The TapRoot. Hollywood producers had snatched Monsieur LeBlanc from The Tappers, so Rita took over his position. Because of Jake's health, Tatyana eased out of dancing and took on the responsibilities as vice-president of The TapRoot Corporation.

Hospice Care

Chapter 59

Grandpop lay on the hospital bed. The head nurse, now familiar with Joey and Lucia, made her patient as comfortable as possible. She informed them that when Roger's temperature spiked, he experienced hallucinations and spoke to imaginary spirits. "This is not unusual for someone so close to leaving us."

§ § §

One Saturday morning, Joey and Lucia decided to talk with their children about their grandpop's grave condition. Gathered together in the living room, Lucia sat between their daughters, 13-year-old Giana, and Zita who was 11. Her arms around each. Rogie, the oldest who just turned 16, took the ottoman. They waited in silence as their father paced up and down the room.

Finally, he faced his family. "You know your grandpop once again is in the hospital. I have … I mean, your mother and I have sad news. It's about his condition."

Young Zita burst out, "Dad, don't be sad. We already know."

"You know about his condition?"

"Yes, dad, and we cried a lot knowing he is going …"

"Shh, Zita," demanded her older sister. Then Giana faced their parents. "We just didn't want to tell you. We didn't know how you'd handle it."

Tapping the top of a box of tissues on her lap, her mother asked, "How did you know?"

Giana gave a nod to her brother. "It was Rogie. He said the last couple of months when they went biking, they had to slowly walk the bikes back home. Grandpop had a hard time catching his breath."

Zita added, "And a few weeks ago, Rogie found another one of his bloody handkerchiefs thrown in the garbage can."

Giana stared down her sister. "Oh, Zita. Come on! Remember what we promised?"

Rogie stood, rubbing his brow. "Zita, we said we didn't want to tell them that. It might make them sad."

Joey walked to his son and tousled his hair, an obvious genetic inheritance, and with a hug said, "It's okay. And I don't think grandpop wants us to be sad, either." He studied their mournful expressions. "We had so many happy times with him. Let's … let's…" At a loss for words, he turned to his wife, the one he depended on to offer a solution.

Lucia thought for a moment and then said, "How about this. Let's tell grandpop about a special happy time he spent with each of us."

It didn't take Rogie long to come up with his idea. "I want to thank him for riding bikes with me and showing me how to fix them, you know, like taking care of the brakes, checking tires, cleaning and lubing the chains. Grandpop took time to teach me lots of things. I'm happy about that."

Giana waved her hand to be next. "I want to thank him for teaching me how to play gin rummy and how to shuffle a deck of cards. I'm pretty good at it now. I mean, the cards don't fly all over the table. And we used match sticks to bet on the games. Sometimes I would win. It was fun and I'm happy about that."

They all looked in Zita's direction. "Well, I want to tell

him I'm sorry."

Her sister, with an exaggerated huff, said, "Oh, come on, Zita, this is serious. We're thinking of what will make grandpop happy."

"Mom, is it okay if I want to talk about the Space Gypsies jigsaw puzzle we worked on together?"

"Sweetheart, use the words you feel most comfortable and honest with."

"Well, you see, it had over five hundred pieces and we needed just one more piece to finish it. Grandpop kept looking for it, under the sofa, between the pillows, on the bookshelves, all over, and he kept searching."

Giana rolled her eyes. "Soooo?"

Undaunted, Zita continued. "You see, I wanted to be the person to finish the puzzle. So, I hid the corner piece, but I couldn't remember where I hid it. I was too embarrassed to tell him. I'm really sorry I did it, and I want him to know that." She wrinkled her nose at her older sister. "That's soooo. And I'll be happy he knows that."

§ § §

Rabbi and hospice chaplain, Judith Saiger, was a longtime friend of the Atkin's family. Joey and the rabbi spoke softly as Lucia stroked her father-in-law's face. Each of the grandchildren came forward with their honest farewell. The attending nurse held a box of tissues.

Zita pulled out one. "Why does grandpop keep talking about an angel?"

The nurse looked for her parents approval before offering an answer. Joey gave his nod as did a tearful Lucia. "I believe your grandpop is making ready to go to heaven. He may believe a little angel is waiting for him. He keeps repeating, "my Angioletto, my Angioletto."

Before Rabbi Saiger began the end-of-life arrangements,

the parents gave their final kiss to the family patriarch. Their youngest offered a moment of spiritual comfort. Zita walked over and whispered in his ear, "I hope many little angels are waiting for you, my sweet grandpop."

A Blessed Family

Chapter 60

By 1977, Saint Brigid's religious community eased into the modern era as an outcome of the Second Vatican Ecumenical Council and the feminine movement. Now in her forties, Sr. Zita traded her traditional habit for a short veil, modest street clothing, and laced-up Oxford shoes with chunky heels. She accepted new assignments and embraced each as a new opportunity to serve the Lord.

Currently a third-grade teacher in Detroit, Michigan, with Saint Xavier Elementary School, she stood in front of the classroom window and pulled her shawl tight around her shoulders.

Snow drifted down, not yet enough to form a snowball. A heavier accumulation was predicted overnight. By morning, full-size snowmen would stand in front of many homes.

Sr. Zita watched the pupils boarding the school bus. A few of them turned and waved, knowing she watched over them. After the bus pulled out, Sr. Zita walked past the neatly lined rows of desks, stopping in front of the wall calendar, and turning the page from November to December. *Where has the time gone?*

On the side of her desk, she looked at the patched statue of San Pasqual, cupped his prayerful hands, her usual show of respect. Then she sat behind the desk, arranging her lesson plans in a folder. Footsteps alerted her to the sound of someone running toward the classroom. Leaning her ear to the hallway, she made the sign of the cross calling upon St. Christopher, patron of travelers, to see her students safely home.

Breathless, the secretary ran in. "Sister, you have a long-distance phone call. He says he's an old friend of yours. His name is Joseph Atkins."

Sister's walk down the hall quickly turned to a run, her short veil flapped behind her. Once inside the faculty lounge, conversation among her peers came to a whisper. A teacher, running material through the loud mimeograph copy machine, stopped and gathered her papers. Others put on their coats, boots, hats, and gloves preparing for their ride home. One by one, they tiptoed from the room allowing Sr. Zita privacy. A colleague handed her the phone and waved goodbye.

Sr. Zita held the receiver to her chest and after a quick prayer. "Come Holy Spirit," she said before holding the phone to her ear. "Hello, this is Sister Zita."

A smile stretched across her face. "Oh, Joey, it's so good hearing your voice after all these years." She flopped into a worn, but comfortable easy chair positioned next to the telephone. "Oh, no! You lost your father." Twisting the phone cord, her face turned somber. "I'm so sorry, so sorry and sad. May he rest in eternal peace."

Joey hadn't wanted to burden her, but he needed to talk to someone who knew his pop. Lucia suggested he reach out to Sr. Zita since Mr. Jake's stroke left him unable to speak. He didn't want to disturb Tatyana, Jake's caretaker and the one overlooking the affairs of The TapRoot Corporation. Rita returned to California and was working on the third or fourth new man in her life. Joey lost count.

"My dear friend, I appreciate your contact. God bless Mr. Atkins' soul! Such a kind man, he was." She dug into her pocket and took out three ceramic bells. She pressed them close to her tear-streaked cheeks, kissing them slightly. The memories of Mr. Atkins remained strong in her heart. She was comforted in her belief that God called him to his eternal resting place, most assuredly, in heaven and by His side.

Briefly, they entered into a conversation on a variety of subjects. Joey introduced her to the names and ages of his children. Sr. Zita smiled. "Joey, I will keep them all in my prayers."

"Sister, tell me about Miss Mo, one of my favorites at the hospital."

"After Miss Mo's father died, she traveled to Ireland looking for her mother. She never found her. Miss Mo passed away and was laid to rest on the Emerald Isle."

The janitor entered, tipped his hat to Sister Zita, and pushed the broom around the room.

She paused for a moment, then said, "Joey, I pray you keep all the wonderful memories of your pop and they bring you continued comfort. I am here when you need me."

Before Joey and Sr. Zita ended their conversation, both promised to keep in contact.

The phone line clicked dead. Sr. Zita couldn't move. She sunk deeper and deeper into the chair and into sadness. She stayed seated, deep in memories, until the janitor's broom accidentally hit the chair. He tipped his hat and apologized for the disturbance. She got up and smiled. "The Lord works in strange ways. I've just been reunited with an old friend. Praise the Lord!"

§ § §

Sr. Zita sat at her desk for hours reading, rereading, and comparing greetings over the years. She arranged each letter, card, and photo in a special album she named, A Blessed Family. Picking up the latest photograph of Rogie, Giana, and

Zita, she kissed each of their pictures. "I pray for all of you little darlings."

When the Heavenly Father called Sister Marie to her eternal home, she included a copy of her liturgy inside her annual correspondence to Joey. The following year, Dooley passed peacefully to the Lord. She inserted the newspaper article with his obituary in that letter, too. Several paragraphs were dedicated to Dooley's efforts in creating the first fundraising committee of Saint Brigid Hospital. Dooley's quotation was revealing.

I saved the medical facility from closing its doors. My family from Ireland stands with their heads held high.

The lengthy account detailed the cleric's last assignment. After his tenure at the hospital, Dooley served as the visiting priest covering the vast territory of Elko county, the fourth largest county, land wise, in the continental United States.

Fr. Dooley traveled in an RV and used Jackpot, Nevada, as his home address. The congenial priest was remembered for auctioning personal possessions and distributing funds to various causes.

Sr. Zita sealed and mailed the material to Joey. *I will remember Fr. John Dooley for his good intentions. May he rest in peace.*

Joseph Atkins, Ph.D.

Chapter 61

Over time, Joseph Atkins, Ph.D. distinguished himself among scientists studying the effects of nuclear warfare. Sr. Zita followed his accomplishments in the newspaper and added articles to the family's album.

In 1980 the U.S. Congress summoned Joseph Atkins, Ph.D. to serve as expert witness in front of the Select Committee/Hearing to study government operations/with unauthorized storage of toxic agents.

While the taxi waited for him at his home, Lucia complained to no one in particular, "Joseph, always running late, never organized." She rummaged through file folders on top of his desk, looking for an empty attaché case.

Lucia spied Roger's old leather case resting in a corner. She wiped the layer of dust on its top, unlatched its closures, and inserted stacks of her husband's documents and evidentiary material into its pockets. She did not lock it, but tucked the key in the desk drawer, fearing Joey might lose them if she handed them to him.

Joey hurriedly threw his coat over his arm, put on his hat, and grabbed the briefcase handles. With a hug, Lucia sent him off. "Stay safe. We love you."

§ § §

Joey arrived at the senate office building in Washington, D.C., and pushed opened the tall bronze doors. He smiled, checking the time on his inherited Omega Seamaster wristwatch. As he clutched his father's briefcase, a comfortable awareness swept over him. He felt Roger's presence.

With a few minutes to spare, Joey purposely chose to climb the grand marble staircase to the third floor. *Magnificent and prestigious. Our congressmen do things with style.* He paused often to catch his breath. Years of pasta dinners and endless hours sitting at his desk reflected on a thick waistline.

On both sides of the long, wide corridor, small groups of professionally dressed individuals, with name tags around their necks, huddled at the entrance to each hearing room. A large easel identified the location:

U.S. CONGRESS/SELECT COMMITTEE
1981 - OPEN HEARING
CHEMICAL AND BIOLOGICAL WARFARE

The security officer at the door checked Joey's identification and handed him a special lanyard. With his VIP pass as expert witness, his escort led him to a wooden table. He pulled his modest vinyl conference chair closer to the table, took out his written statement, and tucked his pop's briefcase underneath.

In advance of the day's proceedings, committee members received Joey's written statement. Once the formal proceedings began, Joey was allotted fifteen minutes for his oral summary, a limited amount of time to present his extensive research and findings. Hopefully, during the question/answer period that followed, he would have the opportunity to produce subsequent evidentiary material.

Joey faced the senate seal affixed to a tall white and gray marble wall with walnut paneled sidewalls. It offered a backdrop for a two-tier platform with an extra-long walnut wooden circular desk.

Once again Joey thought, *Magnificent and prestigious, even intimating*. Leather high-back chairs, accented with nail-head trim, were spaced along a two-tier platform. Gradually, senators filtered in front of their seats, a solid walnut name plate identified each committee member.

The chairman delivered an opening speech, after which he referred to notes for Joey's introduction. "We welcome Dr. Joseph Atkins, research scientist, authority on toxic agents, and author of scientific books and articles on the subject of biological and chemical warfare. Today Dr. Atkins will address Russia's unauthorized storage of toxic agents."

Joey stood and was sworn in. Cameras flashed, temporarily blinding him. The chairman instructed him to be seated. "Dr. Atkins, what is your position regarding the alleged anthrax epidemic on the Soviet city of Sverdlovsk last year?"

Cameramen jockeyed for positions in front of Joey, hoping to catch that one shot displaying the essence of the day's events. Eager to share his findings, Joey brought the microphone closer. "I strongly disagree with the conclusions offered by the Soviet news agency, TASS."

Buzz from those in attendance became audible as did clicks and flashes from the cameras. Joey maintained his focus. "To date, evidence indicates those deaths were not caused by consuming tainted meat from anthrax-contaminated cattle." Once again, a wave of indistinct babbling traveled throughout the room.

The chairman struck his gavel, demanding quiet. With order restored he asked, "And what do your findings suggest, Dr. Atkins?"

Joey informed the committee that his research demonstrated it was the result of military activity at the suspected Soviet biological warfare facility. "Specifically, this occurred at Compound 19 and is a violation of the terms on the 1972 biological weapons convention signed by the Soviets and the U.S." Cameras clicked and flashed.

§ § §

While their children slept, Lucia kept vigil waiting for her husband's return. She greeted him with a loving hug and ordered him to relax on their love seat. She opened his briefcase, carefully layering material in proper piles as she listened to him describe the minute-by-minute details of the hearing.

Lucia checked inside the briefcase, making sure she had collected all the materials. As she closed the case, a folded piece of paper, stuck inside the flip pocket, caught her eye. Pulling it out, she saw it had yellowed and was brittle to the touch. Carefully, she unfolded it and froze.

Joey was still describing the events of the day when his wife blurted out, "Joseph, Joseph!" Breathing hard, she walked slowly to him and handed him the page. He immediately recognized his pop's penmanship.

On the top half of the page Roger had written, *Cherub Loaf Project, dedicated to the cherished love of my life, my sweet Giana Puglia, my little angel, my Angioletto.* Glancing at the bottom half of the page, Joey's eyes filled with tears seeing his mother's name scribbled again and again, surrounded with drawings of loaves of bread.

Joey froze. His tears fell onto the page, so Lucia gently took it from him hands. "Time moved on for your pop, but his thoughts and feelings for your dear mother never left him."

The simple tick tock from the wall clock offered a dramatic backdrop to the solemnity of the moment. Joey and

Lucia found comfort in each other's arms, each in their own way, processing their new discovery.

§ § §

Joseph Atkins Ph.D.'s picture was spread across the morning's front page. He was still sleeping when Rogie, discovered the article in the *New York Times*. Excited, he read it to his siblings over the breakfast table. Even though Lucia reminded them their father had been up late the night before, keeping them quiet was difficult. Their mother promised a celebratory dinner and told them their father would share exciting news with them.

Lucia gave her children a kiss before they piled into the car. The three of them outdid each other with guesses as to what the news would be. Their chatter continued until Rogie dropped his sisters off at their high school and he continued to his college classes.

Joey, remembering what he learned, danced down the stairs wearing the look of wonderment and kissed Lucia. For the first time, he paired the name of his parents in an amorous and charming relationship. "My mom was his little angel, his Angioletto. My pop loved my mom." He couldn't stop grinning and laughing. He sat at the kitchen table, and suddenly, he turned to Lucia, looking dazed.

"What is it, Joseph?"

Nodding back and forth, he paused. "I'm just thinking … my pop? A romantic? Oh, Santo Cielo! I could never, ever have imagined that."

Hospital's Image

Chapter 62

In April of 1984, Joey scheduled a side trip to Henderson. At McCarran International Airport he hired a taxi for the day and sat in the passenger's seat. The former desolate dusty road between Las Vegas and Henderson changed with the times.

Joey stared at street and business signs dotted along Boulder Highway. Mix-use commercial properties, trailer parks on either side of the road, fast food chains, drug stores, gas stations, an Indian Trading store, printers, auto parts and repair, a visual reflection of the accelerated growth of the area in a random fashion.

He hit the dashboard with a folded newspaper. "Wouldn't Pop be surprised to see the growth and changes!"

The driver kept his eyes on the road as Joey mumbled to himself. "Amazing! Look at that … Girls A Go-Go Club right next to the business, U In? We Get U Out Jail Bond."

He stretched his neck searching for the bigger-than-life billboard of Tam O'Shanter wearing knickers hitting a 3-D golf ball into the air. There was no trace of the once historic landmark announcing the gateway to Lake Mead/Fishing-Boating-Skiing and to the city of Henderson.

The cab driver, weaved in and out of traffic, and glanced over to Joey. "Got too big, too fast." He accelerated and passed a trailer with a California license plate. "See that? Too many kooky types moving in."

"You mean from California?"

"Don't need 'em here. Got our own strange ideas." He stopped for a red light. "Can you imagine 'em politicians thinking of running a woman for our mayor." He slammed his hand against the steering wheel. "A woman mayor here in Henderson!"

Joey let the statement alone. *Can't change a person's belief during a short cab ride.*

The driver broke the silence. "What kinda meetin' you say you at?"

"Conference on the politics of chemical and biological warfare."

"Jesus! Most tourists come to Vegas for fun … gambling, women, drinking, not that warfare thing." He took a right turn and drove past the hospital's old entrance showing years of growth with tall, red oleander trees stretching past windowsills.

Flashing warning lights and the sound of a siren slowed the cab. An ambulance pulled ahead, turning into the area marked Emergency Entrance.

The taxi drove into the new, large circular entrance. He passed several aisles designated for Physicians Only, 15-minute Patient Parking Only, before rolling into the Visitors parking area.

Joey looked amazed at the health-care facility design to handle the explosive growth of the community. He stretched his head out the window drinking in the landscaped entrance. The palm trees, decorative rocks and stones, drought resistant plants and shrubs looked completely natural. He put aside the newspaper, musing to himself, *Twenty-five years.*

"I'm not sure how long I'll be so just park."

The driver found a space and turned off the ignition.

Joey slowly ambled to the entrance and turned back to the driver. "I want walk around and buy a few loaves of bread."

The driver cupped his hands over his mouth and shouted back, "It's a hospital, not a bakery." He shook his head. "What a nerd!"

Joey experienced an internal *wow* entering the large, well-appointed reception area. Looking to the right, he saw the workspace dedicated to admitting services. Hospital personnel, name tags hanging around their necks, sat behind each desk assisting individuals with medical intake forms. *I wonder how Pop would have reacted if Miss Crawford demanded such a long process?*

Colorful patterned sofas and chairs offered comfortable relief to those in the Waiting Area. Behind that, three large picture windows overlooked a well-cared for garden. The gardener was busy cutting back faded blooms from a variety of rose bushes.

He faced three elevators across the spacious waiting room with visitors, patients, and personnel in front of the elevator doors. One door parted and two nurses in surgical scrubs hurried out. Gone were nurses wearing identifying pins on their white caps, white uniforms, white shoes and stockings.

From another elevator door, two women exited engaged in a conversation. Each wore a midi length skirt, a large cross hanging from a modest blouse, a short black veil, and sensible shoes. *They must be members of the modern religious community*. He favored traditional religious habits but realized those, too, were relics of the past.

Joey resisted some of the sweeping changes initiated within his church. He longed for Mass celebrated in Latin with a priest facing the Tabernacle, not the congregation. He favored some changes, though.

With girls of their own, Lucia and Joey were proud seeing their daughters serving as altar girls, a position once reserved for young boys. Other professions were opening to women, a thought that pleased Joey. His youngest, Zita, aspired to enter flight training school to become a commercial pilot.

Suddenly a young child bellowed out, "I want it back," and gave chase to his bigger brother. He wanted his toy and he wanted it right then! The mother ran after the boys, separated them, and apologized for the noisy outburst. *Doesn't his mother realize this is a hospital, a Catholic hospital, and no running is allowed?*

Smiling, Joey turned directly to his left and saw the gift shop. A volunteer took inventory of the flowers housed in a small refrigerator. He walked from section to section, greeting card section, candy shelf, stuffed animal ledge. *This is an upscale operation.*

"May I help you?" asked the volunteer.

"I just stopped to purchase some bread, some Cherub Loaf."

"Excuse me? Bread?" The woman paused for a few seconds. "If you're looking for something to eat, we have a new cafeteria." She pointed to the left of the elevators and looked back to a puzzled Joey. "I know they sell sandwiches on rye, white, wheat. Not sure they have … what did you say that was?"

Joey fixed his stare at the cashier who reiterated, "But they don't sell loaves of bread."

He thanked her and walked away. Instead of heading to the cafeteria, he spotted a walkway in the opposite direction. The space, about twenty by forty feet, connected the new addition with the original hospital and was converted into a photo gallery.

One of the first pictures Joey spotted hanging along the wall was an enlarged black and white photo. It pictured seven sisters in their black and white full traditional habit, lined up behind Father Dooley. He sported a broad smile as if he had just won a seven-card stud poker hand.

Immediately Joey identified Sister Marie and Zita and blew a kiss in their direction. *My friends, my friends. We shared interesting times.*

He took a few moments to imagine Miss Crawford in her office refreshing her makeup while Miss Mo busied herself baking Cherub Loaves in the kitchen. *God Bless them, my friends.*

He followed the chronological photo gallery path toward the old hospital. He stopped and examined a large photo, a group of men he instantly recognized. Joey read the names of each member engraved on the brass name plate identifying them as the hospital's First Fundraising Foundation.

Something is wrong. There was no mention or tribute to his pop who ignited the real first fundraising project, the Cherub Loaf Foundation. Joey was not willing to allow that part of the struggling hospital's history to be tossed aside, to dismiss his pop's effort.

A stream of people filed past Joey. He paced back and forth, his Italian temper getting the best of him. He reached into his pants pocket and pulled out a pack of gum and put a few sticks in his mouth. He chewed until the sugary substance became stretchy. In his mind, he quoted his version of a proverb on justice: The Lord detests dishonest and deliberate omissions in history, but finds favor with him who corrects the data.

With the coast clear, Joey took out an appropriate size of masticated gum and methodically stuck a wad after wad over the face of each man.

He stood back, admired his work, and gave an Italian salute. *Cazzata!*

Joey decided not to walk through the rest of the hallway into the original part of the hospital. He had work to do on behalf of his pop.

New Clinic

Chapter 63

On a bright, windy January day in 1987, Joey helped Sister Zita into the rental car, a red '56 T-Bird, with a front license plate that read: CLASSIC CAR FOR HIRE. They headed from the original Saint Brigid Hospital to the congregation's newer medical facility.

In the passenger seat, Sr. Zita folded the newspaper on her lap with the headline:

Nevada Designated Garbage Bin
for Nation Toxic Nuclear Waste

Their conversation flowed easily. Two old friends comfortable in each other's presence. Rubbernecking during the ride, Sr. Zita interrupted more than once. "Would you look at that!" "Can you believe it!" "Oh, my-oh-my. It's not a small town anymore!"

A line of cars slowed at the hospital zone. Joey inched his way to the parking area, a large architectural sign mounted over the complex:

SAN PASQUAL HOSPITAL

A covered walkway connected the medical clinic, Cherub Clinic, with the main hospital.

The security guard directed cars to designated white-lined spaces. When he saw the red '56 T-Bird, he motioned for it to stop. Joey rolled down the window and gave a cheek-to-cheek smile as an older Officer Hafen approached them.

"Good afternoon to the both of you." He pointed to a reserve parking space. "I've been waiting a long time. I want to thank you for making our city a better place to call my home."

Joey gave a thumbs-up to the officer and parked the car. He walked around to the passenger side and extended a helping hand to Sr. Zita. She took a moment to readjust her skirt and jacket, stood tall, and rolled back her shoulders. She chuckled, "Wear and tear of old age."

They headed for the Cherub Clinic, dedicated to research and treatment of war-related burns. Joey exclaimed, "Now, would you look at this!" He grinned, knowing his letter to Sister Elizabeth, current administrator, citing the omission of his pop's efforts hit a nerve.

A black '87 Fleetwood D'elegance Sedan with tinted windows slid parallel to the sidewalk and stopped next to Joey and Sr. Zita. The vehicle's nameplate identified it as from The Taproot Hotel and Casino. A chauffeur, distinguished and tall in a three-piece black suit, collared white shirt, straight tie, jumped from driver's seat. He hurried to the side door and extended his black leather driving-gloved hand to the passenger.

Tatyana stepped out, sun bouncing off her emerald-diamond cluster necklace from which a diamond cross hung in the design of a Russian Orthodox Cross with the image of a bottom footrest.

Joey and Sr. Zita embraced and thanked her for her generous participation with the addition of the Cherub Clinic.

Tatyana said, "I am sorry Jake can't be here with us and be the one receiving the recognition." Holding Sr. Zita's hand while they walked to the event, she continued, "I cannot stay. I release the nurses and feed him myself." She squeezed Sr. Zita's hand. "But he's here in spirit."

Inside the new addition, a team of volunteers stabilized a large green and white balloon arch and stood back to admire their work. Another group directed guests toward the auditorium, site of the celebration.

Mittie, the hospital's public relations director, held several files. She stood next to newspaper photographer, who scanned the list of dignitaries for his photo shoot. The photographer asked, "Who's this germ warfare guy?"

Mittie slipped the program over her mouth and whispered, "Dr. Joseph Atkins." She referred to notes in the margin of her program. "You can't miss him; mop of fluffy white hair, looks like your typical scientist."

"And this nun, Sister Zita?"

"For Sister." She held up a blue corsage. "I'm told she's wearing a blue suit and coming with Dr. Atkins."

"And this Tat-ay-na … can't pronounce her last name. What gives with her?"

"VIP. That's the shot we want, Steve. She's responsible for financing the hospital. Shoot away when you get a chance. She's stopping only for a few minutes and will leave after receiving a certificate."

Steve jotted down his assignment when the director reminded him. "We plan to use these pictures inside our next campaign fund letter. So, get as many as possible."

Guests, mostly seniors, continued to file in, including an older Red and Miss Crawford in a dated getup with a veiled hat. Her alteration skills minimized her dowager's hump. She clutched her purse close to her body.

Miss Crawford's sewing expertise could not camouflage Red's rotundity, his semi-precious gemstone belt buckle barely sneaking out from under his full belly. His western outfit was accessorized with an abundance of American Indian jewelry pieces.

They edged toward the back of the auditorium. Miss Crawford left her brace at home and slowly wiggled into a comfortable sitting position. She squinted, scanning the audience recognizing a few individuals from her past.

Sr. Elizabeth, advancing to the dais, escorted the honorees to their places. She began the program with a prayer, followed by traditional welcomes to honorees, community leaders, hospital staff, volunteers, and guests. Sr. Zita kept her eyes lowered. Joey looked out at the audience and smiled seeing the crowd. He caught Miss Crawford's eyes, she immediately looked down.

With camera equipment swung over his shoulder, Steve made his way to the dais. Applause from the audience swelled when he captured the moment Sr. Elizabeth presented Tatyana with a framed certificate, which she held close to her heart. A tear trickled down her cheek with the mention of Jake's name. It was through the influence of The TapRoot Hotel and Casino that several Strip properties contributed to the new addition. Tatyana blew a kiss in the direction of Joey and Sr. Zita and made her exit.

Applause died down and Sr. Elizabeth invited all to the new dining facility after the presentation for refreshments and a sample of Cherub Loaf.

Sr. Zita looked up; the slight movement of a white handkerchief caught her attention. Her eyes rested on a woman familiar to her.

Sr. Elizabeth continued with her presentation. "1987 is a very timely year for our celebration. Over thirty years ago, in 1957 ..."

Renewal of Friendships

Chapter 64

Miss Crawford's eyes grew distant as her mind traveled back to Roger. He never was far from her memories. Sr. Elizabeth's voice faded "A publicist was a patient…"

Joan lifted her hat's veil and wiped tears from her eyes, reflecting on that day in her office, the same flashback she experienced time and time again, word for word. If only she could change the circumstances and events of that fateful day when Jim and Patrick had barged into her office.

Jim began, "Just remember, you and Father started it and now we're counting on you to finish it."

Patrick added, "You got Father jittery. And now you've gotten to their superior."

"The tide turns quickly," Jim interrupted and forced a pencil into her hand. "Too bad about unintended consequences."

She slammed the pencil on her desk, breaking its point. "But what about Roger?"

"What about him? He's a big boy." Jim winked at Patrick. "We've got to turn off the oven and have the flame die down, if you catch my drift."

She stared at both men too upset to speak at first. Then with a voice choked with emotion and tears streaming from her eyes, she blurted out, "But I made that up about Roger and Sister. And you ... you know I did."

Jim ignored her pleadings. "Since the community knows the financial needs of the hospital, we've hired a contractor and a professional fundraiser who understand how to work with us."

She pleaded, "And the bread and ... Sister?"

Jim laid the journal on her desk. "Sisters get new appointments annually. They've been taken care of. We've seen to that." He forced a new pencil into her hand. "Just remember what you're expected to do, that is, if you like and want to keep your job."

"Please. Please. There must be another way. I didn't want-"

Patrick made it sound simple. "You need to make it seem like the Cherub Loaf effort is failing; no, that it failed. Just a few changes under different columns; that's all we're asking."

Jim said, "It's best for all. Both you and Father will be taken care of." He directed her that under the column of 'loaves sold,' she was to erase the number 29,000 and write in 13,000. She was to make sure the financial column corresponded with the new information.

Once done, Patrick added, "In the meantime, I'll make sure their superior knows the Cherub Loaf Foundation has evolved into the First Fundraising Foundation. She will understand and appreciate all we've done to keep her hospital open."

Jim lost patience. "Can't turn back now. If gossip ..."

Patrick explained, "When gossip gets back to her that a womanizer is on the loose, she'll act in the best interest of all."

"But I didn't expect it to go this far and so fast. What about Roger?"

A recognized voice jarred her back into real time. Sr. Elizabeth closed the ceremony, "A different time … a different place … a legacy."

Miss Crawford mumbled to herself, *"I only did as I was told."*

Guests ambled into the dining room. A trio played Spanish melodies. A bartender served champagne punch. Large trays of appetizers rested on long, skirted tables. Steve pushed his way through the crowd with his camera at the ready.

On entering the room, Joan pulled Red's elbow. He barged ahead, intended to get first shot at refreshments. More people filed into the decorated area. She inched closer to Red, opened her clutch purse, and looked at a letter, copied on thin onion skin paper.

She whispered, "Get ready to leave."

Red, with filled plate, seemed not to heed her words. He moved down the table to the crab dip.

The Women Committee decorated the two front walls with drawing from third-grade students, their interpretative drawings of the Cherub Loaf story. The most descriptive ones were selected and incorporated into a twelve-page booklet.

In the middle of the main table, Joan spotted a white frosted cake in the shape of the Cherub Clinic. Curiously hesitant, she walked over, eyed the souvenir booklets fanned out on the table. On its cover was a line drawing of a happy face patient holding up a slice of bread, a wiggly black one floating up into the air. She opened it. The dedication on inside cover read:

To: Roger Atkins
Creator of the first
Fund Raising Committee
of Saint Bridgit Hospital
Hearing rumblings of a small entourage of well-wishers

following Sr. Zita and Joey, she immediately set the pamphlet aside. Easing her way to Red, she nervously eyed the door. "I need to hand this to …"

Red attempted to stuff her mouth with an unwanted selection when she whipped her head and caught sight of the crowd moving closer to the middle of the room.

She pulled out the letter, "Follow me, and *now*." She yanked his arm.

Red dropped a cracker topped with sour cream, left it on the floor. He moved on down the line. "Just some shrimp dip. I won't need any dinner tonight."

Between clenched teeth, Joan said, "We need …"

The old cowpoke lost his balance on the mess he previously left on the floor. A loud crash alarmed everyone as the porcelain plate fell from his hands and shattered into pieces. Guests stared at the commotion.

Mittie ran to Steve, ready to nail down the mishap. She whispered, "Only cheerful moments."

"Mortified, Joan bent down trying to hide behind Red's big frame. She tucked the letter back in her purse and began picking up glass fragments.

Joey and Sr. Zita exchanged glances. Joey said, "Could it be Miss Crawford?"

They excused themselves and headed in her direction at the same time a waiter grabbed a broom and followed them.

Joey reached Miss Crawford and Sr. Zita knelt to help her. "Miss Crawford?"

Joan sucked blood dripping from her cut finger then admitted, "Yes, ah, yes. It's me. I want to give you… I only came to ask for your forgiveness."

Joey extended his hand toward Red who stared and laughed at him. "Turns out while the little nun was baking the bread, guess who was cooking the books?"

Joey made an Italian gesture, "Stronzo!" and mouthed, "Asshole." He left a stunned Red and knelt to help the women.

Sr. Zita dug in her pocket to free a handkerchief. Joey took and wrapped it around Miss Crawford's injured finger.

Joan choked up. "Thank you, Sister. Thank you, Joey. Oh, excuse me, Dr. Atkins."

"It's Joey, and always Joey to you."

The three assisted each to stand. Miss Crawford sobbed between apologizes. "I have so many regrets. I'm so sorry … I …" She opened her purse producing the onion skin copy of the letter she mailed to the superior a few years earlier.

Joey returned it without reading it. "We've been informed about your correspondence. It took courage to write such a confession and intimate letter."

"We thank you for clearing up the misunderstandings," Sr. Zita added.

"I just didn't know what I was doing, and it took me so long…"

"Miss Crawford, we are happy you are here with us."

Clutching her purse to prepare to leave, she said, "I do not want to be a distraction on your special day."

Sr. Zita reassured her, "But, Miss Crawford, you are part of our history and the Cherub Bread Loaf project."

"Perhaps, not the part of history… you wish to remember." Tears rolled down her face.

Sr. Zita grabbed a cloth napkin and gently cleared her up. "History is what it is … and look at us now … a bit older and a lot wiser."

Joey looked over the crowd milling around the room.

"Do you recognize any of these faces?"

"Joey," answered Miss Crawford. "We all are older and that makes a difference."

"I mean, these people are supporters of the hospital. But we're the only ones who worked behind the scenes of the Cherub Loaf project with all its struggles. Those were our moments. I haven't forgotten and can't share with many people. And I don't want to forget them."

He took the women by their elbows and escorted them to a seating area bordering the wall. Joey settled his friends into cushioned chair and sat between them.

Holding their hands, "Do you remember Roger's excitement when he read about the Abbey's effort and their Amen, Amen enterprise?"

A waiter sat down three drinks on the table between them. "If you need something more, just give me a wave."

Guest strolled by and smiled at the trio absorbed in conversation.

Once again, Steve prepared to capture the moment when Mittie pulled on his sleeve. And whispered, "This is an eye-catching setting. The lady sitting with sister and father was an employee of the hospital during the start of the Cherub Loaf Fund. Take several shots. We'll use one as the opening for my article, titled Remember When."

Undeterred by the guest milling around Joey reminisced. "To think, a legacy grew from simple ingredients of flour, yeast, sugar, oil, water and salt to get things rolling."

"And a dedicated Sister to make sure she had it right," Miss Crawford nodded to Sister Zita.

"And, Joey, I remember when Father Dooley suggested we call it Leprechaun Bread." Sr. Zita chuckled.

"And, in my youthful arrogance, I said it sounded like Irish talk to me."

Miss Crawford with raised eyebrows was amused, "Joey, you didn't!"

"But Father got even with my suggestion, Yum, Yum Bread. He said it sounded like baby talk to him."

Sr. Zita continued, "I remember when I was so scared in front of the committee to explain why I liked the name of Cherub Bread."

"Sister, you were very persuasive because …"

A harsh sound of Red snoring detracted and momentarily held their attention. He fell asleep in the chair and oblivious to the attention.

Guests strolled by and chuckled at his whimsical presence.

Miss Crawford leaned into her friend. "He's my chauffer, guess you're stuck with me a little longer."

"Lucky for us," Joey replied. "I 've got more stories."

Sister Zita said, "I remember when Father Dooley…"

The End

AUTHOR INFORMATION

While chair of the Women's committee of St. Rose de Lima Hospital, Henderson, Nevada, members gathered oral history from residents who witnessed their desert town leapfrog into the second-largest city in the state. Their material is included in the Library of Congress 2000 Local Legacy Project, offered background for FORGET-ME-NOT.

Joan McSweeney contributed material to the Southern Women's History Project:
SKIRTS THAT SWEPT THE DESERT FLOOR, 2018
UNFORGETTABLE NEVADA WOMEN,2020